MW00874167

Kathy,

Thank you so much for your support!

You are awesome!

Go Herd!

Your friend,

[illegible signature]

The Judge's Wife

PATRICK CLEVELAND

ISBN-13: 978-1724278159

ISBN-10: 1724278150

Thanks to my wife

whose love and patience make dreams come true

CHAPTER ONE

If he had been asleep, he would've awakened when the woman pushed against him and rolled off the pool table. But he wasn't asleep—he was unconscious. And it takes more than a push to bring one to life after drinking a half-handle of bourbon and a ridiculous number of tequila shots. What it takes is a high-pitched shriek, which didn't register in his consciousness, but somehow managed to arouse him enough to hear her next words.

"What the hell!" she yelled. "What time is it? Sheila! Sheila! Where the fuck are you?"

Nolan Getty groaned as he reached up and waved his hand around until he found the chain to the lamp above the pool table. For all he knew it could be high noon and sunshine, but it was impossible to tell because there were no windows in the basement of his office. He cupped his hand to shield his eyes from the lamp and squinted to see what the commotion was about. "Easy with the F word. And stop yelling for God's sake."

She was completely naked, scurrying around the table and snatching up articles of clothing. Now able to see, she jerked her wrist up to look at her watch then let out another round of obscenities. "Damn it, damn it, holy shit! Sheila!"

The hidden door on the floor-to-ceiling filing cabinet squeaked open and another woman appeared with Nolan's assistant behind her.

"What's wrong?" the woman asked, pulling a pink pajama top over her bare chest.

"I'm late! We've got to go now!" the judge's wife screamed.

Nolan's head fell back onto the felted slate and he closed his eyes, but the lamp was still too bright for comfort. He pawed around, found a small piece of clothing . . . perhaps a sock, then covered his face and eyes with it. Face up and spread-eagle on the pool table he was completely ambivalent to the fact that he was naked and wearing the woman's underwear on his face.

"Give me those," she barked, snatching them.

Nolan groaned again as the light from the lamp pierced his throbbing brain. He rolled over and tried to bury his face into the corner pocket—like an ostrich.

"Why are you yelling?" her friend asked.

The judge's wife hopped a few times as she slipped on her bottoms, then her slippers. "Let's go. Now!" she barked.

"No need to run away, ladies," Rick's voice was next to the pool table. "I don't have jail call 'til nine."

"Fuck off," the judge's wife yelled as she grabbed Sheila's hand and jerked her to the stairs. As they stomped up the stairs, Nolan managed to croak out one more time, "Stop with the F word." Nolan then heard their footsteps across the main floor and the sound of the front door banging shut.

As he was trying to recollect how he had passed out on the pool table in the basement of the Public Defender's office with the judge's wife and how they had become naked, he heard Rick chuckle next to him.

"Ah, I don't know if you realize this, boss, but you're butt naked."

"Get me my pants," Nolan mumbled into the corner pocket.

Rick was Nolan's right hand man. He was short, perhaps 5'8", but he was very stocky with huge biceps, which were the product of obsessive trips to the gym. Nolan had hired him six years earlier and in that time several assistants had come and gone but not Rick. Rick was the loyal type and he would never leave as long as Nolan remained the Chief Public Defender. More importantly, Rick had caught on to the system quickly and in his own quirky way he represented all his clients in a zealous manner.

Rick found his pants on the floor and threw them across the table. "Here you go, boss."

Nolan rolled off the pool table and fumbled getting them on. "Holy crap, my head hurts. Why do you always have to make a contest out of drinking?"

Rick held his arms up in a strong man pose, flexing his massive biceps. "It's the pipes boss, they can soak up gallons of liquor."

"Put those things away, you frickin' freak."

Rick laughed. "Looks like you and the judge's wife got along. By the way, how do those implants feel?"

"Like about ten grand . . . just what the good judge paid," Nolan answered as he stumbled into the secret room behind the swinging filing cabinet.

He had set up the room shortly after becoming the Chief Public Defender so that he and his boys had a place to relax and hang out, whether it was during work hours or not. There were three thickly padded chairs aligned in front of a big screen TV, a gaming console, a bar stocked with liquor and most importantly, a sink with running water. It was the water that interested Nolan the most. He leaned over the sink and began filling a glass.

"I'll have a glass of that if you don't mind, I'm feeling just a tad parched myself."

"Oh bullshit," Nolan quipped. "Big Boy doesn't get hangovers . . . Big Boy's just fine. Besides, there ain't enough water in the city for both of us right now."

To say his mouth was dry would've been a colossal understatement. The combination of hard liquor and cigars had created a unique condition that couldn't be that much different than a cat crapping in his mouth, stubbing a cigarette out in it, then scratching sand on top for a finishing touch.

"Oh no you don't," Rick jostled Nolan out of the way to get to the sink. After they had drained and filled their second glass, they plopped into the easy chairs and began to piece together the evening while sipping the old-fashioned goodness of cold water.

"Why the hell were they wearing pajamas in the bar?" Rick asked.

Nolan laughed. "You asked that about three times last night and the answer never changed—they were at a pajama party at the old train depot and skipped out to have a few cocktails."

"Pajama party?" Rick squinted and cocked his head. "Since when do grown women go to a pajama party?"

"It's a charity thing . . . a bunch of rich women in town pay big bucks to spend the night at the old train depot in their pajamas doing things that high-class women do, I guess. You know, facials, manicures, all that stuff."

"What about you then? I can't believe you did the judge's wife . . . and you just had that felt replaced!"

"Easy now. For the record, I don't think we did anything. Oh, and by the way, what happened last night never leaves this room. Nobody . . . and I mean *nobody* ever hears about this. Not even Danny Boy." Nolan was referring to his other Assistant Public Defender.

"Oh, man, that's a good idea, I would've never thought of that. So, you're saying we shouldn't tell everyone the judge's wife was naked in our office. That's such a great idea!"

"Okay, enough smartass," Nolan stopped him. "Besides, you're the one with the great ideas. How about you talking them into . . . what did you call it, progressive billiards?" Nolan changed his voice to sound like Rick, "Oh yeah, everybody's doing it in Hollywood, it's all the rage."

Rick chuckled. "Sounded good to me."

"Well, we're a long frickin' way from Hollywood and even if we weren't, the only people playing strip billiards last night were us clowns."

"Don't forget the shots of tequila, Mr. Most Interesting Man in North America," Rick countered. "You were the one who came up with the belly shots."

Nolan chuckled. "Now that was a good idea!"

They both heard the chiming sound at the same time. "What was that?" Nolan cocked his head.

Rick shrugged. "Don't know."

Nolan pushed himself out of the easy chair and stepped through the filing cabinet door into the billiards room—the direction from which the sound came. He stood next to the pool table and cocked his head. The chime occurred again, this time close. He looked under the pool table, then walked around until he found the source in the side pocket. He pulled the pink cell phone from the pocket and held it up.

"Uh-oh," Rick shook his head. "I'm going to guess it belongs to Mrs. Judge."

Nolan sighed. "Yup."

"Now what?" Rick asked.

Nolan touched the phone to make the screen come alive. The chime had alerted to a new text message.

Where are you? I'm waiting.

Nolan put the phone back to sleep and turned to Rick. "Now nothing," Nolan answered. "When she figures out it's missing, she'll be back, or maybe she'll call the office."

CHAPTER TWO

One month earlier

It was another beautiful fall day in Big Shanty, Virginia, especially on Regal Drive where Judge Chancey and his young wife lived. On each side of the divided avenue large mansions sat far back from the road, protected by walls and perfectly trimmed hedges near the street. One could get a full view of each mansion only where the hedges parted at the elaborate gates and cobblestone driveways that led to them. In between the driveways, the only structures visible were slate roofs and towering brick chimneys, the latter being the status symbol du jour. Here, wealth was measured by the quantity and quality of a mansion's chimneys and anything less than four was pedestrian at best.

On this street lived those who were more fortunate than most. There were a few doctors, a few lawyers, a real estate mogul, a hotelier, a guy who owned almost all the car dealerships in town and, of course, one judge who could only muster up three chimneys, none of which were as architecturally ornate as his neighbors'.

Judge Chancey turned his car into the driveway, drove up the hill and took the circle leading to the front of his house. He recognized the old pickup with the ladder rack parked in front and blocking his way.

Stopping his car behind the pickup, the judge stepped out and slowly walked by it, tapping the rear quarter panel as he passed, then glancing at the faded paint on the door that read, "Old Dominion Construction." Underneath the red letters there were smaller ones in italics that read, "We do it all – no job too big or small."

Apparently my job is too big, he thought. Jim from OD Construction had been working at the house on and off for over a month. He was supposed to build a wine cellar and install a security system, but so far he wasn't making much progress on either project. The wine cellar had been framed and electrical installed but that was about it. Jim had claimed that the brick makers were back ordered and slowing him down. As for the security system, Jim said he had to send back the master controller because it was faulty.

The door of the truck should read, "No excuse too big or small," he thought as he entered his front door and called out, "Hello, I'm home."

No answer. He glanced at his watch. It was 12:10 p.m., the exact time it said every day that he came home for lunch. He took off his hat and hung it on the rack next to the door before stepping into the kitchen, which was just off the foyer to his right. There was a toppled bag of groceries on the kitchen island.

"Hello? Torey?" he called out again. Still no answer.

He wasn't too surprised that lunch wasn't ready. Torey had been hit or miss lately, but mostly miss. Just like Jim, she had her excuses too. "My tennis lesson ran over . . . our ladies' lunch ran late . . . it was the only time I could get my hair done . . ."

He walked through the kitchen and saw the side door to the garage cracked open. Just then, Torey pushed the door open carrying two more bags of groceries.

"Hello," he said, grabbing one of the bags from her arms.

"Oh, thanks," she said. "You're home early."

He glanced at his watch again. "No, same time every day."

"It's after 12 already?"

"What's for lunch?" he asked, ignoring her feigned surprise.

"How about a bologna sandwich?" she asked.

He shrugged. "I guess that's fine. Where's Jim?"

"I don't know, I suppose either upstairs or in the basement." She brushed past him and set her grocery bag on the counter.

No kiss, no hug . . . nothing. Times had definitely changed since their marriage five years earlier. Back then lunch not only included a kiss, but activity in the bedroom as well; or the foyer, or the living room—wherever she met him when he got home.

He stared at her as she placed items in the fridge. Still in her thirties, she was over two decades younger than he and as spunky and fit as the day he had met her—no doubt due to playing tennis just about every day and working out with a personal trainer three times a week.

His friends had the usual questions when they started dating, mostly fueled by jealousy he figured. Deep down not a one of them would've passed up a chance to be with her if they could've. Then when they announced the marriage, his closer friends tried to talk him out of it. They all thought it was too soon after Agnes had died in the car accident. But for him, the timing was just right. If it wasn't for Torey he would've spiraled into a deep depression. She brought new energy and purpose into his life, like nothing he had ever felt before.

His eyes dropped to her tanned, firm legs, but then he heard footsteps and saw Jim appear in the foyer.

"I thought I heard someone up here. How are you sir?"

"I'm fine and yourself?" he set his grocery bag down on the counter. "You get the brick yet?"

"Yep, should be delivered this afternoon. I was just getting things ready in the cellar."

"How about the security system?"

"Still waiting on that master controller. I called this morning and they said it's on back order. They have no idea when it will be shipped."

Torey continued to load groceries into the fridge, ignoring their conversation.

"I see you installed the camera over the front door at least."

"Yeah, but it ain't gonna work until the controller gets here. You still want the other camera installed over the garage doors?"

"That's right."

"I'll try to get to that later today before the brick comes. Right now, I need to run down to the city office and pick up some permits."

"And you're coming back?"

"Yes, sir, I'll definitely be back. I'd like to get some brick laid before the end of the day."

"Sounds good, maybe we'll see you later," the judge began unloading his bag of groceries.

"Ok then, see you later," Jim turned and exited the front door, closing it behind him.

"He been here all morning?"

"I don't know, he wasn't here when I left about two hours ago," she shut the fridge and began making him a sandwich.

"That could probably wait, if you know what I mean," he reached around her and squeezed her lightly. He felt her flinch under his arms.

"It's that time of the month," she said without hesitation.

He knew it was a lie. But he didn't push it.

"Fine," he said, taking a seat at the island counter. "Can you at least toast the bread?"

"Whatever you want," she shrugged.

When she was done making his sandwich, she turned and plopped the plate in front of him. "I've got to change."

"Thanks," he nodded. He took a big bite of the sandwich and watched her turn the corner in the foyer to go upstairs. Things were far from what they used to be, he thought as he chewed on his bologna. Very far.

When he had finished, he rinsed his plate and set it in the sink. "Goodbye," he yelled up the stairs as he put on his hat and opened the front door. He paused, waiting for a response, but received none. "I love you too," he added, stepping out and closing the door behind him.

CHAPTER THREE

At 8:53 a.m., Friday morning, Nolan Getty opened the door to the Big Shanty Circuit Court and strolled down the center aisle between the seating areas, both sides of which were filled to capacity. Most everyone turned their heads and whispered to each other as he passed. Nolan could hear the whispers but could only make out a few words.

He's the lawyer.

There's his lawyer.

Nolan Getty.

The reporters in the first row nodded at him as he pushed through the swinging gates at the front of the courtroom. He returned the courtesy, nodding to both sides of the gallery.

The deputy in the corner pointed to the side door that led to the holding cells behind the courtroom. "You ready for him?" he half whispered.

Nolan nodded in the affirmative and the deputy keyed the microphone on his lapel, giving orders for the other deputies to bring out the defendant. A moment later the magnetic lock clicked and the door opened.

A black man in orange coveralls appeared in the doorway. The deputy pointed to the defense table and the man followed his direction, sweeping his eyes until they landed on Nolan. He smiled and walked without the deputy's assistance to the table. Nolan stood up and held out his hand to shake but the inmate ignored it and instead, wrapped his arms around him in a bear hug, practically lifting Nolan off the floor.

Nolan chuckled. "Easy there fella, I like my ribs."

"What a day," the orange clad defendant released his strong hold and patted Nolan on both shoulders. "God bless you, Mr. Getty. Praise the Lord!"

"No problem, have a seat," Nolan gestured to the chair beside him.

The defendant glanced at the prosecutor's desk before taking his seat but obviously, he didn't recognize the faces.

"Where's the son of a bitch that put me away?" he whispered in Nolan's ear.

"John Keene was run out of office a few years ago. That guy right there is the assistant of his replacement."

"Fucking weasel. How about the judge? Will it be the same judge?"

"Yep, the one and only," Nolan answered. "Just keep yourself calm though. In less than an hour you'll be out of those coveralls and sipping a malted beverage if everything goes well."

The defendant smiled. "Don't worry about me."

William "Willy" Bisbaine had spent eight hard years in Virginia's Stanton Penitentiary for a crime he did not commit. He was now 28 years old but looked much older than that, no doubt due to the steady diet of cigarettes, breaded chicken patties, and the constant stress of jail house justice. Nolan knew they had to be hard years for the simple fact of the crime—the rape of a 13-year-old girl. Nolan wondered how many attempts had been made on his life; how many gang beatings he had to endure; how many days he had to spend in solitary confinement for his own safety. He knew for sure that he had taken a shiv to the belly two years ago, but luckily he survived. After all that it was a miracle he still had a glimmer of humanity in him.

"All rise!" the deputy barked. "Big Shanty Circuit Court is now in session with the Honorable Yancy L. Chancey, III presiding."

Nolan had the same question every time they announced the judge's name—what kind of parents would name their son Yancy Chancey? And then what kind of parents would do it again? And again? Would the madness ever end?

Judge Chancey stepped into view from the doorway behind the elevated judge's bench, quickly surveyed the courtroom, then took his seat on the throne of justice.

"Be seated," the deputy finished.

The clerk handed the judge a file and stated in a loud voice, "William Horatio Bisbaine."

Judge Chancey took the file and donned his reading glasses.

"Well, this one has been going on awhile and I've read through the motions from both the prosecutor and defense so I know all the details. But for the record, I'd like to hear from the horse's mouth. What say you, Mr. Daniels?"

The Assistant Commonwealth's attorney stood up and read from his notes.

"Your Honor, as you've read, this is a motion for habeas corpus brought by the defense which we originally objected to . . . but now we are formally withdrawing our objection based on the DNA evidence which the defense discovered and which was subsequently analyzed by the State lab. We agree that the evidence absolves the defendant from any culpability in this case and inculpates another party who has since deceased."

"So, for the record, the Commonwealth's Attorney's office is asking this court to order the defendant to be freed from incarceration, correct?" Judge Chancey looked over his reading glasses.

"That's correct, sir."

"You have anything before I make my ruling?" Judge Chancey turned to Nolan.

"Well, yes sir," Nolan stood up. "We would like the court to make it clear in its order that Mr. Bisbaine is innocent of all charges and that they be dismissed with prejudice."

"Very well, Mr. Getty." Judge Chancey removed his reading glasses. "Stand up, Mr. Bisbaine," he ordered.

Willy stood up and held his hands behind his back. "Yes sir."

"Mr. Bisbaine, this court hereby finds you completely innocent of the charges you were convicted of and I am dismissing them with prejudice. That means that you are a free man and have no further obligation to the Commonwealth."

A collective hoorah came from the gallery, which prompted Judge Chancey to hammer his gavel. "Order in this court!" he yelled. The onlookers quickly fell silent.

"This isn't some peanut gallery where you can just yell out like a bunch of animals," he reprimanded the crowd. "Any more outbursts and you'll be held in contempt."

He glared at the crowd, waiting for someone to challenge him. But nobody did.

"Excuse me, Mr. Bisbaine," he turned to the defendant. "Just one more thing. There is nothing I can do to change what's happened to you. There are no words this court can say to repair the wrong you've suffered. But just the same, on behalf of the Commonwealth of Virginia, I would like to offer you an apology for your wrongful conviction and incarceration. And it is my duty to inform you that there is compensation available for you through our Commonwealth. You have the right to hire an attorney to help you obtain this compensation and I would suggest that you do. That said, do you have any questions for this court?"

Willy shifted in his shoes and cleared his throat. "Yes sir. Back when I went to trial, eight years, one month and three days ago, I sat up there in the witness stand beside you and told you that I was innocent. And then my attorney had that bus driver get on the stand and tell you that he saw the man who did it, and it wasn't me. But you ignored all that and decided that one little old white lady who couldn't see a thing was right and we were wrong. So, I've always wanted to know . . . are you a racist or are you just a bad judge of character?"

Nolan visibly winced and turned to his client. "All right now, take it easy."

"That's it. Deputy, you can process him out," Judge Chancey ignored Willy's question. "What's the next case?" he turned to the clerk.

CHAPTER FOUR

Jim was laying brick in the basement when he heard Torey come home from her workout. He heard the floor creaking on the other side of the basement—she was in the kitchen. He set his trowel down and listened, hoping he would hear her at the top of the stairs, coming to see him. After a minute he heard her enter the foyer above him. Was she going to come down? Silence. She knew he was here—his truck was in the driveway and he purposely left the basement door open. He was about to yell out, but then her steps faded away to the second floor.

She was driving him nuts. He couldn't even concentrate on his work anymore. All he could think about was how she rejected him the last two days in a row. He had approached her in the kitchen, just like the other times, but then she refused to play. And she didn't even give him an excuse, just "Please don't," and "Stop it, Jim."

Did I do something wrong? Why is she doing this to me?

Like many men before him, Jim was suffering from *I can't have her, so I want her more* syndrome. He didn't know it but this was a common symptom of those who had shared their body fluids with Torey Chancey. Like Jim, most men thought it was love. But they were mistaken, because love is a two-way street and Torey's street was definitely a dead end . . . with a suicide curve and a sheer rock cliff that led to certain destruction for those who attempted to conquer it.

Jim's brick laying was on autopilot because his thoughts were far away from the mortar and trowel at hand. One by one, he put bricks down without even knowing what he was doing. In his mind he was staggering through an obsessive fog in search of the secret to Torey's desire.

I can play her game. She wants to play hard to get, so I'll give her a taste of her own medicine. To hell with her. I can have anyone I want. I don't need her.

But as much as he tried, he couldn't shake the thought of being with her and the pleasure it brought. He knew she was probably up in her bedroom at that very second—probably naked and getting into a shower. He imagined himself going up there . . . waiting for her to step out.

His thoughts were interrupted by the squeak of a board at the top of the basement steps. He paused. "Hello?" he called out.

No answer. Was he hearing things? He dropped his trowel and stood up, dusting the mortar off his apron. "Hello?" he called again as he walked to the foot of the stairs.

Nothing.

Screw it. I can't take it anymore.

Jim untied his apron and threw it to the side, then stomped up the stairs intending to confront her . . . ask her what was wrong . . . just do anything that would bring her back to him.

He pushed open the door at the top of the steps with the intention of storming the staircase to the second level, but his plans were abandoned the second he stepped into the foyer.

She nearly knocked him over when she jumped onto him and wrapped her legs around his waist, squeezing her arms around his neck. He stumbled backward, then caught his balance. She was completely naked.

"'Bout time you came up here, stud. I thought I'd have to come get you," she bit his ear as she whispered.

Jim smiled. All was good again. That feeling that he thought was love cascaded over him. He carried her into the living room and they fell onto the large stuffed sofa.

"I love you," he couldn't stop himself from saying it. "I really love you," he repeated, kissing her neck and caressing her hair.

He didn't see her eyes roll when she whispered, "Don't talk, just take me."

But it wasn't that easy. He needed answers about the direction they were heading.

"How long are we going to go on like this?" he pulled away from her, staring into her eyes. "I can't take this sneaking around anymore. I need you all the time . . . not just here and there when he's not looking."

She sighed, pushing him off and sitting up on the couch. "Well, I guess *that* moment's over. I told you it's not that simple. You think he's just going to watch me leave and not do anything about it?"

"What can he do?"

"He'll fucking kill me . . . and you. That's what he'll do!"

Jim laughed. "He's not going to kill anybody."

"You don't know how psycho he is. You have no idea the things he's told me and he's told me that stuff all the time. 'Don't ever screw around on me or I'll kill you and anybody you're with.' Those are his exact words . . . and he means it."

Jim shook his head. "There's no way. He wouldn't risk everything he has—his life, his career, his fat pension. It's all a big bluff to keep you under his thumb."

"It's not!" she raised her voice. "Don't you see? He wouldn't be risking anything. He would make sure he never got caught. He knows the system. He knows how to manipulate the whole fucking system."

"What if I just take you away? He'll never find us—I'll make sure of that."

Torey's smile was condescending, as if she was amused at his suggestion. "And what would we live on? Water and crackers?"

"I'll start a business in another town. Hell, we'll go across the country, maybe out west or up north. There are plenty of jobs in the oil towns. I heard they've got more jobs than workers in North Dakota. We could go there and he'd never find us . . ."

Torey laughed out loud, cutting him off. "I'm not going to live in some ratty little trailer on the prairie, Jim. I'm a Southern Belle, not a farm girl." She stood up and walked towards the foyer.

Jim stared at her swaying body. "Don't go," he begged.

She stopped at the foot of the stairs. "We need a better plan, Jim. And until we think of one, nothing's going to change. But right now you need to get back to the basement cuz he'll be home soon."

As she dashed up the stairs, Jim glanced at his watch and then quickly headed for the basement door.

CHAPTER FIVE

Judge Chancey returned home for lunch that day at his usual time. Torey answered his greeting from the second floor. "Lunch is in the kitchen."

He glanced at the basement door which was slightly open. He knew Jim was down there because his pickup was parked out front again. He thought about checking on his progress but his growling stomach told him to wait until after he had eaten.

After taking his hat off he entered the kitchen and found what Torey claimed was lunch—a peanut butter and jelly sandwich on a paper towel and a sleeve of salted crackers beside it. His shoulders visibly sank as he shuffled ahead and sat down on the island stool. It's come to this, he thought, as he sat and stared at the pitiful display before him.

To anyone else it was a peanut butter and jelly sandwich, but to him it represented so much more. This was the symbol of his declining marriage and growing obsolescence to the one he loved. And there it sat, taunting him in smug silence, knowing it would be eaten and swallowed despite all that it represented.

"To hell with you," the judge breathed, lifting his fist and dropping it down as hard as he could, smashing the bread. Trembling with anger and perhaps self-pity, he hit it again and again until it was smashed into a pulp. Then he stepped over to the sink, wound up his arm and violently threw the pieces into the hole. He flipped the switch to the sink grinder and watched the pieces gurgle down.

When it was gone he returned to his stool and rubbed his face with his hands. I can't do this anymore, he thought. Why can't things just be like they were? His life had been perfect only a few years ago and he couldn't understand how things could spoil in such little time.

Eventually he stopped trembling and regained control of his emotions. As an afterthought he opened the sleeve of crackers and began munching on one in an attempt to calm his churning stomach. As he munched he heard Torey's footsteps on the stairs.

"Hello," she barely glanced at him as she entered the kitchen and went to the fridge. She was still wearing her workout pants and sport top.

"Hello," he answered. He watched as she retrieved a bottle of water from the top shelf, unscrewed the top and took a sip.

"How's your day going?" he asked.

"Good. And yours?" she stared at the screen of her cell phone as she responded.

"Not well. I can't seem to get that Bisbaine kid off my mind."

"Who's he?" she asked.

"I told you about him. He's the kid that I wrongly convicted."

"Oh. What can you do? What's done is done." Her tone was ambivalent at best, as if he had just given her a weather report.

"I'd like to send him some money. You know, get him on his feet until he can get a settlement from the State."

"Un-fucking believable," she stared at her cell.

At first he thought she was referring to something on her screen but then she looked up.

"I can't get a new car because we can't afford it. But now suddenly we just have piles of money to give to complete fucking strangers. You're kidding me, right?"

He knew she wouldn't like the idea but he threw it out there anyway. "I put him away for eight years. I think I should do something."

"Not one fucking dime," she wagged her finger, "unless I have the keys to a new car in my hand."

He didn't understand how and why she had changed so much in five years. She was never that selfish before. In fact, she used to be grateful for all the things he let her buy and do. Now she had reached the stage of entitlement. She demanded all the things that were once considered gifts—clothes, cars, jewelry, personal training, and trips. But it was never enough—she always needed more.

"I'll see what I can do," he relented. "If you promise me one thing."

"What's that?" she put a hand on her hip.

"Be happy," he smiled. "I just want you to be happy. But I don't think you are."

Her furrowed eyebrows relaxed and she smiled as she approached.

"I'm happy," she was telling the truth. Unfortunately, the reason for her happiness had little to do with the judge.

She wrapped her arms around his neck and threw a leg over his lap, straddling him on the stool. "Is my judgey wudgey feeling neglected?" she cooed in a baby voice. "Maybe Torey can fix judgey wudgey," she kissed him on the lips, but only briefly. Then her voice switched to a more seductive tone as she whispered in his ear. "If I can have the car, I'll make it worth your while," she ran her fingers through his thinning gray hair. "I'll do anything you want me to." She kissed his neck and nibbled on his ear. "You know, I still have that nurse uniform. And I think you're long overdue for a thorough examination."

For one fleeting moment the judge was taken back to the early days of his marriage—those wonderful, intoxicating days of spontaneous love. In that second, he went from emotional life support to exhilaration, as if she had slammed a syringe full of adrenalin directly into his heart.

And so it happened. Like all the men before him . . . men that were far stronger than him, the old judge did not have a chance at overcoming the power of God's greatest invention . . . the female anatomical purse. For untold centuries it had been taking on all who attempted to conquer it. From kings and noblemen, to farmers and peasants, it felled them all with indiscriminate force. And once again . . . it remained undefeated.

"I have to check the price on some stock," he stammered, willing to do anything to keep the feeling alive. "It might be possible."

"That's my judgey wudgey," she pinched his cheek. With that she gave his crotch a quick squeeze and hopped off his lap. "Gotta go," she said in a cheery voice.

"I thought you were done working out for the day," he protested.

"Golf lessons," she offered over her shoulder, "and Thad hates it when I'm late."

CHAPTER SIX

Torey Chancey stood at the window in the kitchen, watching and waiting for Jim's truck to arrive. She had already prepped her neck with blush, tussled her hair, and gave her shirt a slight tear at the collar. It was obvious that Jim needed a kick-start. He was cute, but not too bright.

When the truck pulled into the driveway she ran to the foyer and up the stairs to the top step. She quickly sat down and mustered up all the strength she could before winding up her arm and slapping her own face. Then she buried her face in her hands and began sobbing as Jim opened the front door.

"Hello!" he yelled as the front door shut behind him. "Torey? Are you all right?"

She shuddered her shoulders with her face buried in her lap.

"Torey!" he yelled again, bounding up the steps.

Just as he reached her she lifted her head. "Oh, Jim," she cried. "Thank God you're here," she lunged at him, falling into his arms.

He held on to her for a moment then leaned back and looked at her face. The side of it was bright pink, her shirt was torn and she had marks on her neck.

"What the hell happened?" he asked.

She buried her head into his chest and sobbed. "I thought he was going to kill me."

Jim's temper immediately flared. "The judge did this?"

"He was so angry; I've never seen him like that before."

"Why?" Jim pressed, holding her and rubbing her back. He noticed a broken vase on the floor near the landing.

"Because I wouldn't have sex with him," she stuttered between sobs.

"That son of a bitch!" Jim raised his voice. "I'll knock his teeth down his throat."

"Please, no," she objected. "Don't make it worse than it is. I'll be fine," she released her grip and stood up. Wiping her tears away, she began picking up the pieces of the broken vase. "I just need to clean this up."

Jim pulled out his cell. "Well, I'm calling the police."

"No!" she yelled, turning and swiping the phone from his hand before he could react. "We can't get the police involved."

"Why not? He just assaulted you! We can bring him down. Now's our chance."

"What are they going to do? Maybe give him a slap on the wrist, maybe even a night in jail. Then they'll kick him off the bench and then what? How do you think he'll take that, Jim? He'll come back and finish me off. He'll fucking kill me!" she screamed.

Jim shook his head. "You can't live like this. *We* can't live like this. Something has to be done."

"I wish that son of a bitch would just die of a heart attack or something," Torey returned to her task of picking up the glass. "That's the only way I'll get out of this alive."

Jim clenched his fists. He couldn't stand seeing her this way . . . beaten and disheveled. More than anything his honor was at stake. He was supposed to be her protector, but so far, he was failing. How was he going to convince her that he could handle the job if he let this go? No, this could not be tolerated . . . not for a second more.

"I'll kill him," Jim blurted out. "If that's what has to be done to save you then that's what I'll do."

She gave him a quick smile. "Oh Jim, don't even talk like that. I know you mean well, but let's face it, you're just a construction worker, not some knight in shining armor."

Her tone was slightly berating which added to Jim's resolve.

"You don't think I would kill for you?"

She shook her head. "Just stop it Jim, the idea's absurd. I don't even want to hear you say such things."

"Just answer my question. You don't think I would kill for you, do you?"

"I think you love me enough to *think* you could and that's good enough for me."

"You're wrong, Torey. I'd kill him in a second if I thought I could get away with it and be with you."

With that, the seed had been planted, which wasn't as difficult as she thought it would be. Even more difficult would be the cultivation of that seed with just the right amount of passion to make it blossom into action. After all, she already had the plan, now she just needed to convince Jim that it was his idea all along.

CHAPTER SEVEN

Judge Chancey slapped the snooze on his alarm clock and rolled over, reaching out for his wife in the predawn hour. But the bed was empty. Picking himself up on one elbow, he looked around, thinking that she had gone to the bathroom but it was dark and empty.

That's strange. She always sleeps in.

The judge folded back the covers and reached for his robe on the bathroom door. As he stepped into the corridor he heard a noise from the kitchen and saw the light from the kitchen shining into the foyer at the bottom of the stairs.

What in the world is she doing up so early?

Just then he smelled the aroma of freshly brewed coffee and bacon wafting in the air.

Is this a dream? She hasn't cooked breakfast for me in two years.

He stepped lightly down the stairs, not wanting to reveal his presence. At the bottom he poked his head around the corner and saw her working over the stove. Stepping into the light, he greeted her. "Good morning, what are you doing up so early?"

"Good morning," she smiled. "I just thought it's been too long since I've made you breakfast, so here I am . . . making you breakfast."

"Wow, that's quite a surprise."

"Sit down, let me get you some coffee," she went to the cupboard and retrieved a cup.

Stunned, the judge obeyed her and sat down on the stool at the island. He watched her pour the coffee in disbelief.

"Here you go . . . this should get you going."

"Thank you," he lifted the cup and sipped from it. "That's good."

"It'll be a few minutes for the bacon. Why don't you go take a shower and I'll have it ready when you're done."

"That'll work for me," the judge smiled.

"And I have another surprise for you."

"What's that?"

"Take your shower, I'll let you know when you come back down," she leaned over and kissed him on the cheek.

Still in a state of shock, the judge did what she asked. She almost seems normal again, he thought as he ascended the stairs. Was it the promise of a new car? That's the only thing that had changed since the other day. Was she really that shallow that her entire personality would change because of a new car? Whatever the reason, he didn't care that much. He just knew that he liked the change . . . change was good. Her gesture of good will with breakfast was a complete turnaround from how she had been treating him so he wasn't about to complain.

Filled with new spirit the judge took his shower and actually whistled a tune while doing it. As was his mantra, he soaped his face and rinsed. Then he cleaned the rest of his body, scrubbing under his armpits and his crotch. When his body was clean he shampooed his hair.

When he had finished he toweled off and inspected himself in the mirror; first standing at a profile and sucking in his stomach while glancing out of the corner of his eye, then fronting the mirror and holding his chin high to hide the flabby pouch beneath it.

Not bad for almost 60. You still got it!

After he shaved he put on his favorite suit and readied himself for the day. By the time he was done the sun was up and shining brightly. What a beautiful day, he thought as he descended the stairs with a little more bounce in his step than usual.

Torey was just setting his plate down when he entered the kitchen.

"That looks wonderful," he rubbed his hands. "And the breakfast doesn't look too bad either," he said as he put his arms around her and gave her a kiss.

"Oh, thanks," she gave him a peck back.

He hesitated, then slipped his hand inside her robe.

"Hey now, you better not let your breakfast get cold," she pushed his hand away and guided him to the stool.

The judge didn't protest, partly because he was hungry but mostly because he just wanted to keep her happy. He sat down and took a bite of the bacon first, followed by a sip of coffee, then a bite of toast.

"What's this about a surprise?" he asked through his mouthful of food.

"Well," Torey sat down at the island with her cup of coffee. "I've been thinking about the other day. You know . . . when I told you we shouldn't give that boy money because I didn't have a new car."

"Yeah?" the judge's curiosity grew.

"Well," she continued, "I just realized in the last few days how utterly selfish that was of me."

"You just realized?" the judge asked. "And how did you come to realize that?"

"Look, I'm sorry I haven't been acting myself lately. I think it's hormones or something. I just know that what I said was wrong and how I've been acting is wrong too. So, I wanted to make it up to you."

"Thank you," he said, pointing at his plate with the piece of toast. "This is good."

"It gets better," she smiled. "It took me all day yesterday but I finally got a hold of him."

"Who?" the judge asked, confused.

"The boy . . . well, I guess he's a man now, but you know, William Bisbaine."

"Bisbaine?" Now the judge was bewildered. "What do you mean you got a hold of him?"

"I called him on the phone and talked to him. He's really a nice person."

"You talked to him?" the judge set down his coffee. "What do you mean you talked to him? Why?"

"Because of what you had told me. You wanted to give him money, right?"

"Yeah, but I didn't want my wife involved in it. What are you thinking? What exactly did you do?" The judge didn't like the sound of anything she was saying. He couldn't believe she had called

Bisbaine, a man who seemed to be carrying a grudge against him based on his comments in the courtroom.

She looked at the clock. "I told him to come over this morning and that you wanted to give him some money."

The fork dropped from the judge's hand. "Are you out of your mind? What's wrong with you? You told him to come here? To our house?"

She visibly recoiled. "But . . . but, I thought that's what you wanted. How else are we supposed to give him money?"

"The damned mail!" the judge screamed and stood up. "You put it in an envelope and send it to him! You don't invite him to our house and let him know where we live! Do you have any idea what kind of person he is? No, you don't," he answered his own question. "What if he wants to hurt me for what I did? Or something even worse? Did you ever think of that?"

Torey blinked her eyes as the tears welled up. "I'm sorry . . . I . . . I was just trying to make you happy," she stuttered, then she buried her face in her hands and ran from the kitchen into the living room.

Son of a bitch! I can't believe this, the judge thought as he watched her go.

"Torey!" he called her name and followed. "Torey, it's okay. I'm sorry. Everything will be all right." He watched as she flung herself onto the sofa and buried her head into the pillows, crying.

"I'm sorry, Torey," he repeated as he sat down on the edge of the sofa. "I didn't mean to yell."

Her voice muffled, he could barely make out the words. "All I wanted was to make you happy, that's it. That's all I wanted."

"Oh, honey," the judge melted. "I'm very sorry." He bent over and held her tightly. "I know. Your heart was in the right place. It's okay. I just overreacted. Everything will be fine."

She was cute, but not too bright, the judge thought.

"You think?" she showed her face. "What if you're right? What if he is a psycho?"

"No, I'm sure he's fine. After all, he's an innocent man. Why would he want to jeopardize his freedom at this point?"

Torey sniffled. "The money's in an envelope in the kitchen."

"How much?" the judge asked.

"$2,500."

The judge flinched, but held back his emotions. He was thinking more like $500.

"When is he supposed to be coming?"

Before she could answer, the doorbell rang.

"Right now," she said sheepishly.

Judge Chancey snapped his head towards the door. Before he was a judge he had been a lawyer and the combination of the two careers had trained him to keep a clear head under pressure. He stood up and pulled Torey to her feet. "Go upstairs," he ordered. "If anything funny happens call 911."

Torey did as she was told, quickly running up the stairs while the judge retrieved the envelope from the kitchen. He quickly opened the envelope, counted out $1,000, then stuffed the bills into his pocket. After sealing the envelope he returned to the foyer, straightened his tie, then opened the door.

And there was Bisbaine standing on his porch. In his mind, the judge expected to see him in orange coveralls, probably because it was the only way he had seen him over the years. But he wasn't, and the judge was slightly irritated at himself for the brain hiccup. Instead, Mr. Bisbaine was dressed in blue jeans and a tight, sleeveless t-shirt. The ex-convict was about the same height as the judge but his chest and arms were much bigger, no doubt the product of eight years of weight training and a high carb, jailhouse diet. Those arms were filled with tattoos as well—crude carvings in ink that made Bisbaine look like a hardened criminal.

"Mr. Bisbaine," the judge tried to remain cool. "Thank you for coming over," he held out his hand and Bisbaine shook it.

"Please, come in," the judge waved to the open front door. The last thing he wanted to do was show fear or weakness, both of which he was actually experiencing. On the other hand, if he feigned confidence and power then he knew he would have a chance at remaining in control.

Bisbaine nervously glanced in both directions but didn't move. "Ah, well, I wasn't meaning to stay."

His demeanor boosted the judge's confidence. "No, no. I insist. Please, come in." The judge placed his hand on his shoulder, gently guiding him to the door.

"Ah, well, okay, I guess I have a few minutes," he lowered his head and stepped into the house. "Thank you, sir."

The judge closed the door behind him. "Have a seat," he waved to the winged back chair in the living room just off the foyer. "Can I get you something to drink?"

"No thank you," Bisbaine smiled. "That's very nice of you." He shuffled into the living room and gently lowered himself into the chair. The judge watched as his eyes surveyed the room and the staircase leading to the second floor. "Nice digs," Bisbaine added, patting the arms of the chair.

The judge took a seat in the other chair. "I'm glad my wife was finally able to contact you. I've had her trying to find you since the hearing," he lied. "Did she tell you why I wanted to see you?"

"Uh, yeah, something about money."

"Well, there is that. But I wanted to talk to you as well. I can't tell you how sorry I am for what's happened to you. And I can't blame you for what you said at the hearing. I would've had the same questions."

Bisbaine shrugged. "I ain't that mad."

"You probably think I'm a racist but I can assure you I am not. I screwed up plain and simple. And now I have to live with that mistake for the rest of my life."

"I'm sure you'll get over it," Bisbaine scanned the room again, admiring the nice things that filled it. "I ain't gonna sweat it no more though. I've been blessed by the Lord and all the shit that's happened to me is just part of his big plan. He's gonna see to it that things work out for me in the end . . . and you," he added.

The judge shifted in his chair. "Well, like I said at the hearing, I'm sure you're going to get a very nice settlement from the state but I wanted to offer you something in the meantime," the judge pulled the envelope from his breast pocket and handed it across the table.

Bisbaine took it without hesitation.

The judge was hoping that he would leave without opening it but no such luck. Bisbaine tore open the envelope and counted the money inside.

"Well," he started to say something as he stared at the envelope, but then stopped.

The judge studied him to gauge his response—hoping that the ex-prisoner wouldn't do anything irrational. "I know it's not a lot. I was just hoping it could get you by for a little while," he tried to explain.

"Uh . . ." Bisbaine stuttered, then finally looked up. His eyes had welled up with tears. "God bless you sir. Praise the Lord."

Judge Chancey smiled. This was going a lot better than he had hoped. And then he remembered the $1,000 that he had pocketed, which made him feel less than noble. Attempting to ease his conscience the judge added, "And I want you to know if that doesn't get you through, I can always give you some more."

He watched Bisbaine turn his head away and stare. At first, the judge just thought he was looking for words to say but then he realized that he was transfixed on something near the staircase. The judge turned to see Torey slowly coming down the stairs as if she was a contestant in a beauty pageant.

Damn it.

She was wearing pink shorts and a black tube top with her hair pulled up in a pony-tail. "There he is," she called out. "Honey, why didn't you let me know he was here?"

Bisbaine stood as she approached. The judge followed his lead but was momentarily distracted by her shorts. They rode high, tight and snug, leaving nothing to the imagination as to what lay underneath.

"Um, Mr. Bisbaine, this is my wife, Torey," he stammered.

Bisbaine reached out his hand to shake hers but she stepped through it, opening her arms and giving him a hug.

And he hugged back.

"Oh, you poor thing," she cooed. "We're so glad you're free."

The judge noticed the flabbergasted look on Bisbaine's face.

Finally, she released him and turned to the judge. "Now what kind of host are you . . . did you offer him a cup of coffee?"

"Yes," the judge nodded.

"I'm good, ma'am," Bisbaine confirmed.

"Oh nonsense, I'll be right back," she turned and stepped towards the kitchen. "Cream and sugar?"

Bisbaine glanced at the judge who simply shrugged his shoulders.

"Yes ma'am, please."

The two men sat back down. "As you can tell," the judge offered, "she's got a big heart."

"Yes sir," Bisbaine nodded.

Within a minute, which was mostly filled with awkward silence, Torey returned with a tray and cups filled with coffee. She served Bisbaine first, then the judge before sitting on the sofa opposite the chairs and pouring her own.

"Well now, that's better," she perched herself on the edge of the sofa. "So tell me about yourself, Mr. Bisbaine. Do you have family?"

"Oh yes ma'am," he smiled. "There's me and my four sisters, and my Mom."

"Oh, that's wonderful. You're not the baby are you?"

To the judge the suggestion seemed ridiculous, mostly because the man sitting in their living room had large biceps covered in crude tattoos.

Bisbaine grinned, "Yes ma'am, I am."

"They must be so happy to have their baby back," Torey smiled. "I know I would be."

For the next ten minutes Torey hammered him with small talk, asking inane questions and getting the same in response. They talked about his family, where he went to school, if he knew this person or that person, and what his plans would be. Bisbaine was polite and all, but the judge noticed his eyes fall down several times, obviously stealing glances at his wife's surgically enhanced breasts. But who could blame him? Eight years was a very long time and now here he was sitting before a hot blonde in a tight top with a set of high beams who seemed interested in every little detail about his life. And even though he understood, the whole situation was beginning to annoy him.

"Now honey," I'm sure Mr. Bisbaine has better things to do than get his ears talked off, perhaps we should let him get on with his day," the judge stood up and straightened out his suit coat.

"Yes sir, I better get going," Bisbaine stood.

Torey raised an eyebrow at the judge. "Well, did you give him the $2,500?"

Damn it!

A surge of anxiety swept through the judge as he closed his eyes for a moment before turning to Bisbaine, knowing full well that he had counted the money.

"Ah, well . . ." the judge stammered. He was accustomed to thinking on his toes but there was no way out of this one.

"Yes," Bisbaine let him off the hook. "He gave me the money."

Bisbaine stared at him a few seconds. There was no anger behind his eyes . . . no contempt whatsoever . . . just a knowing stare of disappointment, as if he expected no less from the man who had put him away.

Unable to move or speak, the judge simply watched as Torey ushered him to the door.

"Good luck to you, Mr. Bisbaine," she said as she opened the door.

Bisbaine stepped onto the porch and turned. "Thank you again, Mrs. Chancey," he smiled and bowed his head.

"Oh, no you don't. I can't let you go without a big hug," she wrapped her arms around him and squeezed hard.

The hug was annoyingly long.

"Goodbye now," the judge waved from the living room. "Take care."

"I will," Bisbaine answered. "Praise the Lord!"

CHAPTER EIGHT

Torey Chancey wasn't good at many things. Not tennis . . . golf . . . horse riding . . . but she had taken professional lessons in them all. Yet her skills had never reached anything close to average. The problem was that she was always more focused on the lesson giver than the lesson itself. And of course, the lesson giver was always a man.

It's not that she was a sucker for every man that came into her life, rather, every man was a sucker for her because that was the one thing she was *really* good at . . . manipulating men. Obviously, she enjoyed the sex but that was just a small part of her sport. The ultimate goal was to completely dominate their mind and body. For her, there was nothing more exhilarating than breaking a man, which was not much different than a trainer breaking a horse. She looked for the powerful, the high spirited, the adventurous, and the wild ones . . . anybody who appeared unbreakable. Those were the ones that gave her the most pleasure.

She understood that part of her magic was her body and her looks. But she also knew those things alone couldn't take all the credit. Her real talent was reading men and knowing what they wanted. The way she saw it men were like pianos. All women could play them and make sound . . . usually something along the line of chopsticks. But she was different. She knew which keys to press and when. If men were pianos, she was a concert pianist, tickling the high keys and pounding the low, making them respond in a crescendo of passion.

The problem with men unlike pianos is that they were usually only good for one song. And when she mastered that song she became bored.

Her crowning achievement was Judge Chancey. Here was a man who was a pillar of the community. He was powerful, prominent and wealthy. Simply put, he was one of the biggest fish in the Big Shanty sea. It had taken her three years to master his song but now she knew it by heart and the truth be told, she was sick of playing it. So, she found a new piano that could play something different—one who was close . . . in the basement. He was younger than her and muscular, with rugged good looks. He could've been a model, but instead he was a construction worker. And it was just blind luck for her that the judge had hired him to work in their home.

She had been playing him for over a month, cautiously at first. Over time she tamed his free spirit just like the others before him. Now, she knew he was at the point where he didn't even want to glance at another woman. She knew he was consumed by her and willing to do anything to keep her. And that's how she liked it.

When she got home from her workout she stopped at the door to the basement, and changed expressions—she needed to have a frowny face when Jim saw her.

When she reached the bottom of the steps Jim saw her and immediately dropped his trowel.

"Hey there, cutie!" he beamed, coming over to her.

"Hey," she said with a frown.

Jim wrapped his arms around her and intended to give her a deep kiss but she pecked him instead.

"How are you today?" he asked, still holding her in his arms.

"I'm fine," she tried to seem not so fine and distant.

"You don't seem fine," he caught on.

"I need to ask you something . . . something real important."

"Go ahead. Anything."

"Do you really want to spend the rest of your life with me?"

Jim chuckled. "That's it? That's the big question? I think you know the answer. You know I want that more than anything."

"Are you sure?" she gave him her puppy dog eyes.

He hugged her and kissed her on the forehead. "Yes, yes. I would do anything to be with you. Leave him. Come with me. We'll start a new life."

"It's not that easy, Jim. I've told you what he would do. But I've figured out a way that we can be together . . . anywhere we want. We can live on a tropical island and drink Pina Coladas the rest of our lives and I can make love to you on the beach and we can live happily ever after . . . forever, Jim. And nobody will care."

"That sounds good to me," Jim smiled. "How we going to do that?"

"Well, it sounds bad, but," she paused, then turned her head. "Oh, Jim. I'm so crazy about you, I'm willing to do anything to be with you, but I can't hardly bring myself to even say it."

Jim grabbed her chin and turned her head to him. "What is it?"

"Will you hate me if it's bad?" her eyes glistened with tears.

"No, honey. What's your plan?"

"Well, you know, I've told you he made me sign a prenuptial agreement, so if we get divorced I get nothing. Not that he'd let me divorce him but I just want you to know that."

"Yeah, you've told me."

"Well, did I tell you he has a life insurance policy? It's for $500,000 and I'm the beneficiary."

"Wow, that's significant."

"It would be enough for us to start a new life on a tropical island anyway. Jim, do you realize that if he dies, I will get the money and all our dreams can come true?"

"Huh," Jim grunted, the wheels appearing to turn in his head. "So what are you saying . . . you're gonna kill him?"

"Ever since you said you would kill him, I haven't been able to stop thinking about it. And if I told you that I've thought of a way for it to happen and there is no possible way that we would get caught, would you be willing to help me?"

"Well, I suppose . . . probably if it was foolproof," Jim's wheels turned some more. "How would we do it?"

"This sounds bad, I know, but it would be really easy. I mean really easy. You just walk up to his bedroom on a Sunday morning and hit him on the head with something, like a hammer or tire iron. He always sleeps in so I know he'll be there. And you cover yourself from head to toe, maybe even with a ski mask, so you don't leave any hairs or anything behind. And after you kill him you take the safe out of the wall that's behind the big painting in our bedroom."

"Safe?" Jim asked. "What's in it?"

"He keeps at least $20,000 in it. And that will be enough to tide us over until the insurance money comes in."

"Why don't you just give me the combination?"

"Because then they will know it's an inside job," she replied with disappointment.

"Oh yeah, I suppose," he agreed.

"Just take a crow bar or something and break it right out of the wall, it shouldn't be too hard."

"And then what," Jim asked.

"You break into the safe when you get to your house, then bury it and everything else, like the crowbar and the clothes you wore."

"And where will you be?"

"Well, I think you should do it when I go to that fundraiser at the old train depot. I will be staying there on a Saturday night and I won't be home until sometime later the next morning."

"So you will have an alibi, huh?"

"Yeah, but so will you . . . well, at least they will never think of you."

"How's that?" Jim asked.

"Well, I've thought about it quite a bit and let's just say it's not easy, but it's something I'd be willing to do so that we could finally be together and it would guarantee that we'd never get caught."

They both heard the judge's car at the same time. "We'll talk later," she pecked him on the lips before pushing him away.

Jim watched as Torey ran up the stairs. Two minutes later he heard the judge open the front door and the floor creak as he walked to the kitchen. There were words exchanged, muffled words that Jim couldn't quite make out. Then silence, followed by more words. Then the judge raised his voice and Jim could hear his words, "I don't give a damn if he's in the basement!"

They were fighting, this much Jim could tell. Was he going to hit her again? That would be the last straw, Jim thought. If that happened, he wasn't sure he could stop himself from going up there and bashing his head in right now. He walked over to the basement steps so he could hear better.

"What's wrong with you? Just tell me!" the judge yelled.

"What's wrong with you?" Torey screamed back. "You're freaking out because I don't feel like having sex right now?"

"Having sex? You don't even call it 'making love' anymore," the judge whined. "Maybe that's what's the matter."

"I don't feel like making love right now," Torey put special emphasis on the words. "Is that better, asshole?"

"Damn you!" the judge yelled.

Jim heard the slap—like a whip cracking, then Torey screamed. As Jim bolted up the basement stairs, he could hear Torey running through the foyer and up to the second floor. He pushed open the basement door and there was the judge, putting on his hat.

Jim froze, staring at the judge. "Is everything alright?"

"Piss off," the judge replied over his shoulder as he walked out the front door.

Jim waited until the judge had driven away, then he ran up to find her.

He rushed into their bedroom and saw Torey lying face down on the bed, sobbing.

"Are you okay?" He went to her and turned her over. The side of her face was red.

"Yes, yes, I'm fine," she blubbered.

"That son of a bitch. He was out the door before I could do anything."

"That's okay," she smiled, wiping away a tear.

"Here now, sit up." Jim helped her sit up on the edge of the bed. "Tell me the rest of your plan. I'm ready to do anything to end this."

If Jim had been more observant, he would've noticed the slight reddening on the judge's cheek before he had walked out the door and he would've realized that it was Torey who had struck the judge and not the other way around. But he didn't. Like a child watching a magician, he was completely fooled by her illusion.

CHAPTER NINE

He had parked his car almost a block away from the Chancey driveway and now he was just waiting.

At ten minutes after noon he saw the judge's car turn off the main thoroughfare and come towards him. Although he knew he was far enough away that the judge couldn't see him he subconsciously slunk down in his seat. When the judge was almost a block away he made a right and turned into his driveway. He lost sight of the car briefly because of the hedges surrounding the estate, then saw it enter the circular driveway at the top of the hill near the house.

Now he could see three cars in the driveway—Torey's, the construction guy's, and the judge's. He glanced at his watch. He knew it would take patience to get her alone. He figured the judge would be home at least 30–40 minutes and that she probably wouldn't leave until after he went back to the courthouse.

What he didn't know was whether Torey would leave the house first, or the construction guy would. If the construction guy left first he would simply drive to the house and knock on the door. If she left first his plan was to intercept her. He needed to talk to her one way or the other and time was of the essence.

His peripheral vision caught motion at the house and he saw the judge's car moving around the circular driveway.

That's weird, he's only been home five minutes.

He watched and waited. A moment later the judge's car appeared at the gate, then roared and sped quickly onto Regal Drive, slightly squealing the tires.

He's in a hurry. I wonder what's going on?

It wasn't like the judge to be in such a hurry. And it certainly wasn't the judge's habit to spend only five minutes at home for lunch. No, something had happened. Had they gotten into a fight?

His thoughts drifted to Torey . . . thoughts that always landed on her stunning good looks, her smoking-hot body and her tempestuous personality. The combination of all three acted as an intoxicant to him. She was like a drug that made him feel different . . . almost euphoric. And she was as addictive as a drug too.

He had heard the stories of meth heads and how they craved the rush so much that they would do anything to get it even though it was destroying their minds and bodies. But they just kept doing it until there was nothing left of either. That's kind of how he felt about Torey, only there were no visible symptoms of his addiction . . . no sunken eyes, no missing teeth, and no atrophy. Just a rush of adrenalin in his chest and a tingly feeling in his groin.

He had that feeling the moment he had met her. The first time was at the country club when he gave her a tennis lesson. He could tell that she was attracted to him too so it didn't take many lessons for their relationship to go beyond the court. Those were exhilarating times—almost too good to be true. But it all ended when the judge caught them together.

He didn't catch them in the act, but it was close. It was so close that Torey decided to keep it cool for a while. He moved back to Mexico over the winter and when he returned, he got a job at the other country club as a tennis instructor. But the old flame didn't go out . . . it just flickered faintly for a while before turning into a blowtorch again.

Almost thirty minutes after the judge had left he saw Torey's car move in the circular driveway. He immediately jerked upright in his seat and started the engine. He threw the car into gear and sped towards the driveway. As he rushed to intercept her he saw a glimpse of her car through the hedges. This was going to be close, he thought.

Within seconds he made it to the entrance of the driveway and squealed to a stop, blocking it before she could get out. She locked up the brakes on her car just in time to prevent a collision.

He quickly opened his door and approached her.

She rolled her window down and began yelling before he could say anything.

"What the hell are you doing, Stefano?"

"We need to talk!"

"You fucking idiot! Someone could see you here!"

Stefano glanced around before leaning on her window sill. "Nobody's going to see me. I need to know what's going on. You say I can't text or email you, so how else am I supposed to know?"

"I told you! I'll come see you!"

"When?"

"When I can!"

"Will you come tomorrow?"

"Yes. I'll come tomorrow. Now get the hell out of here!"

He was about to lean in and give her a kiss but she rolled the window up, blocking his face.

"Tomorrow," he mouthed, before turning and getting into his car.

* * *

Up at the house, Jim stood at the kitchen window watching everything. He saw Torey drive down the driveway. He saw the blue car block her path. He saw what appeared to be a guy of Hispanic descent approach her window.

The encounter between them lasted only a moment but it gave him an uneasy feeling.

Who was that guy and what did he want?

CHAPTER 10

Present

Montgomery Mutz sat in his office waiting for a call from Lieutenant Childress, who was supposed to let him know what had happened at Judge Chancey's house. All he knew at this point was that police and emergency services had been dispatched at 10:14 a.m. This he knew from the police radio that sat behind him on the credenza. Luckily, he just happened to be in his office on that Sunday morning to finish up some paperwork. When he heard the dispatch he immediately called Childress, who indicated that he was on the way. But that was almost two hours ago. Why the hell hasn't he called me yet? Mutz wondered.

The old man probably had a heart attack, Mutz thought. And then he giggled to himself as he pictured Chancey huffing and puffing on top of his young, hot wife before clutching his chest and keeling over. Not a bad way to die, he thought. His imagination began to run as he pictured the judge in a variety of weird, uncompromising situations.

Mutz enjoyed his childish sexual fantasies, but they didn't come close to what had actually occurred in the judge's home just a few hours earlier.

Mutz's cell rang. It was Childress.

"Hello, what's up?"

"It's a murder," Childress said in a flat tone.

"A murder?" Mutz asked. "The judge was murdered?"

"No. It's the judge's wife."

"Oh my God. What?" Mutz couldn't believe what he had just heard.

"I said she's been murdered!"

"When? How?" Mutz stuttered, still unable to fully comprehend.

"This morning. Looks like she was probably raped before somebody bashed her head in."

"Oh my God! In their house?"

"Yeah. The judge was out jogging and found her on the kitchen floor when he got back. She had been at some fundraiser overnight down at the old train depot. It looks like she was attacked when she got back home."

"What about the Judge? Is he all right?"

"Yeah, he's shaken up quite a bit, but he's all right."

"Are you still there?"

"Yeah, been here a few hours."

"I'll be right there." Mutz ended the call. There was no need to waste time asking questions on the cell when he could learn firsthand what had happened at the scene. He grabbed his jacket and rushed to his car.

Who the hell would murder the judge's wife? Mutz thought to himself as he drove out of the parking garage into the crisp fall day.

Mutz had been Big Shanty's chief prosecutor for just over two years. At 32 years old, he was probably one of the youngest chiefs in the history of the town. That's because his rise to the top wasn't due to his legal acumen, rather, it resulted from a mistake by John Keene, the town's former prosecutor . . . a mistake that Mutz had capitalized upon.

It was the last big murder case that had gone to trial in Big Shanty. Mutz was Keene's assistant then and they were trying to put a killer behind bars for life. The only problem was that Nolan Getty pulled a fast one near the end of the trial and exposed their lead witness as a liar. The witness was indeed a liar but that didn't necessarily mean the defendant was innocent. Keene pressed on with the case and eventually pissed the whole thing down his leg, but not before physically assaulting his own witness in a conference room. And that's the mistake that Mutz needed to rise to the top. A month later, Keene had a criminal record for assault and Mutz was the new chief prosecutor.

The thought of Torey Chancey's death began to sink in as he drove through town on that Sunday morning, weaving his way through mini-vans filled with soccer moms and their kids, and old people headed to church. He had just seen her a few weeks earlier hanging on the judge's arm at a dinner for the local Police Benevolent Association. She was smoking hot and friendly as usual. He knew she had a reputation for being flirtatious but that night there seemed to be a genuine spark between them. It was nothing obvious, just the types of questions she asked, the slight wink here and there, and the lingering handshake that let him know she was a player.

He couldn't wait to get to the judge's house. Most people wouldn't enjoy this part of his job but he loved it. There was something about seeing people in death that piqued his curiosity, especially now that it was someone he knew. He wondered if she would be naked but then quickly concluded that she would. Would she be mutilated? Numerous scenarios played out in his mind as he made his way to Regal Drive, each one more gruesome than the last.

As he got closer his fantasies eventually waned and were replaced by the typical reaction of someone in his position who faced such a tragic and horrible event. Not sorrow or grief, but instead, the thought of opportunity.

Finally he would get a chance to prove himself. The last two trials he had handled himself didn't even make the front page of the paper. One was a drug dealer whom he had put away for nine and a half years. The other involved a female teacher at the high school who thought it would be okay to have sex with a 15-year-old student. He nailed her for sexual assault and now she was doing fourteen months in jail followed by at least two years of probation.

Those were the most significant cases he had handled since he had become chief prosecutor. There were other crimes and trials on a constant basis but his minions handled those. There were drug cases, child abuse, domestic assaults, DUI's, larcenies and burglaries; all very typical of a medium sized city in the south.

Big Shanty's official population was just under 62,000, but if you counted the surrounding area, it had to be around 90,000, which was just big enough to keep him and three assistant prosecutors busy every day. Murders were few and usually far between so they attracted a lot of press. This was a good thing because it meant free campaign advertising for him.

The timing of this one couldn't have been better. He would be facing his first election and he needed as much campaign support that he could get. He also knew that a conviction against a high-profile murderer would silence his critics and seal his first real victory at the polls.

He turned onto Regal Drive and saw the flashing lights of emergency vehicles a hundred yards ahead. There was a fire truck, an ambulance and five patrol cars parked on the street near the judge's house. Obviously, they had sealed off the entire estate, not wanting to disturb any evidence that could possibly be found in the driveway or yard.

He pulled into an open spot behind the fire truck and exited his vehicle. "Where's Childress?" he asked the first officer he found.

"Up at the house," the officer pointed through the massive columns that outlined the cobblestone driveway. "Let me call him to see if it's okay if you go up there."

"That won't be necessary," Mutz brushed his suggestion aside, stepped over the yellow tape and began walking up the driveway to the house.

"Fine," he heard the officer grunt behind him.

Mutz surveyed the estate as he walked, which he figured was about three acres. Tall hedges surrounded the entire perimeter with a four-foot chain link fence imbedded within the dense shrubbery. Large oak trees lined the driveway which led to a circular drive in front of the house with magnolia trees and a fountain in the center. As he entered the circle he saw the garage on the right side of the house which was connected to the house by a short, covered walkway. The garage door had been shattered, as if there had been some sort of explosion. Wood from the door littered the lawn and surrounding area in front of the garage. He also noticed a can of paint thinner lying in the grass next to the driveway.

"Huh," he grunted aloud. "I wonder how that happened."

Continuing to the house, he paused and looked up at the two-story Georgian brick manor. There were two chimneys jutting up above the main part of the house and a third on a smaller wing attached to the left side.

Nice place, Mutz thought. It must be good to be a judge.

As he approached the front door he saw a group of officers on the other side of the circular driveway, one of whom was Childress. He walked to the group and saw that they were surrounding the judge who was seated on a lawn chair.

"Okay, you ready sir?" he heard Childress say. "Smith can take you down to our office."

The officers helped the judge out of his chair. He looked shell shocked and had a distant look in his eyes, as if he was in a dream state.

"I'm sorry sir," Mutz offered as he walked by, but the judge didn't even notice him.

Childress came over to Mutz and shook his head. "This is one fucked up situation we have here." They both stared at the judge as he shuffled his way to the front gate.

"What's with the garage door?" Mutz asked.

"I don't know. The judge said it must've happened when he was out jogging."

"I'd like to see her," Mutz stated when the judge was out of earshot. "Uh, I mean the crime scene."

Childress scratched his head. "Well if you want to see her she's already at the morgue. If you want to look in the house then we can do that right now." He turned and Mutz followed him.

As they approached the front porch Mutz immediately noticed the security camera just off to the right and above the door. He stopped and pointed.

"What about the camera?"

"Not working," Childress answered without turning around. "The judge said it was just installed but it's not hooked up to anything yet."

Mutz stayed on the porch as Childress entered the house.

"Who installed it?"

Childress stopped in the foyer then turned around. "I don't know. Why?"

"Just curious. What does it feed, a computer or a DVR?"

Childress shook his head. "Fuck I don't know. The judge just said it wasn't working."

Mutz stared at the camera. "Well, maybe we should check anyway."

Childress stared at Mutz. "Yes, obviously we'll check. Do you want to come in or not?"

Mutz shrugged. "Just thinking out loud."

Inside the front door, Mutz stopped and gazed about. The open formal living room was on his left and the kitchen to his right. Between the two rooms and directly in front of him a sweeping staircase led to the second level.

Childress turned and looked into the kitchen but didn't go in.

"He raped and killed her in the kitchen here. At least that's where her body was found. Right there on the floor," Childress pointed to a pool of blood beside the kitchen island. "Her head was bludgeoned with some sort of blunt instrument."

Unlike in the movies Mutz didn't see a chalk outline or anything to indicate she had been there.

"What makes you think she was raped?"

"Her pants . . . well, I guess they looked more like pajama bottoms, were removed and torn. And it looked like there was some trauma down below. The tech collected swab samples inside and out so maybe that'll tell us more."

"I take it you have lots of photos."

"Only about three hundred so far."

"Good. I'll need to see them. When you get done here I'd appreciate it if you send over copies right away."

Mutz was disappointed he wouldn't be able to view her body in real life . . . or death, rather. But he took solace in the fact he would eventually be able to see her in photos.

"No problem," Childress looked up the stairs. "We're still snooping around up there for any clues. They found a hole in the wall in the bedroom—looks like the killer pried a safe out of the wall. I haven't asked the judge what he had in there yet."

"What about a search warrant?" Mutz asked.

"Don't need one. The judge gave us permission to search everything."

"Hey Lieutenant!" a voice came from the second level.

Childress looked up. "Yeah."

"Come check this out."

Childress and Mutz ascended the stairs to the second-floor hallway. At the end, they saw an officer standing at a closet with the door open. They approached and looked over his shoulder. The closet was big enough to walk in.

"Looks like this is where the video cameras are fed," the officer pointed.

Inside, several wires hung down from the ceiling, leading to a DVR machine on the shelf with a flat panel monitor resting on top of it. The light on the DVR was glowing green.

"Huh," Childress grunted and glanced at Mutz.

"Looks like it may be working," Mutz glanced back.

Childress pointed to the monitor. "Turn that on."

The officer reached with a gloved hand and pressed the "on" button. The monitor lit up, showing a video feed from the exterior of the house on the porch. The judge's car could be seen in the driveway.

"I'll be damned," Childress put his hands on his hips. "He said they weren't working."

Mutz smiled. "Looks like I called this one."

Childress ignored him. "Rewind that thing if you can."

The officer bent down and studied the controls on the front of the DVR. After a few seconds, he pushed a button and the video screen blipped. They watched, not seeing anything at first. Finally, a human figure backed out of the house then a second figure followed a moment later. The officer pushed the button again and regular play resumed, showing Mutz and Childress entering the foyer.

"It works!" Mutz yelled. "Rewind it! You have to go back a few hours!"

Childress chuckled and shook his head. "Unbelievable. This is too much."

The officer hit the rewind button, then tapped it twice more. The rewind symbols went to full strength and a clock appeared in the lower right corner. The minutes sped by in a blur and every 10 seconds, the hour would click one number backward. All three of them watched as the hour number clicked its way down . . . 11 . . . 10 . . . 9. Various human figures blipped their way onto the screen then disappeared as the clock kept ticking until it reached 8:00 a.m.

"That's good," Childress blurted. "Stop it."

The officer quickly reached out and clicked the play button.

Childress and Mutz leaned in, both wanting a front row seat.

"Now do a slow fast forward," Childress directed.

The officer pressed another button and they watched the video feed while keeping an eye on the clock in the corner. The minutes ticked by. 8:01, 8:02, 8:03 . . . 8:12, 8:13, 8:14 . . . 8:32, 8:33. Finally, the first human figure appeared at 8:37 a.m. The officer immediately backed it up to 8:36 and pressed play.

On the screen, Judge Chancey appeared on the porch. He was wearing a white t-shirt and red running shorts. They watched as he lifted a leg and braced it against the railing on the porch. He leaned into his leg, obviously stretching before his run. After a moment he lifted his other leg and placed it on the railing, continuing the process. They watched as he did some deep knee bends then finished by shaking out each leg. When he had completed his stretching routine he hopped down the steps and jogged off camera.

They went through the same process as before, watching the clock click ahead and waiting anxiously for someone to appear. The clock ticked away in fast forward as the shadows on the screen dissipated from the rising sun. 9:10, 9:15, 9:20 . . . 10:00, 10:05. By now Mutz knew the killer had not entered the front door because he would've showed up by then.

At 10:10 the judge sprinted into view, bounded the front steps and rushed through the front door.

The next people who appeared on the porch camera were police officers.

"Huh," Mutz grunted. "I guess the killer entered through the back door or somewhere else. Any sign of forced entry?"

"Nothing," Childress answered.

"So is that the only camera that was working?"

"Looks like it," an officer pointed out. "All these other wires are not hooked up."

"Well," Childress backed away from the closet. "An officer is taking the judge down to the station where he's going to give us a more formal statement. I'm going to go conduct the interview while the boys finish up here. You know . . . get his full statement. You comin'?"

"Sure, "Mutz nodded. "I'll meet you there."

CHAPTER 11

At the police station Childress suggested that Mutz watch the interview with the judge from the video feed in the control room. Mutz was fine with that, mostly because he didn't know what to say to the judge.

After grabbing a cup of coffee Mutz entered the control room and took a seat beside the officer running the video equipment. He watched Childress and the judge enter the interview room and sit down at a small table. It was weird seeing the judge in a t-shirt and running shorts instead of a suit and robe. He looked strangely average . . . almost vulnerable.

"I just need to ask the standard questions," Childress explained as they sat down.

The judge nodded. "Yes, I understand."

"Do you mind if we record this on video? I just want to make sure I don't miss anything."

"That's fine," the judge mumbled. "I understand." He barely got the last words out before his face contorted and he began to sob. He buried his face in his hands and his shoulders shook.

"I'm sorry," Childress reached over and patted him on the back. "I know this is not a good time for you but I hope you understand that this has to be done while everything is still fresh in your mind. You know, to see if you can help us find who did this."

"Yes, yes," the judge regained control. "I'm sorry. I just can't believe she's dead." He wiped a tear away with the back of his hand. "She meant so much to me."

"I understand," Childress comforted him in a soft voice. "Here's a tissue."

The judge wiped his eyes with the tissue. "I'll be okay. Go ahead and ask away."

"All right then. I'll try to make this as brief as possible. What time did you leave the house this morning?"

"Um, well I know exactly when I left because I was timing my run. My phone said 8:39."

"And where was Mrs. Chancey when you left?"

"She wasn't home yet. She was at that overnight fundraiser at the old train depot. So she must have returned while I was out running."

"And what time did you return from your run?"

"Well," the judge shifted in his seat. "Let's look." He pulled out his phone. "I have an app that keeps track of this." He punched the screen. "I ended my jog at the bottom of my driveway, and that's when I stopped it. It says 10:11 a.m."

"Mind if I see that?"

"Sure," the judge handed him the phone.

Childress confirmed the details on the app.

"And tell me about when you got home. What did you first see?"

"The first thing I saw was the garage door. It was completely destroyed. And so I ran in there and looked around and didn't see anything out of the ordinary. So I ran to the front door to check inside the house."

"Did you find her right away?"

The judge nodded and grimaced. "Yeah, right when I ran in the front door . . . I could see her in the kitchen . . . and the blood."

"Did you touch her?"

The judge nodded again. "Yes . . . yes I did. I felt her pulse and knew that she was dead."

"Then what did you do?"

"I called 9-1-1."

"And then what did you do?"

"Well, I bent down and I just held her until the paramedics arrived."

"Any recent threats against you or Mrs. Chancey?"

The judge shook his head. "No, not that I'm aware of."

"So when was the last time you saw her alive?"

The judge teared up again. "It was yesterday afternoon . . . I guess at about 4:30; that's when she left for the fundraiser."

"I see," Childress scribbled some notes. "I know you already answered this at the house but you don't have any idea who would do something like this?"

"No idea," the judge shook his head.

"Did you ever go upstairs while you were waiting for EMS?"

"No, I stayed in the kitchen . . . with her."

"I guess you wouldn't know this then, but whoever did this, it looks like they pried a safe out of your wall. Did you have any valuables in there?"

"Yes. Just money," the judge answered.

"How much?"

"About ten thousand."

Childress paused. "You had ten grand in your safe? Why not the bank?"

"That's just a little emergency money. Of course, I keep most of my money in a bank."

Mutz glanced at the officer beside him. "Wow, ten grand in his safe."

"Did anybody know about that safe besides you and your wife?" Childress continued.

The judge thought for a moment. "No. It was covered by a painting."

"Well, it's not that surprising that it was found. Thieves tend to check behind paintings for just that sort of thing. I was just curious if you could think of anyone who actually knew about it."

"No, nobody knew but Torey and me."

"So what about those video cameras inside and outside the house? You said they weren't working. What makes you think they weren't?"

"Well, my construction guy said he was waiting for some controller or something."

"We found the system running in the closet upstairs and the camera over the front door was actually operating and recording," Childress said.

"What?" The judge gasped. "Did it show the murderer?"

"Ah, no," Childress answered. "It just showed you going out for a jog and then returning."

"So that means whoever killed my wife came through the back door or the side door from the garage. But after I checked out the garage, I tried to get into the house through the side door and it was locked. Did you see if the back door was locked?"

"The back door was locked too," Childress answered. "So that means the killer had a key or he was someone your wife knew and let in. Who's your construction guy?"

"Um, Jim is his name. Old Dominion Construction is the name of his company."

"Does he have a key?"

"Yes."

"How long has he been working at your house?"

"Oh, well, for a few months now. He's also making a wine cellar in the basement."

"Yeah, I saw that," Childress tapped his pencil. "When is the last time you saw him?"

"Um, let's see. I guess it was probably Friday. Yeah, it was Friday. He was working on the wine cellar."

"Did you talk about the security system Friday?"

"Uh, no. I didn't bring it up. He had said he would let me know when the new controller came."

"Do you have his number?"

"Uh, yeah let me see." The judge retrieved his cell phone and looked it up. Here it is," he showed Childress the screen.

Childress jotted down the number and then looked up. "As long as you have that out, would you mind if I look at it for a second?"

"My phone? Why?" the judge asked.

"I just want to look at it for a second. Did you call 9-1-1 from this phone?"

"Yes."

"Okay, I just want to verify the time."

The judge shrugged. "Suit yourself." He handed over the phone.

Childress clicked on the recent calls and noted the time of the 9-1-1 call. He then clicked on the message button and quickly glanced at the list of recent text messages. He was a detective and he couldn't help himself—he wanted to see if the judge had any contact with Mrs. Chancey since yesterday when he claimed she left. There were no messages.

"All right. Thanks," Childress handed the phone back to the judge. "What about her phone? Where is that?"

"Well, I don't know. It should be in her pocket or purse."

"We didn't find her phone. It wasn't on her and it wasn't in the house or her car. But she had one, right?"

"Yes, yes, she had a cell phone."

"What's the number? We're probably going to have to subpoena the records."

"That's fine." The judge recited her number as Childress jotted it down.

"Did she go to the fundraiser with anybody?"

"Ah, yes. Her friend, Sheila."

"Sheila who?"

"Sheila Stenson."

"And do you have contact info on her?"

"Um, no. But I'm sure she's in the phone book."

"All right. I'm sure we can find her, Childress shifted in his chair. "I have to ask you some sensitive questions now because it appears that she may have been sexually assaulted. You know, we need to account for the evidence . . ."

"Yes, I understand, just ask."

"When was the last time you engaged in sexual activity with your wife?"

The judge shifted in his chair. "Yesterday afternoon, before she left."

"Did you use a condom?"

"No."

"How would you describe your relationship with your wife?"

"What do you mean?" the judge asked.

"Were you on good terms? Did you fight?"

The judge bristled. "Yeah, we were on good terms. And yeah, we had our arguments, but nothing that all married couples don't go through. Why do you ask?"

"I'm sorry judge, but I don't like asking these questions any more than you enjoy answering them. We just have to rule people out. So, you weren't thinking about or going through a divorce or anything like that?"

"No, no, not at all. Our marriage was good."

"Did you ever suspect her of cheating on you?"

The judge shook his head, now resigned to simply answering the questions. "No, no I didn't."

"Okay, I just have to ask," Childress apologized. "I'm sorry."

In the control room, Mutz shook his head. *Poor bastard. He's probably the only man in town who didn't think Torey was cheating on him.*

"You have a daughter, right?"

"Yes, Abigail."

"She still live out in the country?"

"Yes, her and her husband have a little farm."

"Well, you won't be able to get back in your house for a few days. We'd like to keep it secure until the lab results come back. You think you could stay with her?"

"Yes, I suppose."

"Yeah, that would be best. If you want I can have an officer escort you over to your house so you can pick up any personal items you may need."

"Okay, that's fine."

"That's about all I have right now. If you can think of anything else that may help I'd appreciate a call."

"How long until you get lab results?"

Childress shrugged and stood up. "We'll put a rush on it. It shouldn't be more than a few days."

When the judge stood, Childress shook his hand while patting him on the shoulder. "I'm sorry about all this. We'll do all we can to find the person."

"I know. Thanks."

Once they had disappeared off camera, Mutz pushed his chair back and exited the control room. He waited in the corridor until Childress met him there. By his line of questioning, Mutz knew that Childress hadn't ruled the judge out as a suspect.

"What do you think?" Mutz asked as Childress approached. "You think he may be involved?"

"Well, I'm not going to rule him out yet. It's just that I can't see the judge doing something so cold hearted—you know, raping her and then bashing her head in. Hold on a second," he said retrieving his cell phone.

Childress dialed a number then spoke. "Anderson, this is Jack. I'm going to text you a number. It's the judge's wife's cell phone. Give it a call and see if you hear it ring anywhere in the house or garage. All right, thanks." Childress hung up and texted the number.

"Now we just have to wait for the lab results, and hopefully we'll get some answers. In the meantime I'm going to see if I can track down this Sheila friend. Maybe she can shed some light on what was going on. And you should subpoena the phone company for Mrs. Chancey's cell records."

"Yes, yes, I know," Mutz seemed perturbed. "But you know that's going to take weeks."

"And one more thing," Childress added. "Let's not tell the press about her head injury. We're going to want to weed out all the nut cakes that come out and give fake confessions."

"Good idea," Mutz agreed. "What should we tell them, then?"

"Let's go with strangulation."

CHAPTER 12

On the Monday morning after his big night with the judge's wife, Nolan Getty arrived at the chateau just after nine. That's what he and his assistants called their office, anyway—the chateau. It was a joke, because the Public Defender's office was an old rickety house more than a hundred years old with a curb presence that was quite far removed from the image one should get upon hearing the word *chateau*.

He still wasn't feeling quite up to par despite spending most of Sunday in a hibernation-like state on his sofa where he caught glimpses of football in between long periods of sleep. He wasn't in a particularly good mood either, partly because of the guilt he was feeling about being with the judge's wife Saturday night. The one saving grace for his conscience was the fact that he was almost certain he hadn't done anything sexual with her—at least nothing more than drinking tequila from her belly and the nudity they shared as a result of strip billiards. But still, the fact that he was with her all night would be quite the embarrassment if anybody found out. Worse yet, if the judge found out . . . well, that was one possibility he didn't want to explore.

On top of his poor decision making over the weekend he had also lost to Rick in their fantasy football league, which added to his grumpiness. The last thing he wanted to hear was Rick gloating over his big win. If only Darion Henderson had caught that pass, Nolan thought as he opened the front door of the chateau.

Vicki, his secretary and office manager, glanced up from the telephone as he entered. "I've got to go," she said into the phone before hanging it up. "Crazy stuff, huh?" she commented, pointing at the newspaper in front of her.

"Uh . . . what's that?" Nolan asked as he picked up the folders in his mail basket.

"Oh my God, you haven't heard?"

"Haven't heard what?" Nolan was in no mood for games.

"The judge's wife. She was murdered yesterday morning!" Vicki handed him the newspaper.

Nolan turned it around and saw the headline, "Judge's Wife Murdered!"

He stared at the paper, unable to speak. "What the . . . ?"

He tried to read the story but his mind raced with images of the judge's wife on Saturday night. "Torey Chancey," he said out loud as he read, unable to comprehend any other words in the article, though his eyes continued to go through the motions of reading it. And then his eyes drifted up and met Vicki's.

"When? How?" he muttered in a state of disbelief.

"Yesterday morning it says. Between nine and ten a.m. Some guy raped and strangled her."

"Wow," Nolan clutched the newspaper. "Unbelievable."

Nolan's external demeanor exhibited the standard reaction that one should have upon receiving such shocking news, but inside, his stomach churned from a plethora of emotions that came together in a frenzied mosh pit, each one trying to fight its way to the forefront of his conscience. Guilt and shame seemed to surface above the others but those feelings were quickly extinguished by his lawyer-trained brain, which honed in on an inescapable fact that could threaten his own livelihood.

I was with her in her last hours and probably one of the last people to see her alive.

Still clutching the newspaper, Nolan turned and ascended the rickety stairs to his office on the second floor where he closed the door behind him. He plopped into one of the chairs facing his desk and let out a big sigh before opening the newspaper and reading the article.

According to the paper, the police suspected that she was sexually assaulted before she was beaten and strangled to death in her own home sometime between nine and ten a.m. Sunday morning. Her husband, Judge Yancy R. Chancey, III, found her when he returned from his morning jog. There were no suspects identified and no other details but the investigation was ongoing. The writer suggested that if anybody had any information they should call the crime hotline.

Like most people it took Nolan a few minutes to fully grasp the concept that the judge's wife had been murdered. Things like that didn't happen in Big Shanty. Every once in a while drug dealers killed each other and every now and then a robber pulled the trigger and somebody ended up dead, but the murder of a judge's wife was a whole different story.

He knew they would find the person, whoever it was. The hunt would be relentless for the simple fact that it involved a judge's wife. He also knew the initial focus would be on those closest to her. And her husband, the judge, would be at the top of that list. That's just the way things worked in a criminal investigation. Once they had ruled out the judge they would turn their attention to others that knew her, expanding the web through interviews and interrogations, eventually touching everyone who had ever known her until they found the person responsible. Nolan knew, just like the police knew, that the chance of this being a random act was extremely remote. She knew her killer . . . or at the very least the killer knew her.

Once he had absorbed the initial shock, Nolan began to analyze the situation in a more lawyer-like manner. Not the *who* or the *why* aspect of the tragedy but the *how am I going to cover my ass on this one* aspect. The facts were the facts. He was with the judge's wife up until the last hour or so of her life. He knew he could not change that. But was there any reason for anybody to know? After all, he knew he wasn't the murderer.

Only two people had any knowledge about it—Rick and the friend. What was her name? Sheila. Would she tell anyone that her and the judge's wife were with two Public Defenders all night? Not if she was smart, Nolan thought. But maybe she's not so smart. He knew he could count on Rick but Sheila was another story. Would the police somehow find out anyway?

Nolan's thoughts raced through numerous scenarios of how the investigatory web could eventually reach him and how he could extricate himself from the situation, all with one thought in mind:

whatever the cost, whatever it takes, nobody can know about Saturday night.

What if somebody saw them together at the bar? That would be easily explained, Nolan thought. They saw her at the bar with her friend Sheila. They chatted briefly, that's all. They may have even left the bar at the same time but that was it. Nothing more. They certainly didn't wake up naked together on a pool table just an hour before she was murdered. No, that didn't happen. Rick would back him up on that one. The plan would work as long as Ms. Sheila didn't spill her guts.

Just as he was starting to feel comfortable about his story Nolan's eyes drifted to his desk and landed upon the one little thing that could expose his lie.

Oh no! Her cell phone! I have her damned cell phone!

There it sat upon his desk in front of God and anybody else who would care to look. It was just a cell phone—an inanimate, electronic tool for communication to many. But to him it was absolute disaster.

"Damn it," Nolan jumped from his chair and swiped it off the desk. "That's great. That's just great, Mrs. Chancey. First you leave your cell phone then you go and get murdered. Awesome. Just awesome."

I'll just throw it away, Nolan thought as he paced the room, pausing to stare at it every few steps. Just throw it in the garbage and forget it was ever here.

No, I can't do that. I can't be destroying evidence. I know. I'll take it back to the bar and drop it on the sidewalk. That's it. She must've dropped her phone when she left the bar.

And then he remembered the text message. What did it say?

Nolan clicked the button to wake up the phone but nothing happened. Dead battery.

He remembered the gist of the text, he just didn't want to think of the consequences.

"Where are you? I'm waiting." That's what the text had stated. And it came just before she had been murdered.

"Jesus, this is a frickin' mess," Nolan breathed to himself, still pacing the office. But his thoughts were interrupted by the sound of footsteps running up the staircase then Rick's voice booming outside his door.

"Boss, you up here?"

Yes, I'm up here. Just taking a nervous crap in my suit pants. I'll be out in a minute.

As he finished the thought, Rick flung the door open, stepped into the office and quickly shut the door behind him, his eyes wild with panic.

"They're coming for you, boss!"

CHAPTER 13

Nolan slipped the cell phone into his coat pocket. "Who's coming for me?"

"Mutz and Childress," Rick panted. "I was up in court this morning checking on a case and they pulled me into a side room. They were asking me questions about the judge's wife and if I had seen her Saturday night!"

"What did you tell them?"

Rick walked over to the couch and sat down. "I told them we saw her at the bar. That's it. Then I told them I got drunk and walked over to the office alone and slept it off."

"Damn it," Nolan stepped to his desk and sat down, relieving the pressure off his suddenly shaky legs. It was too early in the investigation for them to have found a random person at the bar. He knew they must have talked to Sheila, who had led them to Rick. Had she told them everything? Nolan knew the answer. She had absolutely told them everything, otherwise they wouldn't have questioned Rick.

"What have I told you about talking to the police?" Nolan questioned Rick.

"Um, that you should never answer any questions and always plead the Fifth," Rick answered.

"Yeah, don't say anything! You know that! I mean, that's what you tell your clients right? So why not follow the same advice for yourself?"

Rick shrugged. "Yeah, I guess you're right."

"Damn right I'm right. Eighty percent of the time the only way someone gets in trouble is if they talk. Either it's a lie or a confession, but either way it gets them. And in your case it's a lie," Nolan sighed.

"They talked to her friend . . . I'm almost positive. Otherwise, they wouldn't have questioned you."

"Sorry, boss. I didn't know what to say and I didn't want them to know about you and the judge's wife."

"I know. It's my fault. I should've never let it happen to begin with."

"Just tell them what I told them," Rick added. "Even if her friend told them, it's our word against hers."

"No, I can't do it. There would be no reason for her to make up a story like that. They'll sniff right through that smoke."

Just then the phone buzzed and Vicki's voice came over the intercom. "Lieutenant Childress wants to talk to you. Line 2."

Nolan stomach gurgled. "Thanks." He paused for a moment, trying to clear his head and think of a plan. Finally, he clicked the blinking line. "Hello."

"Mr. Getty, Lieutenant Childress here. Do you got a minute?"

"Sure," Nolan glanced at Rick.

"I was wondering if you wouldn't mind coming up to the station. It's about your whereabouts this weekend."

"What about it?" Nolan feigned surprise.

"Well, we just have some questions for you. It's important."

"When?"

"Right now if you could."

"All right. I'll be there in ten." Nolan clicked the button and ended the call.

"Wait, didn't you just say don't talk to the police?" Rick asked.

Nolan smirked. "I'm not going up there to answer questions. I'm going up there to ask questions."

"You're not going to tell them I lied are you? I mean, they could tag me with obstruction of justice or something, couldn't they?"

"Nah," Nolan stood up. "I don't plan on saying anything but if I have to, I'll just tell them you were so drunk you didn't remember what happened. You'll be fine." He was about to walk out but then he remembered the cell phone. He retrieved it from his pocket and showed it to Rick.

"You have a charger for this phone?" Nolan asked.

"Yeah, hold on." Rick exited and returned in a minute. "Here you go."

Nolan plugged the phone in then powered it up.

The first thing he saw on the screen was a missed call from the Big Shanty Police Department. "Huh," he grunted out loud before swiping it away and finding the text. "There it is," he said. He read the text one more time.

Where are you? I'm waiting.

The time of the text was 9:17 a.m., which was before she was murdered. He reached for the phone and called his investigator, Eric.

"Hello boss," Eric answered on the first ring.

"Hey Eric, I need you to look up a number for me and see who owns it. You got a pen?"

"Yeah shoot."

Nolan recited the telephone number from the text.

"Why, where did you get it?" Eric asked

"Ah, that's not important right now. I just need to find the owner. It's a cell phone number."

"No problem, boss," Eric said before he hung up.

Nolan then tucked the phone behind a stack of papers in his desk drawer.

"Wish me luck," he smiled.

CHAPTER 14

At the police station, Nolan told the receptionist behind the glass that he was there to see Lieutenant Childress. A few minutes later, Childress opened a side door and waved Nolan through. "Come on back."

Nolan followed Childress down a hallway. They took a right turn, then a left, until they reached a steel door with a tiny window. Childress opened the door with an electronic badge and motioned for Nolan to enter.

It was a small room with a table and two chairs. Nolan noticed the video camera in the upper left corner immediately. "So this is where the magic happens," Nolan quipped as he took a chair at the table. He recognized the room from the numerous videos of his clients being interviewed over the years. But his view all those times was from the corner of the ceiling . . . not the hot seat next to the table.

Childress stayed at the door, holding it open. It appeared that he was waiting for someone else. After a few seconds Mutz entered the room.

"Hello Getty," Mutz grinned at him. "Nice to see you," he added in a condescending tone.

"The pleasure's all mine," Nolan quipped.

Childress shut the door and took the other seat at the table while Mutz leaned against the wall with his arms crossed.

"Just for the record you have come here voluntarily and you are not in custody, is that correct?"

The statement seemed innocuous but it had an important purpose. If Nolan's presence was voluntary and he wasn't in custody then Childress had no duty to read Miranda warnings. In any other case this fact would be important because Childress would not want to tip off the interviewee that he or she had certain rights, one of them being that they didn't have to talk at all. But in this case it was the product of habit because Nolan already knew his rights and Childress knew that Nolan knew them, so there was no point fussing over it.

"That's right," Nolan answered. "I'm not in custody. But for the record you do not have my permission to obtain any recordings of me and I object to any video, audio, or photographic recording of any type while I'm here."

Childress dropped his pen. "Well, that's fine, I guess. He looked up at the camera in the corner. You heard him, stop the camera."

Nolan smiled. He knew the camera would continue to roll and that they would figure out a way to use it later if they needed it. That didn't matter though because he didn't intend to say anything of substance. He just wanted to let them know that he was in charge.

"Just sign this paper saying you are here voluntarily and you understand all of your rights," Childress pushed the paper to Nolan.

"No thanks," Nolan pushed it back. "Did you have some questions for me or did you just want me to do paperwork?"

Childress bristled. "Where were you Saturday night?"

Nolan ignored the question. "My Assistant has already told me that you cornered him up at the courtroom and asked him a bunch of questions regarding the judge's wife. And yes I know she's been murdered, I read the paper this morning. So, the logical conclusion is that you think either he or I was with her at some point before she was murdered, right?"

Mutz grunted. "We *know* you were with her, Getty. We just want to give you a chance to explain yourself."

Childress frowned at Mutz then turned back to Nolan. "What time did you first see her Saturday night?"

"So by your response, Mr. Mutz, I believe it's safe to say that somebody told you that Mrs. Chancey was with either me or him Saturday night?"

"Listen," Childress interrupted before Mutz could answer. "I'm asking the questions here not you."

"No, you listen," Nolan leaned ahead. "What we're having here is a conversation, which means this is a two-way street. You tell me what's going on and maybe I'll tell you what I was doing this weekend."

Childress dropped his pen again. "What if I told you that we have information that you and your little office buddy were with Mrs. Chancey all night long Saturday night?"

"Well, first of all, if you're referring to my assistant, he's not little, so obviously you have some bad information."

"Oh cut the crap," Childress seemed to be losing his patience.

"Second of all," Nolan continued. "Did you ever think that the source of the information could have been involved in the murder? And by the way let's think about that. If you're saying that I was with Mrs. Chancey all night, wouldn't that be something that would piss off a wife's husband? I would say so . . . yes, that would really piss off a wife's husband, maybe even enough for that husband to kill his wife." Nolan stopped staring at Childress and turned his gaze to Mutz. "Have you thought about that Mutz?"

"Well, for your information we're not ruling anybody out at this point," Mutz crossed his arms. "Including you. Are you going to tell us or not?"

Nolan shook his head. "I'm not going to answer your questions. Not because I have anything to hide, but because the Constitution gives me a right not to. It's really for my protection," Nolan smiled. "That way you can't fabricate a criminal charge and then mold the evidence to fit my answers in order to wrongfully convict me, like what you did to the Bisbaine kid and others before him. It's a good system if you exercise your rights," Nolan stood up. "For the record I plead the Fifth. But just so you know, I had absolutely nothing to do with Mrs. Chancey's murder."

"The lab already told us the semen they found at the scene originated from two different males," Childress interrupted Nolan's departure. "One of them is most likely from the Judge. What if the other is from you?"

Nolan chuckled in an attempt to hide his anxiety. "Well now, that wouldn't be a good thing, would it?"

"That's right," Childress smiled. "So if one of those samples is from you then it could have only gotten there in one of two ways—either the night before, or when she was raped and murdered. So, which was it? Was this a voluntary encounter the night before or did you follow her home and rape and kill her?"

Lieutenant Childress had excellent interviewing skills, using a classic method of obtaining information. First, tell the suspect you have evidence against him then give the suspect two possible scenarios; a seemingly innocent scenario and an inculpatory scenario. The suspect will always choose the innocent one, but at the same time, it's an admission to being involved which can later be used against him.

Nolan shook his head. "You know I wouldn't do a thing like that."

"In time we will find out," Childress picked up his pencil and tapped it on the table. "The lab is running comparisons as I speak. We'll be able to separate the judge's semen and then all we have to do is run the other sample against the databases. Have you ever been arrested?" Childress added.

Nolan flushed. Many years earlier before he had even thought about being an attorney there was that fight in the bar. Some girl had approached him and began carrying on a conversation. Then a few seconds later a drunken guy, most likely the girl's boyfriend, started pushing him. Nolan had turned and walked away but the guy wouldn't let it go. The next thing he knew he felt a hit to the back of his head which pushed him forward into a table, where he caught himself before falling. He turned in time to see the guy lunging at him. Nolan ducked, then delivered an upper cut to his chin that dropped him like a sack of potatoes. On the way down the guy's head hit a chair, then the concrete floor. From there the guy went into convulsions and Nolan went to jail. The charges were later dropped because all the witnesses had confirmed that it was in self-defense, but still, he had been arrested. Had they taken a DNA sample upon his arrest? If so, his DNA would be in the database. He vaguely recalled them sticking a needle in his arm but he thought it was to test his blood alcohol content, which would've been high that night, which was also the reason his memory was foggy at best.

"Like I said, I'm pleading the Fifth. So, you guys go and do what you need to do."

"Well, perhaps the first thing we need to do is get a search warrant for your office," Mutz chimed in.

Nolan's stomach flipped. "Why would you do that?"

"Mrs. Chancey's friend . . . you know her, Sheila Stenson . . . she gave us a detailed description of your office, especially the basement, and it would be a good way to verify that she's telling the truth, wouldn't it?"

"I suppose it would," Nolan responded, knowing that they would search everywhere and easily find the cell phone. He needed to end this quickly so he could get to the cell phone before they could.

"Listen," he braced his hands on the table and stood up. "You do what you have to do but you know as well as I do you're chasing after the wrong dude. Do yourselves a favor and go find the killer."

With that Nolan waved to the door. "May I?"

He knew he could.

CHAPTER 15

Nolan's air of confidence at the police station was an attempt to disguise his true anxiety. It was as if he was a small child who had done something really bad and now he was waiting for his father to come home, extremely nervous about the type and severity of the punishment that awaited. Even if he refused to confess that he was with Torey Chancey all night, they still knew, he thought to himself. Would they tell Judge Chancey? If Chancey found out that he had been with his wife, that could be explained away. But if his DNA was in her . . . that was another story. He could care less whether Mutz and Childress knew, but if the Judge found out he may as well pack his bags and move out of state because his career would be over. He also didn't want Judge Chancey to know because all it would do is cause him emotional harm on top of the pain that he was no doubt experiencing because of his wife's death. And the last thing he wanted was to cause any more harm to the judge. So, the first thing he did after the interview was place Mrs. Chancey's phone inside sealed, triple bags and drop it in the tank of the toilet. He didn't think anyone would look there, but just in case, he put a blue colored, sanitary tank disk on top of it, knowing that it would cloud the water and prevent anyone from seeing anything at the bottom of the tank.

Within an hour, he heard a commotion downstairs and loud voices. He then heard people ascending the stair.

"Oh, boy," Nolan sighed out loud.

Childress appeared in the doorway, then entered his office with papers in his hand. Mutz followed close behind.

"I've got a search warrant here, Mr. Getty. It's to search your entire building."

Nolan stood up and approached him. "Let me see," he asked.

Childress handed him the warrant and Nolan read it. The warrant had been signed by the local magistrate and authorized the police to search for and seize a cell phone belonging to Torey Chancey and any other items that may belong to her. The search warrant also authorized interior photos of the building to corroborate a witness's testimony.

Nolan began chuckling and shaking his head. "Well, before you begin, you may want to get a valid warrant."

"What do you mean?" Mutz piped in.

"You're an idiot," Nolan continued to shake his head. "Don't you know that in order to search an attorney's office, the warrant must come from a Circuit Court Judge and not a magistrate?

"Says who," Mutz replied.

"Um, well, I don't know the statute number off the top of my head, but we can look it up quick," Nolan answered as he went to his computer. After clicking the keyboard a few times, he found what he was looking for. "Ah, here it is, 19.2-56.1. Take a look," he waved Mutz to the screen. "Any warrant sought for the search of a premises or the contents thereof belonging to or under the control of any licensed attorney-at-law . . . shall be issued only by a circuit court judge," Nolan purposely skipped over a few words, hoping that Mutz would gloss over them too.

"Huh," Mutz grunted. "But wait; this states 'evidence of any crime solely involving a client of such attorney'. So that doesn't apply here because Mrs. Chancey was not your client."

"She actually was my client," Nolan lied, knowing that nobody could ever prove differently now that she was deceased.

"Client for what?" Mutz asked.

"Can't tell you. Attorney-client privilege."

"Well, too bad. We'll just sort it out later." He turned and nodded to Childress. "Search the building."

"I wouldn't do that if I were you," Nolan interrupted. "That would be the easiest lawsuit in history now that you know the search warrant is invalid—not only against the police department, but against you personally."

"Ah, yeah. That's enough information for me," Childress replied. "I'm not doing any searching until y'all get this straightened out," he turned and walked towards the door. "We're out of here."

Mutz shook his head and followed, but then turned for one last comment. "You can bet your ass we'll be back!"

"Ah . . . ba-bye!" Nolan waved his hand as if he was waving goodbye to a child. "Ba-bye, Mutzy!" he yelled one more time after Mutz had left the room.

* * *

Over the next few days Nolan's thoughts centered on his exploits and how he wished he could go back in time and change the events as they happened. There wasn't anything he could do about it but that didn't stop him from worrying. Although he shuffled through his papers and attempted to get work done his entire conscience was consumed by the impending persecution and shame that would be brought upon him when Mutz dropped the hammer.

Three days later as he continued through his motions of being a Public Defender, the sound of footsteps interrupted his worries.

Rick came in with files under his arm and looking completely pissed off.

"You're not gonna believe this shit," he said, shaking his head. He threw the handful of files on one end of the couch and plopped down on the other.

"Try me," Nolan replied.

"I just had a guy on an assault and battery in Domestic Court. You know how they have those four conference rooms in the hallway outside the court room?" he asked.

Nolan nodded.

"Well, I got there early and I'm sitting in the end room all alone—just going through my files. Nobody else is around and I have the door shut. I'm in there a few minutes and then I hear the door open in the room beside me and I hear Mutz start talking. Well, I'm a lawyer so

I'm naturally a curious person," he said, holding his hands out and shrugging his shoulders. "So, I lean over to the wall and maybe I put my ear up against it to see if I can hear what he's saying. Well, I realize right away he's talking to some witness. 'What happened . . . what did your Dad do to your Mom?' he asked. Then, a young girl's voice says 'He didn't do anything. Mom was the one that was hitting at him." Then I hear Mutz the Putz say, 'That's not what you told the police on the night this happened.' And the kid says, 'Mom told me to tell the police that Dad was hitting her.' The kid actually tells Mutz that she lied the night when the police came to her house!" Rick exclaimed.

Nolan could tell that Rick was just getting warmed up.

"Mutz then says to her, 'Did you know that lying to the police is a crime?' And then Mutz tells the kid that he will charge her with filing a false police report and that she'll be in a lot of trouble if she tries to change her story. Can you believe that?" Rick asked.

Nolan shook his head and grinned. "Unfortunately, yes."

"Well, guess what," Rick continued. "One of my cases is a domestic assault and battery and so I put two and two together, thinking that it may involve my client. I go out in the lobby and find my guy. He tells me that the prosecutor just went into the side room with his little girl and that his wife is not only making up the entire charge against him, but she's convinced their daughter to lie too. So, I now know that Putz is talking to the victim in my case."

"Now, in your opinion," Rick continued. "Would you or would you not consider the witness's statement in the conference room to be exculpatory information?" Rick asked.

"Let's see," Nolan answered, pretending to think out loud. "The alleged witness to a crime says that she lied and that her father didn't actually do anything to her mother. If true, such a statement would definitely help your client. At the very least her statement appears to be inconsistent with her earlier statement to the police," he continued, tapping his finger against his jaw. "If I'm not mistaken the ethical rules recognize that an inconsistent statement made by a victim is exculpatory information and the prosecutor is required to disclose such information. Yes, I'm pretty sure that's how it works," Nolan feigned as if he was actually analyzing the situation. "So I'm going to say *exculpatory.*"

"Wrong!" Rick shouted. "Not according to Mutz! He doesn't say a thing to me before the trial. And evidently he was able to scare the kid, who testifies that my client hit her mother. There's no marks, no photos of any injuries, just her testimony that my client hit her."

"Is that right?" Nolan asked. "What did you do?"

"This is where it gets good," Rick leaned forward on the couch. "This is my first question on cross. 'Isn't it true that just a few minutes ago when you were in the conference room with Mr. Mutz, that you told him nothing happened that night and you made the whole thing up because your mother told you to lie?'"

"What did she say?" Nolan asked, truly interested.

"This is great," he continued. "She doesn't say anything. She just looks at Mutz and asks, 'Should I answer that?'" Rick giggled, barely able to control his excitement.

"Beautiful," I smiled.

"And then before Mutz can say anything, the judge says, 'Answer the question Miss.' So, she looks at the judge and says 'Yes.' Then I follow up with the spike. Isn't it true that after you told Mr. Mutz nothing happened, he threatened to put you in jail if you didn't stick to the original story that you told the police?"

"Hello!" Nolan exclaimed. This was good. "What did Mutz say about that?"

"He squawked like a chicken!" Rick exclaimed. "'Objection! Hearsay! Blah blah blah.'"

"Well the judge shuts him down on that and so then he tries to explain his way out of it. He goes on this long soliloquy about how children can get scared of abusive fathers and how defendants talk them into changing their story at trial. And then, get this . . . he actually tells the judge that domestic violence would escalate out of control if defendants were allowed to coerce victims into changing their stories."

"Nice," Nolan replied. "So let me get this straight. Mutz is speculating that the father coerced the kid into retracting her story, but in reality, Mutz is the one that's doing the coercing?"

"Yes!" Rick squealed. "But the judge tries to let Mutz off the hook and he turns to me and asks me if I have any other questions for the witness. Well, I say to the judge, 'She hasn't answered the last one!' He just looks at me and says 'I think we know the answer, but I guess you're entitled to hear it anyway.' So, I ask the victim again, "Isn't it true that after you told Mr. Mutz nothing happened, he threatened to put you in jail if you didn't stick to the original story that you told the police?" And she finally says, 'Yes.'"

"Nice," Nolan commented. "What did the judge do?"

"Oh," Rick said in a nonchalant manner. "Of course he avoided the whole thing and simply found that the evidence was insufficient to prove that my client had committed an assault and battery."

"Well, that's a win," Nolan exclaimed.

"Yeah, but it let Mutz off the hook," he said. "I should file a bar complaint against him."

"You should," Nolan agreed, knowing that he wouldn't. Filing a bar complaint would only stir the evil prosecutorial giant, possibly making it tougher on the other clients. It would also soak up valuable time that could be spent on other clients. In this case, he represented his client and won. That was as far as his duty in the real world went. End of story.

"What's all the ranting about in here?" Vicki asked, poking her head in the door.

"Rick here is finding out that prosecutors are cheaters," Nolan explained. "He's talking a bunch of nonsense—wanting to actually do something about it. Can you tell him he's not allowed to do that?"

"You're not allowed to do that," she answered flatly, coming into the office with a stack of papers under her arm. I was coming up here anyway, so I thought I'd tell you in person. Mutz is on line two for you."

A wave of anxiety flooded Nolan's chest.

"Thanks," Nolan nodded to her, then reached over and pushed Line 2, then the speaker button.

"Hello, this is Nolan," Nolan was surprised that his voice cracked as he tried to get his name out.

"This is Montgomery. I just wanted to let you know that you're off the hook . . . at least for now."

Nolan paused before responding. "What do you mean?"

"I mean you don't have to worry that your DNA may be in Mrs. Chancey."

"And why would I be worried or not be worried about that?" Nolan feigned confidence.

"We've made an arrest."

"Who?" Nolan couldn't contain his excitement.

"Check your in-box at the court house tomorrow morning," he stated before the line clicked and went dead.

"Son of a bitch," Nolan breathed. A feeling of relief swept through him. But mostly hope . . . a small glimmer of hope that Judge Chancey would never learn about Saturday night.

CHAPTER 16

When Montgomery Mutz received the DNA results from the state lab, the seemingly senseless rape and murder of Mrs. Torey Chancey suddenly made very much sense. He smiled as he stared at the name of the person whose DNA was found on Mrs. Chancey.

You tried to hide it but you must've been clumsy. And now you're all mine.

The timing of the lab results was perfect. At that very moment his senior assistant was presenting all the month's criminal cases to the grand jury in Circuit Court. Mutz knew it wouldn't take much to get an indictment from the Grand Jury because they only heard the evidence that the prosecutor wanted them to hear and there was no opportunity for them to see any opposing evidence. The old joke was that if a prosecutor wanted he could probably get a Grand Jury to indict a ham sandwich.

With lab results and the defendant's criminal record in hand, Mutz headed to Circuit Court. Once the Grand Jury indicted the defendant, Mutz could get an arrest warrant and then the manhunt would begin. Mutz didn't expect the hunt to be very long, after all, they knew where the defendant lived.

Forty-three minutes later Mutz presented the indictment to the substitute Circuit Court judge who then issued an arrest warrant. Two hours later, the murderer was in custody and Mutz, wanting to be the first to tell him, dialed up the judge to give him the news.

"Hello?"

"Yes, hello Judge, it's Montgomery Mutz, how are you?"

"I'm okay and yourself?"

"I'm good. I was just calling to tell you that we made an arrest. The murderer is in custody."

A moment of silence followed, then, "Who?"

"Are you sitting down?" Mutz attempted to create more suspense.

"Oh for Christ's sake, tell me who!" the judge raised his voice.

"William Bisbaine," Mutz sputtered. "William Bisbaine."

Silence on the judge's end, then finally, "No, I don't believe it. What's your evidence?"

"DNA," Mutz answered proudly. "And DNA never lies."

"Well, that may be but I need to tell you something. Mr. Bisbaine was at my house two weeks ago. He came over because my wife invited him. We gave him money to help him out . . . to get him back on his feet. And I remember she hugged him at the door. So, this DNA could be from anything . . . hair, sweat . . . anything."

"No," Mutz stood firm. "Perhaps you can come down here and I could show you the detailed results. He was definitely the rapist."

"I just can't believe it," the judge continued. "There was no anger in him . . . no sense of revenge. He was happy that we were giving him money and he seemed so forgiving."

"If you want to know the truth, I think he went to your house to kill you and burglarize your home and it was just good timing on your part to be out jogging when he did. There's no doubt in my mind that you'd be dead too if you had been home."

"There has to be some mistake. What if the lab made a mistake and the samples were contaminated?"

"No sir, that doesn't happen. That only happens in defense attorneys' dreams."

"Well tell them to run the samples again."

"Sir . . . the results are conclusive."

"Tell them to run the samples again!" The judge's tone convinced Mutz to obey.

"Okay, sir. I will. I'll ask them to run the samples again."

"Thank you," his tone softened. "I just don't want the same mistake happening to Mr. Bisbaine again. We have to be one hundred percent certain this time."

"I understand, sir."

CHAPTER 17

Nolan couldn't wait to see the files of new cases to which his office was appointed. Usually Vicki went to the courthouse before clocking in at the office, but Nolan had called her and told her to go straight in because he wanted to pick up the new paperwork himself.

He nodded to the security guard who was imploring people to empty their pockets, and then slid around the metal detector gate.

"Have a good one," the security guard waved.

"Thanks, you too," Nolan answered as he turned down the side corridor and approached the clerk's window, which was manned by his favorite clerk, Carol.

"Good morning, Carol," he smiled through the bulletproof glass. "I need to pick up the appointment papers."

"Good morning, Mr. Getty." She smiled and reached her hand below the counter, pushing a button to release the lock on the door beside the window. Nolan opened the door and entered the area behind the courtroom which was a large room filled with cubicles and desks. The two judge's offices were located at the corners and they were the only offices that had walls and doors. Nolan approached the Public Defender's in-box, curious as to who had been arrested the day before. His excitement level grew as he picked up the papers entitled "Indictment – Big Shanty Circuit Court", but nothing could've prepared him for the shock when he read the name on the front.

William Horatio Bisbaine.

Nolan blinked in disbelief. He had seen many surprises in his line of business and intimately understood that life is often stranger than fiction, but this was almost too bizarre to comprehend. Willy Bisbaine, a man wrongfully convicted of rape, incarcerated for over eight years and then freed from prison, was now facing rape and murder charges alleged to have been committed against the wife of the judge who convicted him. This is crazy, Nolan thought. Just plain old, outhouse rat crazy.

"Weird, eh?" Carol placed some papers on the copier beside the Public Defender in-box and pushed a button, before resting her hand on her hip and shaking her head in Nolan's direction.

"Yeah, that's an understatement."

"How's a guy do that when he has the rest of his life ahead of him?" she asked.

"You got me," Nolan shrugged.

"And that's the way he thanks you for doing all that work to set him free . . . it's a real shame. I can't imagine how you represent these animals every day."

She was right. He had done a lot of work and pulled off a near miracle in getting the DNA evidence re-evaluated in Bisbaine's case. All that work for nothing, Nolan thought. All that work so that Bisbaine could get out and kill the judge's wife. And he was responsible for it. As his lawyer, he was the one that had made it all happen.

"I'm not sure myself," Nolan grunted as he shuffled through the papers and confirmed that his client had been arrested and was incarcerated in the city jail, being held without bond.

Usually Nolan liked to let his new clients stew for a day or two in jail before visiting them, but this one was different. This was an old client with a new problem and Nolan was anxious to see what Willy had to say for himself. Perhaps he was looking for an explanation as to why he would throw it all away for the simple joy of revenge. Maybe he just wanted to see his face . . . the face of a man who had been accused and convicted before, and now facing charges of rape and murder again. Would it be different than before? Would he deny this crime, like the first? Nolan had many questions, none of which could be answered until he was face to face with his client.

Outside the courthouse Nolan paused on the sidewalk and stared skyward, soaking in a perfect autumn day. The leaves on the trees had turned red and gold, but they still clung to their branches, offering a rustling reminder that winter was near despite the bright sunshine and warm temperatures. Days like this made Nolan feel glad to be alive and free, something that Willy was certainly not feeling at that moment. Right now, Willy was locked in a steel box and breathing in the aroma of institutional disinfectant with slight undertones of fish sticks and canned corn. What would possess him to give up a day like this for that? Nolan thought about that and other questions as he walked to the city jail just over a block away.

After checking in at the front desk Nolan passed through a sally port where one door closed and locked before the next was opened. Behind the second door he walked a short distance to an elevator lobby and pushed the button to the third floor where the serious criminals were held, one of which was Willy. The elevator made a dinging sound and the doors opened, revealing a clergy person and a probation officer, both of whom stepped into the lobby. Nolan nodded to the probation officer. "Hello Sam, how are you?"

"I'm well, thanks," Sam answered without breaking pace.

Nolan made the trip to the third floor and stepped out of the elevator. The officer at the desk had told him that Willy would be brought to number one. There were six visitor's booths on the third floor and number one was the first in the row. Nolan opened the steel door to the cubicle and sat down at the counter, waiting for his client to appear on the other side of the bullet-proof glass. Within a few moments he heard footsteps and the jangling of keys in the door. The door opened and Willy Bisbaine appeared in his familiar garb of institutional coveralls which looked strangely comfortable on him, as if he was always meant to be in orange.

Nolan nodded to the jailor who shut and locked the door behind Willy.

"What's up, Willy?" Nolan couldn't even muster a smile.

Willy sat down in his chair and shook his head. "They're doing it to me again!" he squealed, appearing to be on the verge of tears.

Well, I guess that answers my first question, Nolan thought. He's going to deny the whole damned thing.

Nolan blinked slowly and opened his folder. "Yes they are, Willy. Yes, they are," he mumbled as he stared at the official charges. "Rape and murder this time. Are you innocent again?"

"Hell yeah I'm innocent!" Willy yelled. "Why would I rape and murder the judge's wife?"

"I don't know . . . perhaps revenge?"

"No sir! I just go out. Why would I want to go back in?"

"Well, instead of you asking me questions about why you wouldn't do it, how about you tell me why you were arrested?"

"I don't fucking know!" Willy screamed. "I have no idea why they arrested me. I thought you would know!"

Nolan shrugged. "I don't know much about anything yet. The only thing I know is that the prosecutor went to the grand jury and the grand jury indicted you on these charges. So, obviously the prosecutor presented some sort of evidence to show you did it."

"That's impossible," Willy huffed. "If I didn't do it then how they gonna show I did it?"

"Well, have you forgotten about how they did it the first time? It's all about witnesses, so let's just try to piece this thing together," Nolan offered. "Where were you Sunday morning when she was murdered?"

Willy rubbed his hands on his face. "Sunday . . . Sunday," he mumbled. "Hell, I was sleeping in my own bed . . . at my mama's house."

"And will anybody be able to say they saw you in bed Sunday morning?"

"Yeah, sure. My mama will tell you that."

"Okay, does she still have the same address and number?"

"Yeah, still the same," Willy nodded.

"All right. Did the police question you when you were arrested?"

"Yeah, they tried. But I didn't say much. I told them that I wanted to speak to you first."

"Nice," Nolan smiled. Finally, a smart defendant.

"What kind of questions did they ask before you told them you weren't talking?"

"Oh, you know. Were you ever at the judge's house . . . have you ever met the judge's wife . . . all that stuff."

"And you denied this?"

"No, I told the truth."

Nolan raised an eyebrow. "What do you mean you told the truth?"

"I told them I was there and everything."

Nolan chuckled and dropped his pen. "So, you were at the judge's house but you didn't have anything to do with the crimes?"

"That's right. A few weeks ago I got a call from the judge's wife and she told me to come over to the house cuz they wanted to give me some money to help me out. So, I went over there."

"Really," Nolan grinned. "And then what?"

"I went into their house, the judge gave me an envelope with money and the wife started hugging on me . . . that's what."

"How much money?" Nolan wasn't actually believing his story.

"Well, there was supposed to be $2,500 in the envelope but the judge had taken out $1,000 for himself cuz the missus asked him, 'Did you give him the $2,500?' But there wasn't $2,500 in there so that tells me the judge took out his cut without the wife knowing nothin' about it."

Nolan leaned ahead. The story was suddenly believable because it contained weird details that nobody would think of unless the events had occurred.

"So, what day was this?"

"It was Friday morning, a little more than two weeks ago."

"You said she was hugging on you . . . what do you mean?"

"Well, she came down the stairs and me and the judge were sitting in the living area there and she just came up and hugged me. Then when we were done she followed me to the door and hugged me again."

"All right, so, if I ask the judge all this he will confirm that you were at his house?" Nolan was testing him to see if he would waiver on his story.

"Yeah, I don't know why he wouldn't."

Nolan jotted down some notes then thought for a moment. "So if they have any scientific evidence, like hairs or fibers or anything like that, it must've come from you when you hugged her."

"Yeah, that's right," Willy nodded. "You ever know her?"

"What's that?" Nolan pretended to not hear his question.

"You ever meet her?" Willy repeated.

"Yeah, I've met her . . . a long time ago," Nolan answered. It seemed like a long time ago to him anyway.

"You know she's pretty hot then, right?"

Nolan nodded. "Yeah, last time I saw her she was hot."

"Well that day she was dressed like a ho'. She had a really tight shirt on and high shorts—the kind of shorts where . . . well, you know, you could see things."

"And why are you telling me this?" Willy's description of the judge's wife gave Nolan an uneasy feeling.

"I'm just tellin' you how she was."

Nolan shook his head. "That doesn't help you, Willy. What are you saying, she was so hot that you couldn't help yourself but to go back and rape her?"

"No, no!" Willy squealed. "I didn't rape nobody. I'm just tellin' you how she is because maybe she dressed like that a lot and maybe somebody else went there because she was always dressin' like that."

"All right," Nolan waved his hand. "I get it. But you understand that the prosecutor is going to spin everything against you, right?"

Willy nodded.

"He's going to say that because you were there you knew where they lived and you came back later to rape and kill her. Everything that happened will be twisted around in a bad way."

"Yeah, I know that," Willy nodded.

"So keep all that talk about her being hot to yourself. Don't give them any more ammunition than they already have."

"I hear ya," Willy nodded again.

"When will you know what kind of evidence they have against me?"

Nolan shrugged. "It may not be for a while. I could file for discovery, but then I'd have to reveal any alibi you may have and I want to confirm with your mom that you were home before I do that. So, the bottom line is that I probably won't know anything until a month before trial."

"Oh," Willy looked concerned. "What about my bond hearing?"

Nolan shook his head. "Forget it. No judge around here is going to give you a bond for rape and murder."

"But I have a right to a hearing!" Willy begged.

"Yeah you do, but you want me working on your case and trying to get you free or do you want me wasting time with crap that won't help you?"

Willy dropped his head. "Whatever man."

"I'll stay in touch. Let me know if you think of anything else."

"All right," Willy nodded.

CHAPTER 18

"What's up boss?" Rick sauntered into Nolan's office, kicked his feet up and placed his hands behind his head in mid-air, before landing on the couch on his back.

"Man, you're hard on furniture," Nolan shook his head.

"Sorry boss, just trying to land comfortably," Rick smiled and closed his eyes.

"You see Danny yet this morning?" Nolan asked. Usually on Friday mornings they all gathered in Nolan's office and told stories.

Danny was his newest assistant who had been there just over a year. He was a millennial with a law degree from the University of Virginia. When not at work, he was the type that wore skinny pants, slip-on loafers, and V-cut t-shirts with ironic phrases. He was a part of the generation of men that had been emasculated by a modern culture and taught from a young age to abhor bullying and violence in any form, including words that may offend others. For this reason Nolan was skeptical that he could truly represent those accused of violent crimes, for the simple fact that he couldn't identify with such a world where people intentionally disobeyed the law by taking matters into their own hands, or in many cases, their fists.

"He said something about stopping at Juvenile before coming in. I'm a little worried about the boy myself. He's spending way too much time down at the detention center with troubled teenage girls. I sure hope he doesn't get manipulated by one. You know how impressionable he is."

Nolan smiled. "He's spending time down there because I'm making him see all of his clients at least once a week."

Rick laughed. "Now that's not very nice! I hope you don't get any crazy ideas about making me do the same. Unlike Danny Boy I have the perfect client visitation system that cannot be tinkered with."

"Oh really? Then why do I see so many complaint letters from incarcerated clients wanting to know if they have an attorney?"

"Because that's the key element of my system. I will not visit any clients unless they ask to be seen. As Confucius says, those who require help will cry out. Those who don't will cry silently."

"I think you just made that up. And I'm going to pretend I didn't hear you because your system is slightly different than the Public Defender Commission's policy . . . you know, the one that says lawyers must see their clients within 48 hours of incarceration."

"Well, that's just insanity. Why would I waste my time seeing clients who are just going to plead guilty anyway? My system is foolproof I tell you. Those who have the gumption to write a complaint letter or have family contact me are the ones who want to plead not guilty, so those are the ones I need to see. On the other hand, those who don't complain obviously have nothing to say to their attorney, so they're the ones who are gonna plead guilty. I'll give you an example—Dashoni Miller, arrested last month for domestic assault and battery. He's been in jail for what . . . oh, about 45 days. I never saw the kid until yesterday, ten minutes before trial. I knew he was gonna plead guilty. If he wasn't then I would've had all sorts of people calling me, like his baby's mama, his girlfriends, his sisters . . . everybody. And that's the Zen of being a Public Defender. Thank you, I'll be here all week."

"Oh, boy," Nolan groaned. "One of these days you're gonna make me look bad."

"I wouldn't do that to you, boss. Trust me, it works. You don't have to worry about a thing."

Nolan leaned back in his chair and swiveled towards the window to gaze upon the Big Shanty cityscape. The chateau sat on a hillside overlooking the two courthouses in town, which were side by side on the street below. The one on the left was General District Court for misdemeanors and the one on the right was Circuit Court for felonies. The Commonwealth Attorney's office was located on the second floor of the General District Court building, so Nolan could see the windows of their office.

Mutz was behind one of those windows diligently preparing for the trial of Willy Bisbaine, which was less than 60 days away. Nolan still didn't have any real information from the case. There was no search warrant on file and the state lab had yet to respond to his request for information. The only other tool for obtaining information was in the form of a discovery motion, but he didn't want to file that until he talked to Willy's alibi witnesses, which he planned to do later that day. If in fact he had an alibi witness then he would not request discovery because the rule stated that if the defense files for discovery, the Commonwealth has the right to receive reciprocal discovery, specifically, the defendant's alibi and the names of any alibi witnesses. And Nolan knew it would be a disaster to give notice of the alibi before trial because the prosecutor would then be prepared to destroy the alibi witness on the stand.

There was still plenty of time to gather information so he wasn't too worried about that. His real worry involved Mutz. Was Mutz smart enough to realize that he was holding the ultimate trump card?

"Whatcha thinkin' about boss?" Rick asked from the couch.

"Mutz."

"Well if you're wondering, the answer is yes. He is an up-skirting enthusiast and he's currently seeking a romantic relationship with a farm animal that has low self-esteem."

"Well, that's common knowledge, so I wasn't thinking about that," Nolan chuckled. "I was thinking about that thing he knows about you and me."

"What about it?"

"It's his chance to bring me down, that's what."

'What . . . you think he'll tell the judge? I don't think he has the guts."

"I don't think so either because the judge may be just as critical of the messenger. But what if I'm the messenger instead?"

"What do you mean?"

"He could subpoena me because I'm a possible witness. And if he does that, then I'm screwed. I can't represent a client and be a witness in the same trial—it creates a conflict of interest. So not only would he be able to get rid of me as Willy's attorney, but he would also make me expose our little secret. He'd call me to the stand and ask me about Mrs. Chancey spending the night with me and the time that she left on Sunday morning. Won't that make some juicy headlines?"

"Hmm," Rick seemed to understand. "Why not just invoke the 5th Amendment and refuse to testify?"

"Well, the 5th Amendment gives you the right to not incriminate yourself. It protects you from having to provide information that could be used to prosecute you. So, all Mutz has to do is grant me immunity from prosecution, which dissolves a person's right to refuse to testify. When he does that, the judge can make me answer his questions."

"That's f'd up if you ask me," Rick sat up on the couch.

"It may be f'd up, but it's the law. So, as you can see, things may not go very well for me in the next few months . . . or for Willy, because you know what'll happen to him if I have to remove myself from the case."

"Yeah, he gets the Hammer."

They were referring to Burford Hammer, a local private attorney with a notorious reputation for being inept at criminal defense. Almost always indigent clients were provided a lawyer through the Public Defender office, but when a Public Defender couldn't do the job the court turned to private attorneys who had agreed to be on the court-appointed list. Burford Hammer was usually at the top of that list. And when he was appointed to represent someone the result was almost always a guilty plea in exchange for a sub-par deal. The prosecutors loved him because they always got their way and the court loved him because he didn't waste any time with annoying trials. Even some of his clients loved him because they thought they were getting a fancy private lawyer for nothing. But in the end the clients were just nails getting driven home by the Hammer.

"So what are you going to do?" Rick asked.

"I guess just keep plugging away on the case until I get the subpoena. Who knows, maybe he's not smart enough to think of that."

Danny appeared in the doorway. "I hope you're not talking about me." He entered Nolan's office and sat down in one of the stuffed chairs facing Nolan's desk.

"You get yourself a girlfriend at the detention center yet?" Rick pushed him. It seemed that Rick wasted no chance to harass Danny, probably because he knew that Danny wasn't as loyal as himself and that the Public Defender's Office was just a stepping stone for him. Or maybe it was just because it was easy to get under his thin skin.

Danny ignored the comment. "Vicki wanted me to give you this," he held out an envelope, which Nolan took. "Looks like it's from the state lab."

Nolan glanced at the return address. "It is." He tore it open and unfolded the papers. Nolan read aloud, "Enclosed please find all documents relevant to your request for information in the matter of Commonwealth v. William Horatio Bisbaine."

Nolan studied the papers for a few moments.

"Well? What do they got?" Rick asked.

Nolan chuckled and threw the papers into the air, one page landing on his desk and the other pages hitting the floor. "I frickin' knew it. He frickin' lied to me."

"What?" Rick begged again.

"It's a semen sample and the DNA matches Willy."

"Holy shit!" Rick exclaimed.

Danny picked up the papers and studied them. "Look, it says there is one sample from a swab of her belly that matches Willy and three different DNA's from the vaginal swab. One matches Willy, one matches the judge and the third one is unidentifiable."

Nolan glanced at Rick, who visibly winced and silently mouthed the F word.

Danny turned to Rick who immediately straightened his face.

"What?" Rick asked.

"So how could that be?" Danny asked. "If it's not the judge's sperm and it's not Mr. Bisbaine's sperm, then whose is it?"

"How the F would I know?" Rick sounded overly defensive.

"I didn't expect you to know. I'm simply pointing out that she must've had sex with somebody other than her husband because it's not from him or Mr. Bisbaine."

"Good point, Sherlock," Rick fell back into the couch. "That would actually help if he had only raped her because we could show the jury that she was a slut and she was asking for it. But he killed her, dumb ass. I don't think we have an argument that she wanted him to do that no matter how many men she'd been sleeping with."

"I'm just saying . . . you don't have to get all caustic."

"Caustic? You people from Charlottesville are all like, you can't just speak plain English."

"Whatever," Danny gave up.

"I feel like getting a little caustic myself . . . on Willy," Nolan added. I wonder what lies he'll tell when I confront him with this?"

CHAPTER 19

Before Nolan wasted any time with alibi witnesses he wanted to talk with Willy first. The DNA results could just possibly wake him up and convince him to plead guilty, which would be a nice and tidy way to close the case, Nolan thought. Then again he'll probably have some whacked out excuse for his semen being in her. One would never know unless one asked.

Same floor, same booth, different day. Nolan glanced at his watch and noted that he had been waiting almost ten minutes. The smell of institutional pine hung heavy in the air, almost completely drowning out the aroma of Friday's fish stick lunch.

He wondered what Willy did all day, or any inmate in the city jail for that matter. Did he watch TV? Did he play cards with other inmates? Did he read the Bible? What was he doing right now that was taking so much time . . . reading law books?

Finally, he heard the keys in the door on the other side of the glass and Willy appeared. He rubbed his eyes and yawned before sitting down. Obviously, he had been sleeping.

"You getting enough sleep?" Nolan asked in a completely sarcastic tone.

"Yeah, I'm good," Willy took his seat.

"I didn't mean to disturb your nap or anything but I've got some fairly important lab results that we need to talk about."

"Oh yeah, what's that?" Willy didn't seem to notice the sarcasm.

"Oh, just the DNA results that show your semen was in and on the judge's wife." Nolan passed the papers through the slot. "Take a look. Your old friend, Dexter the DNA molecule is back but this time he's not on your side."

Willy's eyes widened as he grabbed the papers and glanced at them. "This can't be! I didn't rape and kill no judge's wife!"

"Well, I don't know what to tell you. They have lab results that show it, so what do you want me to do, just argue that you didn't do it and hope for the best?"

Willy stared at Nolan in silence, his lip slightly quivering. "They must have made a mistake."

"They didn't make no mistake, Willy. You know it . . . I know it . . . we all frickin' know it. The only mistake was you lying to me. So, you can either let me know what really happened or I'm going to petition the judge to get out of this case because you refuse to cooperate. Then the court will appoint Burford Hammer to represent you and it's bye-bye for life and let's hope there's an after-world cuz you won't be participating in this one anymore."

Willy's eyes dropped and he stared at the papers. "This is full of shit. I never shoulda gone back there."

Finally, he's folded, Nolan thought. "Yeah, no kidding Willy. You shouldn't have gone back there. But it's not over though, maybe I can get some sort of plea deal."

Willy looked up. "I didn't rape and kill her. I was there the week before she died. I went back there and we had sex."

Nolan blinked, absorbing the ridiculous statement.

"Hmm," Nolan pondered. "So you went back there and she invited you in and you had consensual sex with her and that's how your semen got on her?"

"Yeah, that's the only way this all makes sense. I only went there once and I never went back either."

"Do you expect me to believe that you just rang her door bell and she was like, 'Oh hi, Willy, come on in and have sex with me?'"

"Well, I didn't tell you what she did when I was there for the money," Willy rubbed is face with his hands. "Remember I told you she kept hugging me?"

"Yeah, vaguely."

"Well when she hugged me at the front door when I was leavin' she reached around and grabbed me from behind. And she said, 'Come back next Friday, I'd like to get to know you better.'"

Nolan blinked again. "Really."

"Yeah, man."

"I thought you said the judge was right there."

"The judge was standing in the living room and he never came to the door. He didn't see it cuz he was probably too busy thinkin' about how I knew that he had taken money out of that envelope for himself."

"Huh," Nolan grunted. "So what did you do, just pop over there and ring the doorbell?"

"Yeah, basically. The day I went there to get the money I saw two cars in the driveway. So, when I went back I made sure there was only one car in the driveway before I rang the bell."

"What if the judge had been home and the wife wasn't?"

"Then I was just going to ask him for more money."

"But you're saying it was the wife who was home when you rang the bell?"

"Yup. And she answered the door. And the next thing you know we're drinking beer in the kitchen and she's all up into me and the rest is history."

"But it still doesn't make sense. How did that semen stay in and on her for a week?"

"Maybe she doesn't shower?" Willy offered.

A brief image flashed across Nolan's mind. It was an image of him licking tequila off Mrs. Chancey's belly on the pool table, which was less than a week after Willy had allegedly made his deposit. His mouth began watering then. Not the good kind of mouthwatering when you're hungry, but the bad kind that happens before vomiting.

Nolan shook off the image. "Did you use a condom?"

"Yeah, yeah, I used a condom."

"Well I guess it spilled. So now we need to come up with a valid explanation as to why your semen was still there a week later," Nolan muttered, deep in thought. At least Willy had a story and it was one hell of an interesting one. And since he didn't have a felony record, he could put Willy on the stand and he could tell that story. Who knows, maybe he could get the jury to believe she had poor hygiene?

"Okay, Willy," Nolan nodded. "We'll come up with something for the jury. In the meantime I'll go talk to your family and see who can say they saw you at home on that Sunday morning."

Nolan stood up to leave. Then he thought of the text on Mrs. Chancey's cell phone.

"Did you have any contact with her whatsoever, either by phone or text on the day she was killed?"

"No," Willy answered.

"What's your cell phone number?" Nolan wanted to make sure it wasn't he that had texted Mrs. Chancey on the morning of her murder.

"I don't have one," Willy shrugged. "I wasn't out long enough to even get one. Why do you ask?"

"So the police didn't confiscate any phone from you when you were arrested?"

"I just told you, I don't have one!" Willy raised his voice.

Nolan liked that answer . . . a lot. It could be that he was telling the truth. Or another possibility would be that he had a pre-paid phone that was untraceable. Either way, Mutz wouldn't be able to tie him to a text to Mrs. Chancey.

"Okay. See you when I see you."

"Sorry about lying."

"No problem," Nolan turned to leave. In fact, it was a big problem because now he had to somehow convince a jury that the judge's wife invited Willy to her house and she was willing to have sex with an almost complete stranger. That theory may float if he was a witness and testified that she had basically done the same thing with him, minus the actual sex. But to do that he would have to conflict out of the case and throw Willy under the Hammer, not to mention the fact that he'd be throwing away his career in Big Shanty. And even if he convinced a jury that Willy and Mrs. Chancey had sex, he would then have to convince them that Willy's semen was still there a week later. The more he thought about it the more impossible it seemed. It's far more likely that he raped and killed her, Nolan thought. But he knew he would still go through the motions and present Willy's defense as best he could.

When he returned to the office he called Willy's mother and asked her to come into the office on Monday, which would be convenient for him, because that was the day he had set aside for client interviews for the week.

CHAPTER 20

"Mrs. Bisbaine is here," Vicki's voice crackled over the telephone intercom.

"All right, I'll be down," Nolan answered. He could've interviewed her over the phone but he was a better judge of people in face to face situations. He wanted to know if Willy's mom would be willing to testify that he was home Sunday morning and more importantly, if she seemed honest.

At the bottom of the stairs Nolan turned into the waiting room, which was actually the formal living room when the building was a house. She was the only person there.

"Hello Mrs. Bisbaine, how are you?" Nolan smiled and stuck out his hand.

She stood up and shook it. "I'm fine, Mr. Getty. Thank you."

She had a genuine smile and a pleasant aura, just like Nolan remembered her from Willy's first trial. Amazingly, her faith in God and him had never wavered over the years he fought to free Willy. And in the end she was rewarded by the truth that her son was innocent. But now with Willy being arrested again he had to wonder if she could continue to be strong in her faith and endure another trial in which her youngest son was accused of rape and murder.

"Come on back with me, ma'am, we'll have a seat in the conference room," Nolan waved her through the vestibule and into the former dining room, shutting the pocket door behind them.

"Well, I can't imagine what you must be feeling, knowing your son is accused and facing another trial . . . and right after we had just proven his innocence," Nolan revealed his genuine concern for her.

"Oh, Lord, don't I know it. I still can't believe it. They say truth is stranger than fiction and they'd be right on this one. Lordy, God help us," she exclaimed, taking a seat at the table.

"So thanks for coming down. I just wanted to ask you some questions about Willy, okay?"

"That's fine. I'll answer as best I can."

"Do you remember a few weeks ago on Sunday, October 22nd, where and what you were doing?"

"Well, let's see, on Sundays I get up at seven thirty so that I can make the nine o'clock service at Big Shanty Baptist Church. The service lasts 'til 10:45 and then we have a brunch in the basement. I usually don't get home until about twelve or so."

"And do you have a specific memory of doing that on October 22nd?"

"Mr. Getty I do that every Sunday and I been doing that since I was a child."

"Fair enough. Did you see Willy on Sunday?"

"Well, I already put some thought into that and the devil is tempting me to swear on the Bible that Willy was home in bed and such, but I ain't gonna tell a lie. I went to bed Saturday night at ten and he wasn't home yet. And when I was getting ready for church I knocked on his door to see if he was comin' with and he didn't answer."

"So he could've been in the room, you just don't know one way or the other?" Nolan tried to steer her.

"No sir. When he didn't answer, I opened the door and I saw he wasn't nowhere in there."

Well, that's going to make things easy, Nolan thought. Time to file a discovery request.

"I see. I appreciate your honesty. Did you see him at all that day?"

"All I know is that he came walkin' in the front door at about one o'clock that afternoon and didn't say nothin' to nobody. And I tried to talk to him to see where he been but he just went straight to his room."

"Do you have any daughters or other family members living there?"

"No sir, it's just me and my cat, Mr. Mittens. All my girls are grown and gone out on their own."

"All right. Can you do me a favor . . . well, I guess you'd be doing your son a favor. If the police or any investigators knock on your door and want to ask you some questions, will you tell them your attorney advised you not to speak about it?"

Mrs. Bisbaine blinked. "They already did."

Nolan's shoulders sagged. "What did you tell them?"

"What I just told you. Like I said, the devil was tempting me but I couldn't do it."

Nolan sighed and closed his eyes. He should've immediately gone to her house before the police did so he could've told her to keep her mouth shut.

Why are people so ignorant? The 5th Amendment is over two hundred years old and somehow it's still a secret that continues to escape the common man.

"You didn't expect me to lie, did you?" she asked.

"No," Nolan opened his eyes. "I wanted you to plead the 5th Amendment, which says you have a right to not incriminate yourself. And it's not lying if you simply invoke that right and refuse to answer any questions."

"Oh," she replied.

"You said the devil was tempting you to tell a lie. Did Willy call you from the jail and talk about you testifying that he was in bed Sunday morning?"

"Well, we did talk about it and he was wondering if I had seen him in bed and I said I hadn't and he said he was in bed and that I must've been making a mistake."

"Did this happen over the phone from the jail?" Nolan pressed.

"Well, yes, I guess it did."

Of course, it did, Nolan thought. Now Mutz is going to bring in a jailhouse tape of the telephone call and Willy's going to be exposed for trying to get his own mother to lie for him. That'll be great.

"Let me ask you something," Nolan continued. "Do you think he did it?" He needed to make sure she wouldn't be a witness for the prosecution.

She shook her head. "No sir. My Willy wouldn't do that to nobody. I know that in my heart. He's a Christian, like me," she pointed to the sky and mouthed a prayer.

"Well then, that's about all I need from you right now. I may need to talk to you later though, okay?"

"Yes, whenever you want," Mrs. Bisbaine stood up and straightened her dress. "Thank you Mr. Getty for helping my son again. I appreciate it."

"No problem. I hope I can help him."

"Good day to you," she nodded.

Nolan opened the pocket door and led her into the foyer. "Goodbye now."

"Goodbye," she replied.

Nolan turned and saw one person in the waiting room. He approached Vicki's desk and glanced at the appointment calendar, seeing that Sherman Calhoun was the next interview. He had pulled Mr. Calhoun's file earlier in the morning, so he knew his charge was petit larceny.

Nolan turned to the well-dressed, elderly gentleman.

"Mr. Calhoun?"

"Yes," the man answered, standing.

"I'm Nolan Getty, your attorney. Let's go back to the conference room so we can discuss your case."

"Certainly," he grinned.

Once they had entered the former dining room, Nolan shut the pocket doors behind them, then waved Mr. Calhoun to a seat at the table.

Nolan opened his file and glanced at the warrant again.

"So, they say you stole something from a person named Alice Anderson?"

He shrugged. "That's what they say."

"What do you say?" Nolan asked.

"Well, I didn't really intend to steal it. I was just holding it for her so that nobody else would steal it," he answered.

"What do you mean . . . what were you holding for her?"

"A package that was on her porch," he confessed.

"So, is she a neighbor?"

"Yes. She lives across the street."

"What was in the package?"

"I don't know, I never opened it."

"So this was a package that was delivered to her porch and you just went over there and took it?"

"Yes sir," he answered.

"Then what happened?"

"About an hour later, the police knocked on my door and they said they wanted the package back that I took, so I gave it to them. Then they arrested me."

"And did you tell them you were just holding it for your neighbor?"

"Yes sir, but they arrested me anyway."

"Okay," Nolan continued. "They have you charged with regular petit larceny so I guess you've never been convicted of any larcenies before in your life?"

"Nope," he shook his head.

"Well, that's good. Another good thing is that you never opened the package, so that's evidence that you were just holding the package for her and never intended to steal the contents. Was there a problem in the neighborhood with people stealing packages?"

"Yes sir, just last week my other neighbor told me someone took a package off his porch."

Nolan wondered if Mr. Calhoun had done that too, but it didn't matter. "That's great. You have a rational explanation and reason for taking the package and holding it then. So, let's plead not guilty and see if they can prove that you intended to steal it. Even if you're found guilty, you will most likely just get a small fine without any jail time and then some court costs on top of that."

"Okay, whatever you say," Mr. Calhoun nodded.

"All right," Nolan continued, "your case is at 9:00 a.m., December 1st, in General District Court. Do you know where that is?"

"Is that the same place where the judge said he would have a Public Defender represent me?" he asked.

"Yes," Nolan answered. "Just sit in the gallery of the courtroom and go up to the judge's bench when they call your name. I will be there and we will then have a little trial in front of the judge. Do you have any questions about any of this?"

"No, sir," he responded politely.

As Nolan jotted down the 'not guilty' plea note, Mr. Calhoun continued, half to himself, but loud enough to hear.

"I only wish I hadn't listened to them."

"Who's that?" Nolan asked.

"Oh never mind," he said. "It doesn't matter."

Nolan stared at him for a moment.

"No really, please tell me."

"Well," he explained, "the people from Channel Four News."

"What does Channel Four News have to do with this?"

"Well, to be more specific, it's Catherine Caine and Rex Holt of the Night Team."

The Night Team, Nolan thought. Why did news stations always have to label themselves with such silly terms? He could hear the booming voice in his head. 'It's ten o'clock and you're watching Channel Four News with the Night Team: Katherine Kaine, Rex Holt, and meteorologist, Stormin' Sal Sebastian.' They were just the local news reporters, but in Big Shanty, they were like Hollywood celebrities.

"What does the Night Team have to do with this?" Nolan asked.

"It's a long story," he said, "just forget it."

"No, I can't now," Nolan explained, "as your lawyer I need to know everything."

Mr. Calhoun glanced to the door then leaned forward and whispered. "They've been watching me from the TV."

Nolan was more than a little surprised. After so many years of criminal defense he took a lot of pride in being able to pick out the mentally ill within the first 30 seconds. But this guy almost had him.

"Don't say another word," Nolan whispered back. He stood up from the table and went to the windows where he closed the blinds.

"You can never be too careful," Nolan explained as he returned to the table. "When and how did this start?"

In Nolan's experience, those suffering from paranoid delusions never confide to non-believers. He knew that if you tell them it's all in their head they lose trust and you eventually get categorized as 'one of them.'

"It happened one night about three months ago," Mr. Calhoun began. "I fell asleep in front of the TV. When I woke up the Channel

Four News was on and Katherine Kaine was talking to me. She told me that they planted a chip in my head while I was asleep and that they would be watching me from now on. Weird, huh?" he asked.

"I've heard of this happening to other people," Nolan replied, not completely lying.

He went on to explain that the chip allowed him to decipher secret messages from the TV and that Channel Four people told him to never change the channel or they'd send someone over.

"Well, I didn't believe it at first," he said, "so I turned the channel one night and sure enough, the phone rings and it's somebody from Channel Four telling me to turn the channel back. So, the first thing I do is rip the phone out of the wall. Then when that hurricane hit this summer I try to go to a weather channel to see if we're gonna get some weather here. Well don't you know, ten minutes after I change the channel there's a knock at my door and there's a guy from Channel Four waiting outside. I yelled at him through the door, 'I'm changing it back, I'm changing it back, you don't need to come in!' And he goes away. Well, then I decided to cancel my cable service since I knew I would only be watching one channel anymore."

"What about the package," Nolan interrupted, knowing that a man in his mental state could machine-gun details for hours without cutting to the chase.

"Well, after a while it's not good enough for them just to be watching me and me watching them. Then they start telling me to do things. To tell you the truth I think they just wanted to make sure the chip was still in place. Because the chip is not only a translator, it's a mind controller too."

Nolan nodded as if everybody knew that.

"The first time was when Rex Holt told me to shave my head. Well, it was summer and I was thinking about getting a real short haircut anyway so I didn't mind shaving it off. Then Ms. Kaine starts asking me to . . . well, she had me do some really weird stuff in front of the TV. Again, I think they just wanted to make sure the chip was working. I did it. I knew I had no choice. Then one day Rex Holt tells me there's a package on the neighbor's porch and that I need to get it before someone steals it. So, I walk across the street and grab the package and bring it back home. And the rest is history."

"Are they making you take any medication?" Nolan asked.

"I was taking medication but then they told me to stop," he explained.

"What kind of medication were you taking before they got to you?" Nolan asked.

"Um, I remember the doctor calling it psycho-something . . . psycho . . ."

"Psychotropic?" Nolan cut in.

"Yeah, that's it, psychotropic."

"Do you have any family members that have been watching over you or helping you out?" Nolan asked.

"Yes, my daughter Jeanie helps me out."

"What's her last name?"

"Johnson."

"What's her number?"

Mr. Calhoun recited her number, but grouped the numbers in twos, instead of the normal way of stating the first three numbers, pausing and then stating the last four. It seemed more times than not, if somebody grouped a phone number in two's there was something not quite right upstairs. Perhaps I should just ask clients' their phone numbers right when the interview starts so that I can immediately weed them out, Nolan thought.

"All right, I'm going to call her and tell her to help you get to court, okay?"

"That would be fine," he answered.

"In the meantime go see your doctor about getting back on that medication and do it ASAP. Today if you can."

"But what about the Night Team?" he asked in a panicked tone.

"Well," Nolan explained, "obviously, those idiots weren't aware that you have an attorney. You see, once you get an attorney they're not allowed to communicate with you anymore—not by telephone, not by email, not even by brain chip. So, I'll contact them and let them know that you're completely off-limits, at least until the end of this larceny case."

His eyes lit up.

Poor guy, Nolan thought. He couldn't even imagine the kind of twisted world he had been living in the last several months. A human's grasp on reality was such a thin tendril. One little misfiring synapse and the demons converged like a plague of rats.

"Also," Nolan explained, adding another safety net, "any medication that your doctor gives you will short circuit the chip and they can't control you even if they wanted to. But trust me, once they know you have a lawyer they wouldn't dare get near you, otherwise, I could bring the whole network down."

Nolan knew that in Mr. Calhoun's head, the real battle was with the Channel Four Night Team. He could have cared less about the charge against him. And the fact that Nolan now knew that Mr. Calhoun was insane at the time he took the package didn't change anything. He could plead insanity at the trial, but if it worked then Mr. Calhoun would be sent away to a state hospital for evaluation and he would be held up to 12 months. The better strategy was to just ignore the mental illness, have a trial, and in the worst-case scenario, get a fine.

Mr. Calhoun smiled. "Thank you. Thank you so much."

"Oh, and by the way, don't bring this up during your trial. Just stick with your original story and tell the judge that you were simply holding the package for your neighbor because you didn't want it to get stolen, okay?"

"Okay," he nodded.

Nolan stood up and ushered Mr. Calhoun to the foyer. He opened the front door for him and patted him on the back as he stepped by.

"Have a good day, Mr. Calhoun."

"You too, sir," he answered.

Nolan shut the door behind him then split the blinds with his fingers and watched the schizophrenic seamlessly dissolve into the public.

"How's the witness coaching going?" a voice interrupted his thoughts.

Nolan instantly recognized the voice of his investigator, Eric, a retired Big Shanty Police Officer.

"Not bad," Nolan turned. Eric was standing near Vicki's desk resting his elbow on a filing cabinet. Everything about him screamed retired police officer . . . the khaki slacks and a sport coat with a slight bulge near the hip, the gray hair and mustache, and a pot belly to finish the look.

"That one's going to take some work to get him to lie," Nolan pointed towards the front porch.

Eric smiled and returned to his conversation with Vicki. "Anyway, I still can't figure out for the life of me why some man hasn't hitched you up. It makes me wonder what kind of young men we have around this town."

Vicki smiled. "It has nothing to do with the men in this town . . . it's me. I was tied up once and I tore the hitching post out of the ground running away."

Eric laughed. "I knew you were a wild one."

"Come on, the coffee's still hot," Nolan waved, leading the way up the old wooden staircase.

As they entered Nolan's office on the second floor Eric whistled softly, "Man, that Vicki sure is pretty. I don't know how you keep your hands off her."

"Who says I do?" Nolan closed the door and then made his way to his desk.

Eric raised an eyebrow as he took a seat in front of the desk. "So I guess you're ready to gear up on this big murder case, huh?"

"Yup," Nolan nodded.

"What a screwed-up mess, huh?" Eric shook his head. "I still can't believe she's dead."

"I know, it's weird," Nolan agreed. "You want a real shocker?"

"Sure."

"My client says the reason his DNA was found on Mrs. Chancey was because he had consensual sex with her the week before she was murdered."

Eric blinked, silent for just a moment before bursting into laughter. "Tremendous! That's probably the most fantastic lie I've ever heard. At least your boy has imagination."

"Well, the worst part is now I have to send you on a wild goose chase around town trying to find evidence to support his lie. Sounds fun, huh?"

"Oh yeah, that sounds like a real blast. Who do you want me to start with, her first-grade teacher?"

Nolan smiled. "You don't have to go too crazy. You know the deal, just try to interview her circle of people and ask them about her promiscuity, if she had any known enemies or anybody that was out to get her."

"Yeah, I know," Eric nodded. "You know she had a reputation, right?"

Nolan nodded. "Yeah, so I've heard."

"So Bisbaine must've somehow heard about this reputation and now he's telling a fib that fits right in with it."

"Yeah, I know," Nolan nodded. "But it has to be done. And while you're at it why don't you see if the judge will talk?"

"Oh come on man," Eric shook his head. "Don't make me do that."

"Don't worry, he probably isn't going to. Just document an attempt to talk to him for the file."

"And what if he wants to talk? I imagine you'd want to hear what he has to say, no?"

Nolan nodded. "Sure. Ask him to come in anytime and I'll clear my schedule."

"And you want me to ask the questions though, right?"

"That's right," Nolan smiled. "You know I won't be able to testify as to what he said."

"That's going to be awkward, me asking about his wife and everything. I don't get paid enough for this crap," Eric grumbled. "He better not want to talk."

Nolan laughed. "Sorry."

"Yeah, yeah. What about your defense? Does your boy have an alibi or anything you want me to chase down?"

"I wish. I think he tried to talk his mom into it and I'm sure Mutz will have a jail house recording of it, but no dice. She says he wasn't home the night before or the morning of the murder."

"So are you going to file for discovery?"

"Not yet. I need to talk to Willy again and see if he can come up with a better alibi witness than his mother. If he can't I will."

"All right, well I better get on it. I'll let you know about the judge."

Eric stood up to leave, then turned. "Oh, I almost forgot. I traced that number you gave me," he said, reaching into his pocket.

For some reason, Nolan had forgotten to ask about it too.

Eric retrieved a piece of paper and read from it. "James Sanders, 2312 Orchard Street."

"Huh," Nolan grunted. "Well, that's good . . . it's not Willy's."

"What?" Eric asked.

"Oh, nothing," Nolan hadn't meant to talk out loud. He thought for a minute, then knew what had to be done. "I need you to check him out. I have reason to believe he texted Mrs. Chancey on the morning of her murder."

"What?" Eric seemed stunned. "How do you know that?"

"Ah, that would be better for you not to know right now," Nolan smiled. "You know . . . for your own protection."

"I see," Eric shrugged. "What do you mean by check him out."

"See if you can get anything else on him. You know, personal history, criminal record, anything you can get. And watch his house. See if he's home and when he comes and goes."

"Okay. You think he's involved in this?"

"I don't know, but if he texted her on the morning of her murder, then he's at least a possible witness that could help Willy."

CHAPTER 21

Montgomery Mutz closed the door to his office and returned to his desk. He opened the file on his computer that contained the 389 photographs of the crime scene. In his conscious mind, he was simply preparing for trial, but after a cursory review of some of the photos, his mouse strayed to the one photo that he had opened many more times than all the others.

He scrolled down through the photos until he came to the fifth one in the eighth row. With a click he expanded the image of Mrs. Chancey on the floor with her arms and legs splayed outward. Her pose made it seem as though she was making a snow angel . . . except for the fact there was blood instead of snow.

As usual, he purposely avoided looking at her gaping head wound by zooming and moving the image to exclude her face. With a few more clicks he had enlarged the image so much that only her body was in the frame and the surrounding pool of blood was off-screen. Now he could see what he wanted, without the pesky reminder that she had been brutally murdered.

As he focused in on her body, his eyelids relaxed and his vision faded into a blurry, dream-like state . . . a place where he could play out the twisted fantasy that she was still alive.

He pictured the scene as if they were in a movie, or more likely, a soap opera. The camera in his mind showed the judge's mansion, then panned into the bedroom where they lay together . . . he in the judge's robe and she completely nude beside him, her body flickering in the glow of the fireplace.

What's that? Yes, they are the nicest I've seen.

A loud buzz from the telephone shattered his fantasy, instantly evaporating the scene from his mind. He blinked and jabbed at the top of the screen, closing out the photo.

"What is it?"

"Judge Chancey is on line one for you."

"Thanks."

Mutz absently straightened a few papers on his desk and blinked his eyes rapidly, trying to shake the vestiges of the running soap opera in his mind. After a few moments he straightened his tie, then cleared his throat before reaching over and clicking the speaker button.

"Hello Judge, how are you doing?"

"Hello Montgomery. I'm fine, I guess." The judge's voice sounded distant and weak.

"What can I do for you?"

"Did you have the lab run the tests again?"

"Yes sir. Same result. We have the right guy."

"Huh," the judge grunted. "I guess I just have a hard time believing that he would come back and do such a thing."

"I understand," Mutz tried to act compassionate.

"What about Jim Sanders? Have you tracked him down yet?"

"No sir. We're still trying. We're sending officers over to his house but he doesn't answer the door. We're also interviewing people he knew and we have a BOLO for him. I take it you haven't heard from him either?"

"No. I've called several times and left messages, but nothing. It's not right. He suddenly disappears after my wife's murder and never shows up again. What if he was involved somehow?"

"I agree that it's strange and I suppose that's possible, but right now he's just a loose end that needs to be accounted for."

"Have you searched his house?"

"Well, I'd certainly like to but we don't have enough evidence for a search warrant. We need something more than just the fact he didn't come back to finish your project."

"Yes, I suppose. Has Getty asked for a plea deal?"

"No, nothing."

"I see. Well, at any rate, I wanted to let you know that his investigator has reached out to me. They want to talk."

Mutz thought in silence for a moment. "Not a good idea if you ask me."

"Well, I knew you'd think that but you have to look at the bigger picture. The last thing we want to do is to look like we're hiding something. If I don't talk to them they'll make a big deal out of it at trial. You and I both know that if this thing goes to trial I'm going to have to testify and when I do, I don't want Getty bringing up on cross that I refused to talk to them. He'll play it out that we were trying to hide something, just like you do when the defense witnesses refuse to talk to you."

Mutz thought for a moment. "Yes, I suppose you're right. But you have to be careful."

"What do you mean? I have nothing to hide."

"I mean just make sure you recall the facts as you did when you spoke with Lieutenant Childress. If you are inconsistent with anything Getty will try to twist it around in his favor."

"Yes, yes. Everything is just as clear as the day it happened. This isn't something you can ever forget."

"I don't suppose," Mutz suddenly felt bad. "I'm sorry you have to go through all this."

"Goodbye, Mr. Mutz," the judge hung up.

CHAPTER 22

"You know every call from the jail is recorded, so why would you call your mother and try to get her to lie for you?" Nolan's tone was sharp and angry.

"I just asked if she had seen me in bed," Willy answered with a whine behind the bullet proof glass.

"Yeah, so now they have a recording of you lying about your whereabouts on the morning of the murder. You weren't at home the night before and you weren't in bed that Sunday. Your mother already told the police all this."

Willy's shoulders sank. "Oh."

They sat in silence a few moments.

"Well?" Nolan asked.

Willy looked up. "Well, what?"

Nolan threw his hands in the air and raised his voice. "Where the hell were you?"

Willy rubbed his face with both hands and let out a sigh. "I was with a hooker."

"Go on," Nolan prodded, unfazed.

"I picked her up Saturday night and we spent the night at a motel. Then I went home Sunday afternoon."

Nolan waited a few seconds but Willy didn't continue. He was losing his patience.

"Well, Willy, what do you think I'll want to know now?" he asked with heavy sarcasm.

"Uh, well, I don't know."

"The details, Willy . . . the details. The prosecutor is going to ask for more details so you better have an answer."

"Like what?" Willy asked, still not getting it.

"Like where did you pick her up; what was her name; what did she look like; what did you pay her; how long was she with you; what was the name of the motel; did you pay cash or credit for the motel; did you give your i.d. when you checked in; when did you check out . . . everything Willy."

"Oh, well let's see," Willy thought for a few seconds. "I picked her up about 9 o'clock on Saturday night on the corner of Grace Street and we went to the Shamrock Motel . . . the one at the end of Main Street. I paid her 200 bucks to spend the entire night, and . . ."

"Two hundred?" Nolan didn't let him finish. "And what else?"

Willy blinked. "And some crack."

Okay, that is at least believable now, Nolan thought.

"The prosecutor will ask you where you got it," Nolan said. "What are you going to say?"

"I'd rather not," Willy answered.

"No," Nolan shook his head. "You will be forced to answer his questions so what is your answer going to be?"

"I don't know the dude's name," Willy answered.

"Well then recite the details of how you got it."

"I was just driving around and I asked some people on the streets if anybody was selling and finally, a dude said yes."

"Where were you?"

Willy thought for a few seconds. "On Taylor Street, by the Y."

"Okay, what was the hooker's name and what is her description?"

"She called herself Angel. Black, skinny, no front tooth, orange hair . . . and she had a tattoo on her face—three dots near the corner of her eye."

Nolan liked the description because it was specific enough to believe he was describing a real person. The only question was whether he was with that person on that night or she was a hooker he had been with before he went to prison.

"What about payment at the hotel?"

"I think she gave an i.d. to the guy at the desk and then I handed her the money and she paid the man."

"So you didn't give your i.d.?"

"No."

Of course not, Nolan thought. That would be too good to be true.

"When did you leave?"

"About noon the next day."

"And she was with you all that time?"

"Yes. I dropped her off on Grace Street where I picked her up."

"And then you went home?"

"Yes."

"And I don't suppose you know any more details about her, like her real name or where she lives?"

"Naw," Willy shook his head. "That's all I know."

That figures, Nolan thought. It's hard to know details like that when attempting to describe fictitious people and events. But that's what you get in criminal defense—vague stories and details that cannot be traced. More times than not the balloon of lies just keeps getting bigger until the trial takes place, at which time it's popped.

"Okay, Willy," Nolan sighed. "I'll have my investigator try to track her down."

CHAPTER 23

Nolan checked his watch a second time. It wasn't like Eric to be late. He was supposed to be in the office at nine but it was already 9:15. They were going to discuss the case and make a game plan to question the judge, who was coming in at 10:00. Just as he was about to call Eric on his cell, he heard the heavy footsteps on the stairs. A moment later Eric appeared in the doorway.

"Good morning," he smiled. "Sorry I'm late."

"No problem," Nolan waved to the open chair in front of his desk. "Traffic?"

"It's getting worse every year. Too many damned people moving here if you ask me."

"Willy has a new alibi," Nolan smiled. "He says he was with a hooker named Angel that night. African-American, skinny, orange hair, three dot tattoo near right eye."

"Ah . . . mi vida loca," Eric cut in.

"What's that?" Nolan asked.

"The three dot tattoo . . . it means 'my crazy life'."

Nolan grunted. "That makes sense. Anyway, he picked her up on Grace Street and they spent the night at the Shamrock Motel at the end of Main."

"Great," Eric grunted. "And you want me to waste my time trying to find her?"

Nolan smiled again. "Yep."

Eric shrugged. "It's your money."

"What do you have on this Jim Sanders guy," Nolan asked.

Eric retrieved a paper from his briefcase and read from it. "Construction guy. He owns Old Dominion Construction and does residential remodels and handyman stuff. 28 years old. Misdemeanor record for marijuana possession, reckless driving and an assault. Looks like he's originally from Kentucky and moved here about five years ago."

"Have you seen him?" Nolan asked.

"Nope. There's no vehicle in the driveway and he ain't there. No lights come on at night, nothing. I even knocked on the door a few times and nobody answered."

"Huh," Nolan grunted. "Well, we'll have to ask the judge if he knows him."

Nolan glanced at his watch. "He's still confirmed for ten, right?"

"Far as I know."

For the next forty minutes, Nolan and Eric mapped out an interview plan for the judge. Eric jotted down the questions that Nolan wanted him to ask, mostly about timing and the judge's whereabouts in the 24 hours preceding his wife's death. At five minutes before ten his telephone buzzed and Vicki's voice came over the intercom.

"Judge Chancey is here."

Nolan clicked the button on the phone. "Thanks."

"We ready?" he looked at Eric.

"Yup, let's do this."

They walked down the stairs to the foyer where the judge was seated.

"Good morning, Judge," Nolan smiled and held out his hand. The judge stood up and shook it.

He was wearing a dark blue suit with a red tie, looking more like a businessman than a judge. It wasn't often Nolan saw him without the black robe.

"Do you remember Eric?"

"Yes, hello," the judge shook Eric's hand as well.

"Let's go into the conference room," Nolan stepped aside and waved him into the old dining room, shutting the door behind them.

"Thanks for taking the time to come in," Nolan said. "Please, have a seat anywhere."

The judge sat at the head of the table while Nolan and Eric pulled up chairs on either side of him.

"I'm sorry about your loss," Nolan started. "And I'm sorry we have to ask you about the whole thing. I can't imagine what you're going through."

"Yes, thank you. I understand, though. You're just doing your job."

Nolan nodded. "Well, Eric is just going to run through the standard questions that we have to ask. You know, so we can basically just cover ourselves and document the file that we interviewed everybody possible."

"Yes, I understand. I think we can both agree that we don't want Bisbaine appealing this case on the grounds of ineffective assistance of counsel."

"Yes, that's right," Nolan nodded, pleased with the cordial attitude the judge displayed. "Do you mind if I record?" Nolan placed the small digital recorder on the table.

"Not at all," the judge responded.

"Thank you," Nolan clicked the record button on the player. "Interview with Judge Chancey, ten a.m., November 8th with investigator Eric Wentz and Nolan Getty present." He then turned to Eric. "Go ahead Mr. Wentz."

"Good morning again, Your Honor," Eric began. "I guess we should just start from the beginning. Can you tell us how and when you found your wife?"

"Uh, yes," the judge began. "It was Sunday morning. Torey had gone to a fundraiser at the old train depot the day before. She spent the night there and I didn't expect her back until later Sunday morning. It was . . . well, that morning . . . on Sunday that is, I went out for a morning jog and when I returned, the first thing I saw was the shattered garage door. It looked like someone had set off a bomb—there was wood all over the driveway. I ran inside and didn't see anything out of the ordinary, so I then went to the side door to the house, but it was locked. I then ran into the house through the front door and that's when I found her on the floor in the kitchen."

The judge seemed calm, resting both hands face down on the conference table.

"What time did you leave your house to go jogging?"

"It was almost 8:40 if I remember correctly."

"And what time did you return?"

"This I remember clearly because I was using an app for my run and it said 10:11."

Eric paused. "So sometime after you left for your jog and before you returned, your wife had come home and had been murdered."

"Yes," the judge stared beyond Eric and Nolan. "She wasn't home when I left and I didn't think she'd be home until much later, but then there she was . . . the blood . . . he had hit her on the head with something and there was a pool of blood around her . . ." the judge's voice trailed off.

"I'm sorry," Eric tried to comfort him.

"I'm okay," the judge blinked. "Go ahead. Let's get this over with."

"Sure," Eric continued. "When did she leave Saturday?"

"I don't recall the exact time, but it was late afternoon, before five."

"And what did you do the rest of Saturday and that night?"

"I just fiddled around the house. Pruned some plants in the backyard and cleaned up the garage a bit. Ate dinner, then went to bed early and read a book."

"Did you see anybody that morning around your house? Any neighbors, strangers, anybody?"

The judge shook his head, "No, not that I can recall."

"Did you see anybody you knew while you were out jogging?"

"No, not that I can recall."

"Does anybody have access to your house besides you and your wife, you know, like a maid, pool guy or anybody, really."

"Well, yes," the judge answered. "There is a guy who has been working on my house. Jim Sanders is his name. The name of his company is Old Dominion Construction. And the funny thing is . . . he hasn't been back since that day."

Nolan glanced at Eric, who raised an eyebrow.

"What was he working on?"

"He was installing a security system and building a wine cellar in my basement."

"How long had he been working at your house?"

"Oh, I guess it had been over two months."

"So did he come and go as he pleased?"

"Yes, pretty much. He had a key so he could come and go whenever he wanted."

"So he would work on your house when you and your wife were not home?"

"Yeah, that's what I wanted him to do . . . get the work done when we didn't have to hear the construction noise and all that."

"Tell me about that security system, did you have cameras in the house?" Eric continued.

"Well, he was in the process of installing cameras but only one was working at the time. I didn't even know it was working though. He had told me that he was waiting for a controller. But then Lieutenant Childress discovered that it was working on the morning my wife was murdered."

"And was it recording?"

"Yes, apparently. I haven't seen it but they said it was."

"Did they say what was on it?"

"They said just me exiting the house when I went for a jog, then me coming back. So, that tells me the killer came through the back door or the side door. And both of those doors were still locked."

"I see," Eric hummed. "And you haven't seen or heard from this construction guy since the day of the murder, you say?"

"That's right. Here he is, every day at my house . . . or, most days anyway. Then all of a sudden, he disappears. No calls, nothing. Now that's just weird, don't you think?"

"Yes," Eric nodded. "Do you think he may have had something to do with this?"

"I don't know. Mr. Mutz tells me that all the DNA samples match Bisbaine, so it doesn't make sense that he had anything to do with this. I just find it strange that he hasn't talked to me or showed up again."

Nolan immediately knew that Mutz had not shared the state lab information with the judge about a third person's DNA deposited in his wife. *He said, all the DNA samples match Bisbaine.* That's probably a good thing, Nolan thought.

"Did you ever tell Mr. Mutz this?" Eric asked.

"Yes. I told him the same thing."

"Has Mutz questioned him?"

"Not that I know of. I think he's still trying to find him, but he hasn't yet."

"Did anybody threaten you or your wife at any time before it happened?" Eric changed direction.

"No."

"Do you know of anybody that would have a reason to do this to her?"

"Besides Bisbaine? No."

"Okay, well let me ask you this. Did you ever see Willy Bisbaine around your house after he was freed?"

Nolan had wanted Eric to ask the question in those exact words because he didn't want to reveal Bisbaine's story that he had been to their house, just in case Bisbaine was lying.

"Well, yes, I'm sure he's told you this but I have to explain something. I felt very bad about Mr. Bisbaine's incarceration and so I mentioned to Torey that we should give him some money to help him out until he received the compensation from the Commonwealth. Well, it was she who invited him over, I guess kind of as a surprise for me because she initially didn't think we should do it. But then I think she felt bad and she called him and asked him to come to the house so that we could give him some money."

"So did he?"

"Yes. He came. We had some conversation in our living room and then I gave him some money and he left. That was it."

"How much money?"

"$1,500."

"When did this happen?"

"It was about two weeks before she was killed."

"Did he ever seem angry or upset about the case?"

"Ah, no. He was very pleasant . . . and very grateful for our help."

"Was that the only time you had seen him after he was freed?"

"Yes."

"Okay thank you," Eric seemed to hesitate. "Excuse me, but I need to ask some sensitive questions and I'm sorry."

"I understand."

"Um, are you aware of any infidelity on your wife's part since you've been married?"

"No."

"Have you ever been suspicious of any infidelity on her part since you've been married?"

"Not really. I guess every husband has some worries now and then, especially when you have a young, attractive wife, but I don't believe she ever cheated on me."

"Have you ever thought about or discussed a divorce since you've been married?"

"No."

"Did you have any life insurance policies on her?"

"Yes."

"How much?"

"$750,000. We had that for each of us."

Eric blinked. "Okay, thank you." Eric turned to Nolan. "Do you have anything else?"

"Thank you, Judge," Nolan stood up. "That's all we need right now. Thank you very much for coming in."

The judge shook hands with Eric and Nolan before leaving. They walked him into the foyer and watched as he exited the front door. They then returned to the old dining room.

"I'm going to guess you want me to go full scale on this Jim Sanders guy."

"That's right. I want 24/7 surveillance at his house and business. And track down everybody he knows and anybody he's worked for in the last year."

"Well, I'm going to have to get some sub-contractors involved then. You got the budget for that?"

"I'll pay you one way or the other."

Eric smiled. He knew the Public Defender's office didn't have the budget, so he would be paid from Nolan's pockets. He also knew that

Nolan's pockets were deep. Nolan had told him several years earlier that he had inherited a small fortune from his aunt who had been married to a yacht maker in Florida. Apparently, it was enough to stop working, but Nolan didn't, which was a good thing for Eric because Nolan always paid his bills on time.

"It's your money," Eric turned and exited the front door.

Nolan climbed the stairs to his office and closed the door behind him. He knew there was one other thing that had to be done and he couldn't procrastinate any longer. He had to interview Sheila Stenson to see if she had any information regarding Mrs. Chancey or her murderer.

He pulled up a directory on his computer and quickly found a hit. 'Dr. Michael and Sheila Stenson,' were the first names on the list. The directory gave an address and telephone number.

Nolan retrieved his cell phone and dialed the number. After several rings a female voice answered.

"Hello?"

"Um, hello, is this Mrs. Sheila Stenson?"

"Yes."

"Uh, hello Mrs. Stenson. This is Nolan Getty with the Public Defender's office."

Silence.

"My assistant and I were the ones you and Mrs. Chancey were with the night before she was murdered."

"Yes, I know who you are."

"Well, this is a bit awkward, but I'm representing William Bisbaine and I was wondering if I could talk with you about Mrs. Chancey."

"Yes, I suppose so. I figured you would eventually want to."

"Okay, good." Nolan was relieved. "Um, I could come to your house or you could come to my office, it doesn't matter to me."

"When?"

"Whenever you want. I'll work around your schedule."

"You can come over this afternoon. I'm here all day."

"Okay, great. How about three?"

"That's fine. Do you know our address?"

"Yes, it's on the directory here; Golden Oak Drive, right?"

"Yes, that's right."

"Okay, see you later."

"Bye."

Nolan hung up the phone and leaned back in his chair. He would go alone because he didn't want Eric to know anything about their night together. If she had anything important to add he could always have Eric interview her again later.

CHAPTER 24

As he turned onto Golden Oak Drive from the main thoroughfare, Nolan approached a gate and a guard shack beside it. He noticed a special lane for visitors so he aimed his car into that. He then rolled down his window as the guard stepped out of the shack.

"Hello, can I help you?" the guard asked.

"I'm here to see the Stensons," Nolan answered. "I'm Nolan Getty."

The guard looked at his clipboard. "Okay, can I see your i.d., please?"

Nolan reached in his wallet and retrieved his i.d. for the guard, who studied it, then handed it back.

"Very good," he said, opening the gate.

"Thanks," Nolan said as he rolled his window up.

As he proceeded down the street, enormous mansions emerged on his left and right, each with perfectly manicured hedges and gardens. This was the other rich neighborhood in town. The other one was where the judge lived.

"Whew," Nolan whistled. "Very nice." He wondered how in the world a person of her status would end up in the basement of his Public Defender's office.

His navigation system indicated that the Stenson house was 0.8 miles ahead on the right. The street went up a long hill and each home he passed seemed to be more impressive than the last. Finally, he reached a cul-de-sac at the top of the hill and saw the Stenson house on the right. It was an impressive French Normandy with massive turrets on each end of the house.

He pulled into the cobblestone circular driveway and parked in front of the main entrance. After he exited his car, he straightened his tie, approached the giant double doors and rang the doorbell, prompting the classic tones of Westminster Quarter to emanate from within.

After a few moments, the door opened to reveal a young lady in an apron. She wasn't Mrs. Stenson as far as Nolan could remember.

"Hello," Nolan greeted her. "I'm Nolan Getty. I'm here to see Mrs. Stenson."

"Yes, come in. She's in the study," the young lady stepped aside and waved her arm.

She's in the study, Nolan repeated in his head. Of course she is. Where else would she be . . . the conservatory?

Nolan entered the foyer and stared in wonderment at the scale of it. The ceiling had to be thirty feet high with two grand staircases on each side that curved their way to the upper floors.

"Right this way, please," the young lady led him to the right.

"Mrs. Stenson, Mr. Getty is here," she announced as she opened a double paneled door.

"Hello Mr. Getty," Mrs. Stenson greeted him as he entered the room. Please, have a seat," she pointed to a stuffed chair near the fireplace.

Nolan glanced around the room, which was obviously a library. The walls had floor to ceiling shelves filled with books and a ladder on a rail at the end of the room. A large mahogany desk was the centerpiece of the room and it sat facing the brick fireplace. She sat down in the other chair between the desk and the fireplace and began pouring coffee from what appeared to be a hand-painted ceramic pot.

"Coffee?"

"Um, sure," Nolan answered.

"Cream or sugar?"

"No thanks."

She poured both cups then pushed one to him.

"Thank you," he said, lifting it and taking a sip.

He smiled and shook his head. "Is this as awkward for you as it is for me?"

"Probably more," she answered without smiling.

"Before you start asking me questions, I want you to know that I didn't do anything with your partner that night . . . you know, in a sexual manner. We simply fell asleep."

Nolan nodded as he examined her across the table. She was probably in her early forties but he could tell she was very fit. Her long brunette hair cascaded down to her shoulders, framing a pleasant looking face with kind eyes.

"I love my husband and I would never do anything like that but I guess we just got a little carried away that night . . . the wine, the booze . . . well, it was all that alcohol that made me do things that I would never do . . . like go with Torey to your place."

"I totally understand," Nolan nodded.

"This whole thing is very embarrassing to me, especially when I had to tell the detective what we had done. But he assured me that it wouldn't be necessary to let anybody else know. I mean, I wouldn't know what to do if anybody else found out."

"And I want you to know that it would also be very bad for me if anybody else found out," Nolan chimed in. "Let's just forget the whole thing happened and move on from there."

"Great," she leaned back in her chair, seemingly more at ease.

"I just want to know more about Mrs. Chancey. You know, what she was like, who she hung out with . . . anything that would shed light on this tragedy."

"Ask away," Mrs. Stenson shrugged.

"How long have you known her?"

"Well, I've known her since she married the judge. So, that's been about five years."

"And I guess you were close friends?"

"We were for the first few years. Not so much the last few," she added.

"What happened?"

She shrugged again. "I just decided that I'd be better off if I didn't associate with her so much. As you probably know she was quite the wild one . . . a little too wild for my lifestyle."

Nolan nodded.

"But then we were at the fundraiser that night and one thing led to the other and I was suddenly doing wild things with her again."

"Uh huh," Nolan nodded. "What about her relationship with the judge . . . what can you tell me about that?"

"Well, like I said, I haven't been in her circle for a few years so I don't know anything about how they were as of late. But I can tell you that when we were close, she didn't seem like she wanted to be married to him too much."

"How so?"

"You didn't know she had a reputation?" Mrs. Stenson asked.

"Uh, yeah I've heard rumors. But nothing specific. Do you have anything specific?"

"Well, I don't think it would be appropriate for me to bring out her dirty laundry . . . she can't exactly defend herself."

"Normally, I would agree. But this is about a trial of a person who could spend the rest of his life in prison. And you know what? I don't think he did it," Nolan fibbed about the last part.

Mrs. Stenson thought for a moment before answering. "Well, as you experienced first-hand, Torey was very flirtatious with men. There were numerous occasions where I saw her touching and grabbing men inappropriately. I also know she had at least one affair since she's been married."

"Oh, yeah?" Nolan asked. "With who?"

"With the tennis instructor at our country club."

"How did you know she was having an affair?"

"She told me all about it when it was happening. She also had me cover for her one time. She told me if the judge ever asked if I was with her on one particular night, that I should tell him I was . . . and so I did. And that's when I decided I should distance myself from her."

"When did all this happen?"

"About three years ago."

"And what is the tennis instructor's name?" Nolan asked.

"Stefano Rodriguez. He was from Mexico and he came out here in the summers, then returned to Mexico in the winters."

"So, he's not doing this anymore?"

"No, not since they got caught."

Nolan raised an eyebrow. "The judge caught them?"

"Yes. Well, kind of. He became suspicious after a while and then one day he must have followed her. Torey told me that she and Stefano had drinks at a bar after a tennis lesson, then they drove to Stefano's condo and when they were about to pull into his driveway, she just happened to look in the side mirror and noticed the judge behind them in his car. So, instead of getting out of the car she slumped over and pretended that she was completely out of it . . . like she had been drugged. When the judge confronted Stefano and asked what was going on, Stefano just ran to his condo. And when the judge opened the car door Torey fell out, still pretending to be semi-conscious. She said the judge helped her to his car and he took her home. Later, she pretended to sober up and then suggested that Stefano had slipped her a roofie or something."

"Wow," Nolan exclaimed. "And did the judge ever do anything about it?"

Mrs. Stenson shook her head. "No. She convinced him that it would be too embarrassing for her and the judge. She promised to stay clear of Stefano and never take another lesson from him. And she had a way of getting the judge to do what she wanted."

"And this Stefano guy never came back after that?"

"Not to our club. If I had to guess I'd say the judge probably called him and warned him never to return. But I heard he's now working at the Whispering Pines Country Club south of town."

"Do you know if Mrs. Chancey remained in contact with him?"

"No, I have no idea."

"Do you know of any other affairs?"

"No," Mrs. Stenson shook her head.

"Do you know a person named Jim Sanders?"

Mrs. Stenson thought for a moment. "No, the name doesn't sound familiar. Who is he?"

"He was doing some construction work at the judge's house."

"No, I don't know him. Like I said, I haven't been around her or the judge for about three years . . . except for that night."

"So, how did you get home that morning?"

"I drove Torey home, dropped her off, then drove here."

"Did you see anything suspicious when you dropped her off?"

"No, I didn't. Everything seemed normal. The judge's car was in the driveway at the front of the house and her car was parked right behind his, just like when we had left the night before."

"And she went into the house through the back door?"

"Uh, yeah, I guess. I mean, I didn't wait around, but I saw her headed towards the side door., where the walkway is from the garage."

"Did she say anything to you that night about what was going on in her life or anything else that was out of the ordinary?"

"Not that I recall," Mrs. Stenson shook her head. "She just seemed like the same old Torey to me."

"All right. That's about all I can think of. If you think of anything else I'd appreciate it if you would give me a call," Nolan stood up and handed her his card.

CHAPTER 25

When Danny entered Nolan's office, Rick was sitting on the couch clicking on his laptop while Nolan was at his desk, diligently working at his computer.

"What's happening boss?" Danny asked as he plopped down in the chair beside the couch.

"Not much," Nolan answered without looking up.

"Oh, you bastard!" Rick yelled. "I was going to get Johnson!"

Nolan chuckled. "Fortunately, I was one spot ahead of you on the waiver order."

"So, when can I join your fantasy football league?" Danny interrupted them.

"You can't, Danny," Rick cut in. "I'd like it to happen because you don't know anything about football, which means we would kick your ass, but somebody has to drop out or get kicked out before anybody else can join."

"Well, when will that happen?" Danny pressed.

"When somebody doesn't come up with the $500 entry fee. You got $500 Danny?"

"Yeah, I got $500 Rick," Danny mumbled.

"Well, then you're on the waiting list and you can get in when there's an opening."

"I just got Derick Jones too," Nolan interrupted. Are you guys paying attention here?"

"Who is he?" Rick asked.

"He's the rookie that just ran for 80 yards last week."

"So? That's not that impressive," Rick dismissed him.

"Oh, so you didn't realize that their number one running back went out with an injury in the third quarter and he got all those yards in the fourth quarter?" Nolan smiled.

"Damn it!" Rick yelled. "I guess I do need to pay more attention."

Bored with the conversation, Danny stood up. "Well, I've got to get down to the detention center. See you guys later."

"Don't come back with any diseases," Rick commented without even looking up.

After he was gone, Nolan leaned back in his chair with his hands behind his head.

"You know what's weird?"

"What?" Rick asked.

"You remember the belly shots we did that night with you know who?"

"Yeah."

"Well, I had to put some saliva on her belly, right?"

"Right."

"So why didn't they find my DNA on her?"

Rick shrugged. "Maybe she wasn't licked-ed enough."

"Licked-ed?" Nolan repeated. "Why did you say it like that?"

"Oh, it's just from my old days when I worked in that slaughterhouse one summer in high school. There was a guy who had worked there forever. And I'm not sure what his deal was, but he had a hard time understanding that some words were already in their past tense. One day, I asked him for a cigarette and he said he didn't have any. He said he kicked-ed the habit. So, for whatever reason, I've never been able to forget that and I just say it because it's amusing to me."

"Interesting," Nolan commented. "Let me try one. The Assistant Public Defender could've kept his job if he had just visited-ed his clients at the jail more."

"Yeah, you get it," Rick replied. "Wait. I don't like the sound of that."

Nolan smiled. "Anyway, the weird part of this whole thing is that Willy claims his DNA was on her belly because he had consensual sex with her the week before she was murdered."

"What?" Rick gasped. "Are you kidding me?"

"No, that's what he says. So, if that's true, then they should've also found my DNA . . . from my saliva."

"Huh. Yeah I guess," Rick answered. Then he got the picture. "Oh, gross!" he yelled. Then he started laughing.

"Oh yeah, it's real funny," Nolan shook his head.

Rick continued to laugh as he tried to talk. "You . . . you . . . should've done a . . . a better job at . . . at cleaning your client's DNA from her," he choked out, erupting in more laughter.

Nolan couldn't help himself. He had to chuckle at that.

Rick continued to laugh and try to talk at the same time. "I . . . I knew . . ." He was laughing hysterically but no sound was coming out of his mouth. After a moment, he was finally able to form a sentence. "I knew she was a salty girl!" he blurted out in a high-pitched voice.

Nolan began laughing with him and shaking his head.

Eric appeared in the doorway then.

"Jesus, it's nothing but shits and giggles in this outfit, isn't it?"

Rick continued to laugh as he stood and passed Eric. "I've got to go before I rupture something."

Nolan stood up and closed the door behind Rick, still chuckling. He then sat down at his desk and composed himself.

"What's so funny?" Eric asked.

Nolan shook his head. "There's nothing funny. Rick is just sick." And then Nolan started chuckling again.

"I'm sorry," Nolan shook his head some more, trying to compose himself. "Anyway . . . you see any sign of Sanders?"

"Not a damned thing."

"What about the neighbors?"

"They haven't seen him either. Nobody has seen him."

"Huh," Nolan grunted. "What if he's the one that killed Mrs. Chancey, then skipped town?"

"Interesting," Eric replied.

"Or, what if Willy killed them both? Maybe Jim Sanders is lying there dead in that house, slowly rotting away."

"Same answer," Eric shrugged. "Interesting."

"Were you able to look in the windows?"

"One of them. But I couldn't see anything suspicious. The others had blinds."

"And I guess you didn't smell anything?"

"Nope."

"Something is definitely fishy here," Nolan thought out loud as he stood up and paced behind his desk. "Man, I wish we could look inside that house. He's the only possible person that could give us a lead on anything. I mean, what if he's dead in there? Don't you think we should do a welfare check or something?"

"What would be the reason? So what he hasn't been seen. Maybe he's on vacation," Eric pointed out. "And so what that he texted Mrs. Chancey, he was probably going to meet her somewhere to discuss the construction or something. You still haven't told me how you know he texted her," Eric added.

Nolan was trying to soften up Eric so that he would agree to go check out the house, but Eric was winning. He didn't want to tell Eric about the phone. It was bad enough Rick knew about it, but if he didn't, he would never be able to convince him to go along with his plan.

"I have her phone and I saw the text," Nolan confessed.

"What?" Eric exclaimed. "How the hell do you have her phone?"

"I don't think I should tell you that, yet. Again, for your own protection. Let's just assume for now that I found it in a random spot; you pick it, the sidewalk . . . the street, it doesn't really matter."

"Huh. And what does the text say?" Eric prodded.

"Where are you? I'm waiting."

Eric sat in silence for a moment. "So, it's still possible he was going to meet her somewhere and discuss the construction project."

"On a Sunday morning?" Nolan asked. "If they were going to pick out things, like wine racks or something, it wouldn't be on a Sunday, because most of the stores around here are closed."

"Yeah, I see your point," Eric seemed to relent.

"What if that text was sent from the judge's house?" Nolan continued. "You would have to admit that it's pretty strong evidence that Sanders is the killer."

Nolan could almost hear Eric's brain buzzing.

"And it's at a time when the judge was out jogging," Nolan added. "I really think we should go over there and check it out."

"What do you mean . . . break in?" Eric asked.

"I like the terms, 'sneak in' better," Nolan smiled.

"I don't know about that," Eric shifted in his chair. "That sounds like a B&E to me."

"You need intent to commit a felony for that," Nolan pointed out. "And a B&E has to be at night. So, at the most, it's trespassing."

"You want to do this in the middle of the day?" Eric's tone was one of bewilderment.

"Heck, maybe you went over there to just chase down a lead and you found the back door open, so you wanted to make sure everyone was okay."

"Well, let's assume there's no door open. How do you propose to enter?"

"I haven't really thought about that part yet," Nolan admitted. "I was hoping you had some ideas."

Eric did. But he wasn't quite on board.

"What's in it for me?" Eric asked. "You want me to risk a trespassing charge, it's got to be good."

"What do you want?"

Eric thought for a moment. "A steak dinner at Billy's on top of my hourly rate."

Nolan laughed out loud. "Deal."

"I'll pick you up tomorrow morning at your house. About nine," Eric stood up. "Just wear jeans and a t-shirt."

CHAPTER 26

The next morning, Nolan received the call from Eric.

"I'm here. In the white van."

"Roger," Nolan replied. "Be right out."

Nolan exited the front door of his house and locked it behind him. Although the sun was shining, the air was crisp enough that he could see his breath. He paused on the front porch and noticed the white van idling at the curb. As he approached, he saw the words, "AAA Pest Control" on the side of the van, with a cockroach belly-up under them.

Nolan opened the passenger door and began to enter, then abruptly stopped upon glancing at the driver.

"What the . . . ?" he blinked and stared at Eric. It took a second for him to realize that it was Eric because Eric was supposed to have gray hair and a bushy gray mustache, but this Eric had black hair and no mustache. In addition, his baseball cap was turned backwards and he was wearing large, oval shaped, reflector sunglasses. Altogether it was a distinctive look with a clear message to others: Danger. Sociopath. Do not approach.

Eric smiled. "Been awhile since I've had a bare upper lip."

Nolan chuckled. "And black hair. I guess this is your incognito look, huh?"

"That's right," Eric replied. "Tall, dark and mysterious. Now put these on," he added, throwing coveralls at Nolan.

Nolan unfolded the disposable coveralls and held them up. "Nice touch." He slipped his legs in, then pulled them over his shoulders and inserted his arms before zipping the front.

"I like it," Nolan patted his chest before jumping into the passenger seat and closing the door.

"Nice van. Where did you get it?"

"I borrowed it from a friend."

"Okay, so what's the plan then?"

"We're exterminators . . . obviously," Eric smiled. "Mr. Sanders has hired us to de-bug his house while he's on vacation."

"How are we going to get in?"

"Well, plan number one is to use the key," Eric answered.

"And where did you get that?" Nolan asked.

"I haven't yet. But everybody leaves a key near their front door, as if a thief would never think of that. So, we're just going to look under things, like rocks or porch chairs, or whatever's there until we find it."

"Won't that look suspicious? What if somebody asks questions?"

"I've thought of that too," Eric smiled. "By the way, you're not riding with me. You're driving behind me in your own car."

"Why?" Nolan asked.

"Because if some nosy neighbor gives me any trouble I'm going to say that Mr. Sanders hired me to exterminate bugs while he's on vacation and he was supposed to leave the key under the mat but he must have forgot. I'll feel out that nosy neighbor to see if they have a key and if they do, then I'll call Sanders and he will give them permission for me to have the key."

Nolan seemed confused.

"You're Mr. Sanders," Eric smiled again. "That's why you are going to be in a car about a block behind me—in case I have to call you."

"What if the neighbor knows him really well and would recognize his voice?" Nolan asked.

"Well, that's the part I'll have to wing. If it's a younger person then I won't take a chance. I'll just act like I'm trying to call him and he doesn't answer. If it's an old lady then I'll probably give it a try."

"What if we can't find a key?"

"Then we go to plan number two—check the windows to see if they're open."

"And if the windows aren't open?"

"Then I'll have to go to work on the lock on the backdoor, which is pretty much covered on two sides by hedges."

"Sounds like you put some thought into this," Nolan was impressed. He then glanced in the back of the van and noticed machinery of some sort and duffle bags.

"What all you got there?" Nolan asked.

"Everything we may need. I got a key making machine, laptop computer, camera, exterminating supplies . . . everything I could possibly think of because I don't plan on going back."

"Impressive," Nolan nodded. "Looks like you thought of everything."

"Well, I don't know about you but I plan on eating steak at Billy's tonight, not mac and cheese at the city jail."

Twenty minutes later Eric pulled the van up next to the curb in front of the Sanders house. As planned, Nolan parked down the street but within eyesight of Eric and the house.

The neighborhood appeared to be 1950's vintage, or mid-century modern, as the pretentious folk would say. It consisted of small, one-story homes lined up in straight rows no more than 12 feet apart. Each had a sidewalk that led to a step-up, covered porch. There were no garages but a few of the homes on the street had after-market car canopies planted over their driveways.

The Sanders's house sat in the middle of the block. If someone was home in either of the two houses beside the Sanders's house it would be very easy for them to see and hear them. Although there was some activity on a house porch near the end of the block, the houses immediately surrounding their target were quiet.

Nolan watched Eric exit the van then open the back doors to put the finishing touches on his costume. He first strapped a respirator around his neck and let it dangle below his chin. Then he slipped on a pair of green tinted goggles, perching them atop his head. He then retrieved a pump-up garden sprayer, nodded in Nolan's direction, and approached the house.

Eric didn't even glance around. He just walked straight to the house as if he had been there a thousand times. It almost looked like he was whistling.

Nolan watched Eric climb the front steps of the porch. A dog started barking then. The sound was coming from the back yard of one of the adjacent houses but Nolan couldn't tell which one from his location. It was a deep bark, obviously from a big dog and not a little yapper. That's going to be a problem if Eric has to work on the back-door lock, Nolan thought.

Eric lifted the door mat and looked underneath. Nothing. He then pulled up a cushion on the chair. Nothing. There was obviously nothing else that could hide a key on the porch so he went back down the stairs and glanced around, probably looking for a rock, Nolan thought.

Eric bent down by the bushes in the front and then Nolan watched him stand back up and hold something in front of him that glistened. Eric then went back to the front door, opened it and disappeared inside.

Nolan chuckled. Well, that's a hell of a thing, he thought. All that planning and it was as simple as it could get.

Nolan exited his car and walked to the van. He retrieved a second garden sprayer from the back of the van before approaching the house. He tried to be like Eric but he couldn't help himself. He had to glance over both shoulders to see if anybody was watching. As he stepped up onto the porch he glanced to his left and saw white blinds part in the neighbor's window, then quickly shut.

Uh-oh, somebody's watching, Nolan thought as he entered the front door.

"Well, we made it," Nolan chuckled, "but the neighbor was just peeking through the blinds."

Eric grinned. "That's not a problem. The house is clear. There's nobody here."

Nolan looked around. It was a small house, perhaps 1,200 square feet. The living room was to his left and the kitchen and eating area were to his right. He could see a short hallway beyond the living room which ended at an exterior door to the backyard. The blinds were closed in the living room and kitchen, so the house was strangely dark for it being daylight.

"Turn on the light there," Eric pointed.

Nolan turned and flipped the switch. "What if he comes home?"

"He hasn't been here since I started watching so it's highly unlikely. But if he did, I already have a plan," Eric said as he stepped into the kitchen area.

"What's the plan?" Nolan asked.

Eric retrieved a piece of paper from his pocket and handed it to Nolan. Nolan opened it and saw that it was a contract for services between AAA Pest Control and someone named Mr. Edward Johnson. The address for Mr. Johnson was 2321 Orchard Street.

"You're dyslexic and you read the address incorrectly. You told me we were exterminating 2312 but we were supposed to be doing the house at 2321 Orchard Street."

Nolan smiled. "And what if he knows the person at 2321 Orchard Street and this person isn't Edward Johnson?"

"I already looked it up. The person that lives there is a guy named Edward Johnson."

"Hey, what are you doing in here?" Eric changed his voice, as if he was Jim Sanders.

"We're exterminating."

"I didn't hire any exterminators!"

"Well, you're Mr. Johnson, aren't you?"

"No!"

"Well this is 2312 Orchard Street and Mr. Johnson hired us to exterminate it."

"This is my house and I'm not Mr. Johnson!"

"I act shocked, then we look at the contract and discover the screw up. I then yell at you and you apologize profusely for your gross ineptness. Get the idea how it would go?" Eric winked.

Nolan grunted and held the paper out for Eric.

"Put that in your pocket. I never did confirm the address."

Nolan folded it and put it in his pocket. "So what are we looking for? Where do we start?"

"Well, we're here, so we're eventually going to search everything. Under the beds, between the mattresses, the closets, the dressers, the garbage . . . everything. I'll start here in the kitchen and you start in the bedrooms."

Nolan nodded and stepped through the living room and into the hallway, then he entered the first bedroom on the left. It had obviously been used as an office because there was a desk but no bed. There were a few invoices, some bills and junk mail on the desk, but nothing else. In addition, the closet in the office was barren. In less than five minutes Nolan moved on to the second bedroom.

A queen-sized bed sat in the middle of the room with a nightstand next to it. Nolan looked under the bed and between the mattresses. He then looked in the drawers in the nightstand. He then opened the closet doors and saw that it was barren as well.

"Anything?" he heard Eric behind him.

"No, nothing. It looks like he packed up and left. There aren't any clothes or any personal items of any kind."

"Yeah, that's the impression I got," Eric agreed.

Nolan knew there was a chance that things might go south during their illegal search, but all the planning in the world wasn't enough to prepare his mind and body for the moment that it did. It was not that much different than watching the prank video on the internet that ends with a ghoulish, shrieking face . . . even if you know it's coming, you still jump. And that's what he did when the loud rapping on the front door pierced the solitude.

"Police Department! Open up!"

CHAPTER 27

Montgomery Mutz stood at the window in his office staring up at the Public Defender's house, which was a block away. He knew that Nolan Getty was working diligently behind those walls, doing anything and everything possible to beat him at trial. He had witnessed the trickery before and because of this experience he knew he had to account for every loose end. If he didn't, Getty would expose those loose ends to the jury and convince them that William Bisbaine was innocent.

He thought about getting another search warrant for Getty's office—a valid one this time, but he knew it would be a waste of time as Getty was warned by the first attempt and he would've removed any incriminating evidence immediately thereafter. I suppose I could do it just to harass him, Mutz thought. He pictured himself ransacking Getty's office; throwing law books on the floor, tipping over cabinets and leaving the place as if a tornado had hit it, which gave him some pleasure. Then his mind went other directions.

There was one major loose end that he couldn't ignore any longer and that was the unidentified semen in Mrs. Chancey. He walked to his desk and retrieved the state lab results, reviewing them one more time.

One sample matched the judge, one sample matched Bisbaine, and one was unidentified. Could that unidentified sample be from Nolan Getty? Mutz wondered. He knew from talking with Sheila Stenson that her and Mrs. Chancey had been with Getty and his assistant all night in a private setting. But Sheila didn't know any details about what happened between Getty and Mrs. Chancey. She did know one thing though; neither of them were wearing clothes when they woke up.

Yes, Mutz thought, it had to be Getty's. That's what made the most sense. So, naturally, he would not want to bring it up during the trial. Or would he? Would he be that bold to suggest that the unidentified semen was from the rapist, knowing that the semen was actually his? If he did, then how could I possibly make a counter argument? Mutz wondered.

And then it finally hit him. Mutz laughed out loud as the idea formed in his head. To tie up the loose end he needed an explanation for the unidentified semen and the only person who could do that would be Nolan Getty, whether he wanted to or not.

"He's a witness!" Mutz exclaimed. "I should've thought of this before! It's perfect. And it's the end of that son of a bitch."

CHAPTER 28

Nolan froze, staring wide-eyed at Eric.

Eric quietly approached him and whispered, "Get out of sight and stay in here until it's all clear." He then strapped up his respirator and donned his goggles before stepping into the hallway and slipping silently out the back door.

Nolan pressed himself against the wall in the bedroom and stared through a small gap between the window frame and the blinds. Charged with adrenalin, he couldn't stop his heart from racing madly which also caused his breathing to become shallow, quick pants.

The incessant rapping at the front door continued.

"Police! Open up the door please!" the voice repeated.

Had the neighbor called? Or was it just the daily, random attempt to find Jim Sanders?

Nolan continued to stare through the small gap in the blinds which was a view to the side of the house. He then heard Eric humming and saw him through the gap. He was spraying the ground and making his way to the front of the house.

"Hey!" he heard the officer yell. "Are you Jim Sanders?"

Nolan watched through the gap as Eric stopped just past the window.

"No," he yelled through his respirator. "I'm the pest control guy." Then Eric raised his hand. "Whoa, hold on. You don't want to get close to this stuff without protection."

"I need to talk to you. Put down that sprayer and come out to the front of the house."

"Uh, I can't just take this stuff off. I have to decontaminate in a portable shower by the van before I do, and I've got at least ten more houses to do today. So, if you don't mind, I don't want to go through all that twice in one job. If you got questions, I'll answer them . . . just stay back about ten feet."

"I guess that's fair enough," the officer answered. "Where is Mr. Sanders?"

"I don't know," Eric shrugged.

"Well, when did you last see him?"

"I've never seen him," Eric answered. "He hired our company to come out here every quarter and spray for bugs. So, every three months I do just that and he always pays the bill so I always keep coming back."

"What's your name?" the officer asked.

"Ted McClain. Triple A Pest Control."

"You got an i.d. on you?"

"Well, yeah, it's in my wallet, but like I said, I can't open my coveralls or take my respirator off unless I decontaminate first. Can you wait until I'm done? That way I only have to decontaminate once."

"I suppose I could," the officer answered. "How long will it take?"

"Not more than 30 minutes."

"Ah, okay. How about this. What's your social security number?"

Eric rattled off a number, which the officer repeated when he was done.

"And your date of birth?"

Eric gave him a date without hesitation.

"Ok, carry on. I'll be back."

Nolan watched as the officer turned and headed towards his car. Eric continued spraying, humming a song as he worked.

Nolan was worried to say the least.

Ted McClain? Will the name and social security number check out or will the cop come back and arrest Eric? And if the cop arrests Eric, will he search the house and find me?

Nolan slipped out of the bedroom and pushed the button on the doorknob on the back door to lock it. He then returned to the bedroom and stared through the small opening in the blinds. He could see the rear end of the officer's car parked on the street.

A few minutes later, Nolan heard the officer's voice, but he couldn't see him through the gap in the blinds.

"Okay Mr. McClain, thanks for your cooperation. If you see Mr. Sanders, I would appreciate it if you would give us a call. Here's my card."

"Sure, no problem," Eric answered. "Just put it on the windshield of the van and I'll grab it when I'm done."

Nolan could still see the back end of the patrol car at the street, but it didn't leave. For ten more minutes he stared through the gap in the blinds until finally the car disappeared.

Nolan let out a sigh of relief. He stepped over to the bed and sat down, taking the pressure off his shaky legs.

A few minutes later, there was a knock on the back door. Nolan went to the door and let Eric in.

"I'm going to spend a little more time out front just in case he comes back. I'll call you when I'm sure it's clear, then you can come out to the van."

"Okay," Nolan nodded.

"Lock this back door again before you come out," Eric added.

"Will do," Nolan nodded.

While he was waiting for Eric's all clear signal, Nolan snooped around the house some more. He checked the bathroom and noticed there were no towels or any personal items. Jim Sanders had obviously packed everything up—at least everything that could be packed, and left the big items behind, like the desk in the office, the living room furniture, and the bed.

Just to be thorough, Nolan pulled back the shower curtain and looked inside the tub. Nothing. But when he turned, he noticed the mark on the side of the sink. It was dark, with a trail beneath it. It looked like a blood spot. He bent over and examined it closely. It was definitely blood.

"Huh," Nolan grunted out loud. He thought for a moment, then wondered if he should take a picture. He wasn't sure if he wanted such a picture on his cell phone, but finally decided that he couldn't just leave without documenting it. He retrieved his phone and took the picture.

Nolan then placed his fingers between the vinyl blinds over the window in the bathroom and saw Eric digging in the garbage can beside the house. Nolan watched Eric retrieve something from the bin, then walk towards the front of the house. A minute later, Nolan's phone rang.

"Yeah."

"You can come out now, he hasn't even circled."

"Okay."

Nolan exited the back door making sure it was locked behind him, then walked to the front of the house and out to the van at the curb.

"Jump in the back here," Eric instructed as he stood by the sliding side door.

Nolan followed his instructions and Eric slammed the door shut behind him. Then Eric jumped into the driver's seat and turned around.

"Man, that was a close one!" Nolan exclaimed. "How did you pull that off? And who is Ted McClain?"

"Ted is dead," Eric replied. "Every once in a while there's a glitch in the system and for whatever reason the death of a person is not recorded. So, although Ted McClain died five years ago the system still reports that he is a living, breathing citizen of our great Commonwealth. I even have a fake i.d. to back it up. Yes sir, Ted McClain, 314 Mimosa Drive, Bakersfield, Virginia. Nice to meet you."

Nolan chuckled. "Man, you're good at this. What about the van? What if the cop had run the van?"

"Like I said, I borrowed it from a close friend and we have an agreement. If anybody asks about the van before I get back, his story is that he loaned it to Ted McClain for the day, or whatever name I give him at the time."

"Nice," Nolan smiled. "I think I found a spot of blood on the side of the bathroom sink."

"Yeah?" Eric asked. "Did you take a picture?"

"Yeah. Should we do something else? Like take a sample?"

Eric frowned. "Ah . . . hell no. We'll let the police do that. I found some CD's from the garbage," he added, holding up two disks in his gloved hand. "Use my laptop there and see what's on them. You'll have to connect the external player. I'm going to drive around the block just in case our friendly officer decides to return. Oh, and put those latex gloves on first," he pointed to a box of gloves on the floor. "You probably don't want your fingerprints on these."

Nolan donned the latex gloves and retrieved the laptop and the external drive from the case. He plugged in the player then fired up the laptop. When it was powered up, Nolan slipped the first disk into the player and a movie automatically began playing on the screen.

A kitchen appeared on the screen. It was large, but typical, with a granite topped island in the middle. The room was well lit with sunshine, so obviously the video was taken during the day. But there was no movement of the camera. It appeared to be mounted like a security camera would be. Then Nolan noticed the date and time in the upper left corner. It indicated September 23, 11:58 a.m. Within a few seconds, a woman appeared from the right. As she approached he recognized her at once.

"It's the judge's wife!" Nolan exclaimed. "I think you're going to want to see this."

Eric pulled the van over, put it in park and turned in his seat so he could see the laptop screen.

Mrs. Chancey came from the right with bags of groceries in her arms. She set them on the island, then retrieved a can from one of the bags. She turned and approached the cupboards, then stopped and read the label.

A man entered the screen from the left, tip toeing across the kitchen. He was wearing jeans and a t-shirt, and he had a tool belt strapped around his waist.

"I'm guessing that's Jim Sanders," Eric said.

"Uh-huh," Nolan grunted.

The man sprung on her from behind. He grabbed her arms and leaned down, biting her neck. She dropped the can of food and immediately turned to him. He picked her up and sat her down on the island, spilling the sack of groceries.

"Take me, you big stud," she said, leaning back.

He took her then, and during the taking, she screamed out, "Oh, Jim!" several times.

When they were done, they laid together limp for several moments. Then suddenly they both jerked up and Jim hastily pulled his pants up before running off screen to the left. Mrs. Chancey ran off screen to the right.

A minute later, a voice could be heard on the video. "Hello, I'm home."

Then Judge Chancey appeared on the screen from the left.

"Hello? Torey?" he called out again, walking through the kitchen in the direction that Mrs. Chancey had left.

Mrs. Chancey appeared, carrying two more bags of groceries.

"Hello," he said, grabbing one of the bags from her arms.

"Oh thanks," she said. "You're home early."

He glanced at his watch again. "No, same time every day."

"It's after 12 already?"

"I thought I heard someone up here," a voice boomed off screen. Then Jim Sanders appeared from the left. "How are you sir?"

Jim looked strangely comfortable, as if he had done this before. Ho hum, Nolan thought. Another day on the job. Take the judge's wife, then act like nothing had happened.

"I'm fine and yourself?" the judge set his grocery bag down on the counter. "You get the brick yet?"

"Yep, should be delivered this afternoon. I was just getting things ready in the cellar."

"I don't think so," Eric commented. "But you are a good liar."

"How about the security system?"

"Still waiting on that master controller. I called this morning and they said it's on back order. They have no idea when it will be shipped."

Mrs. Chancey continued to load groceries into the fridge, ignoring their conversation.

"I see you installed the camera over the front door at least."

"Yeah, but it ain't gonna work until the controller gets here. I've got the other cameras installed over the garage doors and in the back yard. You still want the inside camera in the foyer?"

"That's right."

"I'll try to get to that later today before the brick comes. Right now, I need to run down to the city office and pick up some permits."

"And you're coming back?"

"Yes sir, I'll definitely be back. I'd like to get some brick laid before the end of the day."

"I bet you would, Nolan commented. "That and other things."

"Sounds good, maybe we'll see you later," the judge began unloading his bag of groceries.

"Ok then, see you later," Jim turned and exited off camera.

After some small talk, Mrs. Chancey said she had to change and the judge ate his sandwich. When he had finished, he rinsed his plate, then exited the left side of the screen.

"Goodbye," his voice boomed. There was a pause, then, "I love you too."

The screen went blank.

"Wow," Nolan commented as he ejected the DVD and inserted the second one.

Same camera, same kitchen, different day. The date indicated Friday, October 13, 10:14 a.m. But this time Mrs. Chancey came from the left.

They watched Mrs. Chancey place a lap top computer on the island then approach the fridge. She retrieved a small package of yogurt then opened a drawer to grab a spoon before returning to the island, where she sat down on a stool. She was wearing a very short skirt and a tight tank top, as if she was going to play tennis. As she ate her yogurt she clicked her index finger and thumb on the mouse pad of the lap top, but from the angle of the camera one could not see what was on the screen. After a few minutes, she stood up and put the spoon in the sink then threw the empty yogurt container in the garbage below it. She then looked at her watch, then out the window, as if she was waiting for someone. Returning to her stool at the counter, she continued her work at the lap top. A minute passed. Then another.

"Hit the fast forward," Eric suggested.

Nolan clicked the button and the video went into fast mode. They watched the minutes tick by in the upper left hand corner . . . 10:19,

10:20, 10:21 . . . 10:29, 10:30, 10:31. Finally, she stood up and Nolan pressed play again.

Mrs. Chancey quickly stepped over to the window, looked out, then returned to the island and closed her lap top before placing it on the far countertop. She pulled a band from her hair then shook her head and fluffed her hair with both hands. She then re-situated her breasts in her top and then reached down and pulled her skirt a little higher.

"I think she's expecting a visitor," Eric whispered.

The doorbell rang and she strolled across the kitchen as if she was a model on a runway. She went off video but you could hear her voice.

"Well, hello there, handsome!" she exclaimed.

"Something tells me this is not the judge," Eric quipped.

And he was right.

Mrs. Chancey returned on the screen, her arm outstretched behind her, holding hands and leading her visitor into the kitchen.

"It's Willy!" Nolan exclaimed.

"Whoa," Eric grunted. "Unbelievable."

"I'm' so glad you came," she said as she led him to the stool at the end of the island. "I was beginning to think you wouldn't. How have you been?" she asked as she retrieved two beers from the fridge, handing one to Willy.

"Fine," he smiled, cracking the top on his beer. "Just fine."

She lifted her bottle to him. "To you," she said. "And your freedom."

Willy clanked his bottle against hers then took a long pull from it.

"I just can't imagine what you must've gone through . . . all those years in prison, and for something you didn't even do," she commented. "How did you possibly persevere?"

Willy shrugged. "All you can do is take it day by day, and hope the truth eventually comes out."

"You are adorable," Mrs. Chancey cooed. "So masculine, but yet, you seem so sensitive inside. I love your tattoos," she added, stepping close to him. She touched his bicep, drawing her finger around the outline of one. "What is this one, a clock?"

"Uh huh," Willy grunted.

"Why a clock?"

"It's a broken clock. It means I did time, but it was the wrong time."

"Oh, you poor thing," Mrs. Chancey cooed. "Here, finish your beer, I've got plenty more. She tipped hers up and guzzled it until it was empty. When Willy finished his she took the empties over to the sink, then bent over and placed them in the garbage under the sink.

When she bent over, her skirt lifted high and it appeared that she wasn't wearing any underwear.

"Holy Toledo," Eric whistled.

Nolan just shook his head. "I can't believe it. Willy was telling the truth."

Mrs. Chancey retrieved more beer from the fridge and they drank as she did most of the talking. She asked Willy questions from time to time, but the discussion always came back to her. On their third beer she began changing the subject.

"I don't mean to get too personal, but I know how I am, and I don't know how I could go eight years without getting laid. Is it true that men have sex with each other in prison?"

"Some do, I guess," Willy shrugged.

"Did you?" Mrs. Chancey asked.

"No ma'am," Willy quickly answered. "That ain't for me."

"Do you have a girlfriend?"

"No ma'am, haven't really been out long enough for that," Willy answered.

"Oh, you poor thing," Torey repeated. "You must be all buggered up on the inside. That's not very healthy, you know."

And then she made her move, coming up behind him as he sat on the stool. She leaned over and nibbled at his ear as she reached down and grabbed his crotch. "I could help you with that you know."

A few seconds later his pants came down and he lifted her to the kitchen island.

She asked if he had a condom. He didn't. She said she'd get one and jumped from the counter to dig in her purse. After she retrieved the condom she returned and bent down below the island. A moment later she came up, unbuttoning Willy's shirt as she went. When every button was undone, she whipped his shirt apart, as if she was opening a set of curtains, and they immediately began to mate in a furious manner.

"Man, that kitchen island sure does get a work out," Eric quipped.

"Okay, I don't need to see this," Nolan commented. "Let's see if anything else happens afterward." He pressed the forward button and the two figures on the screen rapidly bounced in a comical fashion. After a few minutes, the figures separated and Nolan pressed the play button again.

They watched as Willy put his pants back on and she pulled her top back over her breasts. She took the empty package and the condom, and placed them both in the garbage under the sink. She then led Willy off camera. Within a minute she returned to the kitchen, reached under the sink, then retrieved the condom and the packaging, then left the screen in the opposite direction. The video then went blank.

"I guess she didn't want the judge to find that little surprise in the garbage," Eric quipped.

"Wow," Nolan shook his head. "This is just unbelievable. She was doing everybody."

"And Jim Sanders has it all recorded," Eric added.

"Weird," Nolan pondered. "He must have installed a hidden camera while he was working on the security system."

"Well, at least now you know how Willy's DNA got on her."

"Yeah, that's true. Was this all there was in the garbage? Just these discs?"

"Those were the only suspicious things. There was some junk mail and an empty pizza box, but nothing else."

"I need to make copies of these. How am I going to do that?"

Eric shrugged, "Just use your phone and video the screen as it plays. But if I were you, I wouldn't pan out enough to let anyone know you're filming in the back of this van."

"Good idea," Nolan agreed, retrieving his phone.

Nolan played the videos again and recorded both with his phone. When he had finished, Eric drove the van back to Sanders's house and parked at the curb. Nolan walked briskly across the yard and deposited the discs into the garbage bin at the side of the house, then quickly returned to the van.

Eric circled the block then pulled in behind Nolan's car.
"See you back at the office?" Nolan asked before he got out.
"Absolutely. I can't wait to hear what you're going to do next."

CHAPTER 29

Ordinarily, Nolan would not have time to leave the office and search for evidence in a case, like lawyers do in the novels and movies. In reality, paid staff did most of the field work, but every once in a while, Nolan ignored his time constraints and did it anyway. The problem was that every hour spent out of the office felt like two hours of catching up time.

When he and Eric returned to the office, Nolan glanced at the digital display on his desk phone and saw that there were 14 new messages. Nolan ignored the messages and waved Eric to a chair.

"So, what it looks like to me is that Jim Sanders was nailing Mrs. Chancey, and secretly taping it," Eric said as he sat down. "Then he sees Mrs. Chancey doing Willy, which probably freaks him out. So, he goes over there Sunday morning to confront her, but she's not there. Luckily the judge is out jogging at the time and so he just waits for her. He sends her the text while he's waiting, and when she comes home they get in an argument and he kills her. And it's an angry killing, something a man would do after he saw what was on the DVD."

"Uh-huh," Nolan grunted, deep in thought.

"So now what are you going to do?" Eric asked. Let Mutz know or spring it at trial?"

"I don't know," Nolan muttered. "I need to first think about whether Mutz has any chance at spinning this around and continuing the prosecution of Willy. What do you think?"

"Well, I guess I'd have to think about it for a little bit."

They sat in silence, their brains whirring away with a variety of possible scenarios that could still implicate Willy.

After a few moments Nolan broke the silence. "If you think about it, none of this excludes Willy. I mean, Mutz could argue that it's the other way around. Maybe Willy goes back and finds Mrs. Chancey doing Sanders, Sanders runs, and Willy kills Mrs. Chancey."

"Yeah, I guess there is that," Eric agreed. "Then what are you going to do with the recordings?"

"I don't know. The video will definitely help Willy—it proves he was having consensual sex with Mrs. Chancey. It explains the presence of his DNA on her. But I can't admit how we got it, can I?"

"Right," Eric nodded.

Nolan thought about the cell phone again and how it tied Jim Sanders to Mrs. Chancey on the day of the murder. It seemed that every time Nolan began feeling comfortable about not having to disclose his indiscretions, another reason came up to do just that. It was as if he was trying to walk up the down escalator. He played out in his mind what would happen if he spilled the beans. He would surely become a witness, whether it was in the trial of Willy or in the trial of Jim Sanders. If it was in the trial of Willy, he would have to recuse himself and Burford Hammer would be the defense lawyer. And he knew Burford Hammer couldn't outmatch Mutz on any argument. Worse yet, his career in Big Shanty would be over. He could almost see and hear the exchange at the trial when he took the stand.

What is your name and occupation?

Nolan Getty, Public Defender.

Where were you on the night before and early morning hours of October 22nd?

I was on a pool table in the basement of the Public Defender's office, licking tequila off Mrs. Chancey's naked belly.

Boy, wouldn't that play out nicely for my career, Nolan thought.

Nolan's phone buzzed and Vicki's voice came over the speaker.

"There's a deputy here to see you," she said.

Nolan felt his heart race and a flood of adrenalin fill his body. He looked at Eric and raised an eyebrow. "Okay," he answered, "I'll be right out."

"What the hell," Eric blinked. "I wonder what he wants."

"Whatever it is," Nolan stood up, "it can't be good."

Nolan walked down the stairs to the foyer. He saw the deputy talking to Vicki. There was a woman standing near him who he didn't recognize.

"Hello."

"Hello Mr. Getty," the deputy turned. "I have something for you."

He handed Nolan an envelope.

"What is it?" Nolan asked.

"A subpoena," the deputy answered. "Please sign here," he held out a clipboard.

Nolan signed the clipboard.

"Thanks," the deputy said. "I have something else for you," he said, retrieving papers and holding them out.

Nolan glanced at the woman next to the deputy before he looked at the papers.

"A search warrant?"

"Yes sir. That's a warrant to search your body. More specifically, to collect a swab from your mouth for purposes of DNA analysis."

Nolan's face flushed as the adrenalin coursed through his veins. He read the entire document and realized there was no defense.

"And that's what she's for?" he asked, nodding to the woman.

"Yep. It just takes a second."

The woman donned latex gloves, then opened a sealed package and retrieved a long stick with a cotton ball on the end. "Open wide, please," she instructed.

Nolan opened his mouth and she thrust the swab up and down on the inside of his cheek in a not-so-gentle manner. He felt completely powerless, as if he was a lab animal being studied by the government.

When she was done thrusting and poking she placed the swab in a plastic bag and sealed it shut.

"Thank you."

"Oh, no. Thank you," Nolan feigned politeness as he wiped his mouth with the back of his hand. "I like a good, Commonwealth-sanctioned mouth rape. Maybe we can do this again sometime?"

The woman didn't respond.

"Have a good day," the deputy interjected.

"You too," Nolan mumbled.

"Oh my God, what's going on?" Vicki asked.

Nolan shook his head. "A witch hunt by Mutz." He then turned and climbed the stairs to his office.

"What is it?" Eric asked as Nolan entered his office.

Nolan opened the envelope and saw what he had feared all along.

"It's a subpoena from the Commonwealth," Nolan sighed as he plopped down into his chair.

"For what?"

"For Willy's trial," Nolan stared into the distance.

"Why would Mutz subpoena you?"

Nolan thought for a moment and then concluded that his secret wouldn't matter much longer, so he may as well let Eric know.

"Well, I really didn't want anybody to know this but I guess it doesn't matter at this point. I was with Mrs. Chancey the night before she was murdered."

Eric blinked and smiled. "Really?"

"Yeah, really," Nolan nodded. "Just for the record, I'm pretty sure we didn't have sex but she was with me all night in the basement."

"How? Why?" Eric asked.

"I just ran into her at a bar and took her here," Nolan shrugged. "And a friend of hers named Sheila. Shortly after the murder, Mutz interviewed this Sheila friend and she told him where they had been all night."

"Wow," Eric shook his head. "You got yourself in a pickle on this one, huh?"

"Yeah, I suppose I do," Nolan stared out the window.

"So that's how you got her cell phone," Eric added. "She must've forgot it here."

"Yep," Nolan nodded.

"And so now Mutz is planning on calling you as a witness," Eric concluded. "But why would he do that? I mean, so what you were with Mrs. Chancey the night before. If anything, it just shows that she was promiscuous. How could that possibly help his case?"

"It's not about his case against Willy," Nolan replied. "It's about getting me out of the case and ruining my reputation."

"What do you mean, out of the case?"

"I can't be a witness in a trial of a client I'm representing," Nolan explained. "It's a conflict of interest, or at least the appearance of a conflict of interest. And Mutz knows this. He knows I'll have to recuse myself. And then he gets Burford Hammer and an easy prosecution."

Eric shook his head. "I always knew he was a conniving little bastard. What a son of a bitch."

"Yeah, he's something," Nolan grunted.

"Now what the hell are you gonna do with the videos?" Eric asked.

Nolan shrugged. "I have no frickin' idea. I can't just put them in the file and hand them over to Burford. He'll want to know where they came from."

Eric thought for a few moments before coming up with an idea.

"How about this," Eric began. "You upload those videos to your computer, burn them on a DVD, then send them anonymously to Mutz."

Nolan stared at Eric for a moment, thinking about the consequences.

"That might be the way to go," he smiled. "And then Mutz will tell the judge about it and they'll quickly come to the conclusion that Sanders had a hidden camera. Then they'll search the kitchen, find the hiding spot, and then Mutz will get a search warrant for Sanders's house. And bingo, they will then find the videos."

"And you know Mutz will then subpoena Sanders's cell phone records and eventually see the text from Sanders to the judge's wife on the morning of the murder. Presto whammo," Eric clapped his hands. "There's no way he's going to continue the prosecution of Willy after that."

"Well, I wouldn't say no way," Nolan pondered. "Mutz could ignore the video, as if he had never even received it, and then press on in his dumb, blind way."

"I don't think the judge would let him do that," Eric shook his head. "Once they find that camera, or at least the hiding spot, I think the judge will make him do the right thing, even though Willy was screwing his wife. Besides, it's exculpatory evidence, so he has to disclose it, and he has to know that you will then argue that Willy's DNA is on her because of consensual sex. I mean, that's all they have—just the DNA."

"As far as we know," Nolan added. "But you're assuming he's even going to tell the judge. And you're also assuming he plays by the rules. Maybe he just buries everything. Would that surprise you?"

Eric shrugged. "Not really, I guess."

They sat in silence for a few more moments before Nolan came up with an addition to the plan.

"Hey, how about this," he began. "I also receive the same DVD's . . . anonymously, of course. That way I have insurance in case Mutz cheats and buries everything."

"Brilliant," Eric smiled. "That should do the trick. Only send the videos to Mutz first. If he doesn't disclose them, then you can always send the videos to yourself later. That way it doesn't appear that you were also sitting on them, which may give Mutz the idea that you are behind it."

"Good point," Nolan agreed. "Now the only question is how are you going to deliver these DVD's anonymously?"

CHAPTER 30

That Saturday, Eric drove downtown and parked his car at the end of the block where the post office was located. He could see the row of big blue bins near the curb in front of the post office but he didn't want to take a chance he would be seen on video dropping the packages. And then he waited.

He picked Saturday because kids weren't in school and he needed a kid to help him. He passed the time by surfing the web on his lap top computer. After the first hour with no luck he was beginning to think his plan wouldn't work. There was activity on the streets, but only adults, walking and shopping.

Finally, in the second hour he saw two boys riding bicycles towards him. It would have been better if there had been just one but this would have to do. As they got closer he rolled is window down and yelled out, "Hey, you boys want to make some money?"

They stopped their bikes a few yards away.

"I got a bad back and I can't walk but I need to mail this letter. I'll give you five bucks each if you take this down to those postal bins there," he pointed, "and drop it in the one that says, 'Local'."

"Okay," the first boy said.

Eric handed him the envelope and the kid held out his hand.

"You get the money when you get back," Eric explained.

"What if you just drive away?" the kid was suspicious.

Eric reached in his pocket and pulled out his roll of bills.

"Here's five now. You'll get the other five when you get back."

The kid seemed satisfied with that. "You wait here," he instructed his friend. He took the money then sped down the block on his bike while his friend waited. Eric watched him drop the envelope then pedal back.

"Thanks boys," Eric smiled, handing them the other five.

"Anytime," he replied.

"I might be here next Saturday at the same time. And if I am, I'll pay you the same."

"Okay!" they exclaimed in unison.

CHAPTER 31

Montgomery Mutz sat at his desk with a proud grin. He was thinking about Nolan Getty and the subpoena he had sent him. He wished that he could've seen his face when he opened it up. He imagined him trembling as he held the paper and then falling into depression with the realization that he was trapped and there was no way out.

You're going down, Getty. You always thought you were so smart, but now you know I'm just a little smarter.

Satisfied that he didn't have to worry about Nolan Getty any longer he turned his thoughts to the upcoming trial of William Bisbaine and the evidence against him. John Keene, the former prosecutor, had taught him to leave no stone unturned when it came to gathering evidence against a defendant, and that's exactly what he was thinking about now—which stones had been turned and which ones needed to be.

He had the motive and the DNA evidence but he wanted more. That's why he had sent detectives to interview every member of Mr. Bisbaine's family, all of whom stated that they were not with him on that Sunday. Nolan Getty had not yet sent a discovery request so there was still a possibility that Bisbaine may have an alibi, but he wasn't too worried about it. He was confident he could easily dispose of whatever lie Bisbaine came up with.

He was still waiting for a response to the subpoenas he had sent to every cell phone company in the area. He had asked for the records of Mr. Bisbaine and every member of his family, Mrs. Chancey, Jim Sanders, and even the judge.

The police had executed a search warrant where Bisbaine was staying, but they found nothing inculpatory.

He retrieved a piece of paper and wrote 'Bisbaine – Things to Do' at the top.

He then jotted down the first note: 'Get the telephone tapes from the jail.'

Mutz chewed the end of the pencil and thought some more, before writing down the second. 'Confirm that Childress and the police searched every possible hiding spot between the Chancey's house and Willy's house—clothing, weapons, etc.'

Mutz clicked on his computer then and opened his maps. He inputted the address of Willy and then clicked for directions to the Chancey house.

"5.4 miles," he said aloud. "That's a big haystack." Then he thought about the missing safe which would not be an easy thing to hide. He wouldn't be able to carry that on foot without somebody noticing somewhere along the way, he thought. He had to be driving a vehicle.

'See if Bisbaine had said anything about a car—if he owned one or if he was even borrowing one, etc.' he wrote.

Mutz heard a knock at his door and he looked up to see his secretary.

"Mail," she said, dropping a stack of envelopes in his basket.

"Thanks," he nodded.

He grabbed the stack and began opening each one. There were several Notices of Appeal; a letter from the mother of a defendant, begging him to have mercy on her son; and a letter from that same defendant claiming he had information that would be useful and that he would be willing to make a deal.

Mutz paused then and jotted down another note on the Bisbaine list. 'Interview inmates in contact with Bisbaine.' You never know, he thought. Bisbaine might be bragging.

The next envelope he opened was padded and thicker than the others. He pried open the flap and discovered that it contained a CD. Nothing else, just a CD. And there was no label on it either. Mutz turned the envelope around and noticed there was no return address.

"Huh," he grunted, placing the disc in the slot of his computer. He clicked on the drive and two files appeared. He clicked on the first file and his video software popped up. He then clicked the 'play' button.

The video began playing and he watched as Mrs. Chancey entered the screen. He immediately realized that it was from a camera in Judge Chancey's kitchen. He clicked pause, then got up from his desk and closed the door to his office. He then returned and resumed play.

"Oh my!" he exclaimed as he watched Mrs. Chancey and a guy in a tool belt come together in the kitchen. It's the judge's construction guy, he thought. She was having an affair with Jim Sanders! He became excited as he watched them interact on the kitchen island.

"Oh, you are a naughty girl, aren't you?" he asked out loud. "This is good . . . this is real good," he whispered.

He continued to watch until the screen went blank. He then clicked on the second file and his mouth literally fell open when he saw who was on the next video.

"Willy Bisbaine," he whispered, shaking his head. "Unbelievable."

His eyes widened as the scene unfolded.

"Are you kidding me?" he exclaimed, as Willy took her on the kitchen island. His eyes bulging with excitement, he watched intently as they went at it.

"Unbelievable," he said aloud when the screen went blank.

Like Nolan Getty, Mutz quickly put things together. Jim Sanders was hired to install security cameras, so he must have installed the hidden video camera in the kitchen. He probably wanted a trophy of his conquest, Mutz thought.

Mutz thought for several more minutes. He remembered how John Keene had always told him to put himself in the shoes of the defense and anticipate what their argument would be. Only then would you be able to truly build your own case.

Bisbaine must have told Getty that he had sex with Mrs. Chancey. So, Bisbaine will take the stand and testify to the same, Mutz thought. Then the defense will argue that Bisbaine's DNA was on her because of consensual sex, not because he raped and murdered her.

John Keene had taught him another thing. Don't fall for crazy defense theories, especially if you have someone already charged. He thought about the videos and whether they proved Willy's innocence and he concluded they did not. The date on the video of Bisbaine showed that it happened a whole week before her murder. There is no way his semen could stay on her for a week, he thought.

And then he came to the same conclusion that Nolan had feared. It's just as possible that Bisbaine went to the house again, and caught Sanders and Mrs. Chancey having sex, then got angry and killed her. Maybe Sanders ran and never came back . . . or, maybe Willy killed them both and tried to frame Sanders. The possibilities were many, but there was nothing on the videos that excluded Bisbaine as the killer. Naturally, Mutz then came to the conclusion that the videos weren't even exculpatory in nature. He looked at the envelope then.

"Who in the hell could've sent this?" It certainly wasn't Sanders, Mutz thought. So, somebody else found these videos and this somebody else obviously wanted to expose them in an attempt to help Bisbaine. The videos couldn't have been found in the judge's house—they must have been found somewhere else . . . like in Sanders's vehicle or house, Mutz concluded. So, the person who sent them had to know Sanders or was at least close enough to him to have access to his house or vehicle.

He picked up his telephone and dialed Lieutenant Childress.

"Hey, Lieutenant, it's Montgomery."

"Hey, what's up?" he asked.

"I need to ask you a question. If you get a letter without a return address, is it possible to find out where it was mailed from?"

"Uh, yeah," Childress answered. "The post office scans every single envelope that gets mailed now days. That scan will show which post office received it first and when."

"So, if we really wanted to, we could get a warrant and make the post office produce that information?"

"Well, I'm not so sure you would even need a warrant. There is no reasonable expectation of privacy regarding the outside of a letter. I think you could just send a subpoena."

"Huh," Mutz grunted. "Okay, thanks," he added, hanging up.

If I found out which post office was used, they may have video of the person who mailed it, he thought. *But that would mean I would have to admit that I received the videos.*

He needed to think more about that before he decided whether to bury the disc or disclose it. In the meantime, he would watch the videos again.

And again.

CHAPTER 32

Nolan knew that eventually he would be forced to recuse himself, but that didn't mean he had to do it immediately. Instead, he would wait it out for as long as possible. Eventually Mutz would call for a hearing and bring it up to the judge, but until then, he was still the attorney on record for William Bisbaine. And if Mutz didn't bring it up he would wait all the way up until the day of the trial to do it.

Four days had passed and still no word from Mutz about the videos or the recusal. During that time Nolan had 14 bench trials in General District Court and three guilty pleas in Circuit Court. The wheels of justice never slowed, especially for the Public Defender's office.

The fact that Mutz was sitting on the videos and not mentioning a thing didn't surprise him in the least. He always knew that Mutz cheated when he knew he could get away with it.

On the 5th day, Nolan contacted Eric and asked him to send a copy of the videos to him. Eric went through the same exercise again. Only this time the delivery boys extorted ten dollars each from him.

Nolan had a plan to make sure he opened the envelope in front of Rick and Danny. That way they would be witnesses to the fact that he received it in the mail.

They walked back from morning court together. When they entered the office, Nolan saw the envelope mixed with others on Vicki's desk.

"Any new mail?" Nolan casually asked.

"Uh, yeah," Vicki quickly pawed through and retrieved all the mail for Nolan.

"Let's have a coffee break," he said, turning to Rick and Danny.

"I'm always up for that," Rick smiled.

When they were settled in Nolan's office with their coffee, Nolan opened a different envelope first. Just as he was reaching for the one with the DVD, his telephone rang. He saw that it was Eric and pushed the speaker button.

"Hello Eric, how's it going?"

"It's going. I got a dead end on that hooker. Spent a few days and nights on Grace Street but no sign of her."

"I'm not surprised," Nolan replied. "At least we have the file documented. Did you check with the motel?"

"Yeah, I talked to the clerks at the motel. They don't recall ever seeing a girl with orange hair and a tattoo on her face. They wouldn't let me look at the register. They said they would need a subpoena."

"That figures. Thanks, I'll file for one. Anything else?"

"Nope. You get the package?"

Nolan's face flushed. "Yeah, it's all good. Thanks for getting those mug shots to me. Take care," he quickly reached over and clicked the speaker off.

"Why is Eric looking for a hooker?" Rick asked.

"That's Willy's latest alibi; that he was with a hooker all Saturday night and Sunday morning at the Shamrock Motel," Nolan replied as he reached for the envelope and began opening it.

"Nice," Rick smiled. "Who can blame him after spending eight years in prison?"

"What's this?" Nolan asked, holding up the disc.

"Looks like a CD," Rick answered.

"Yeah I see that, but there's nothing else in the envelope and there's no label on it." Nolan examined the envelope. "And there's no return address on the envelope."

"That's strange," Rick got up from the couch. "Put it in your computer, let's see what it is."

Nolan shrugged and did as Rick asked. He opened the video and played the first file. While it played, he couldn't help but to watch Rick out of the corner of his eye.

"Holy shit! That's the judge's wife!"

Danny got up then and joined them at the computer.

Nolan feigned surprise. "Wow."

"Oh my God, who the hell is that?" Rick asked.

"I think that might be the construction guy the judge hired," Nolan answered.

Rick started giggling like a young girl as they began their mating process on the kitchen island. "Are you kidding me?" he asked through his giggles. "You better shut your eyes, Danny, I don't think you're ready to see how kids are made."

"Funny," Danny grumbled.

"Wait," Rick look perplexed. "Where is this camera?"

"I don't know," Nolan answered. "Must be hidden somewhere in the kitchen. The judge told us that he hired a guy to install security cameras. I'm thinking this construction guy did a little extra work for his own benefit."

"This is crazy," Rick breathed. They watched as the judge's wife and Sanders split apart quickly and ran in separate directions off screen. A moment later, they saw Judge Chancey enter.

"Whoa," Rick exclaimed. "They almost got caught."

When the video went blank, Nolan opened the second file. He couldn't wait to see Rick's reaction on that one.

"Whooa!" Rick screamed, pushing Nolan on the shoulder. "That's your boy!"

"I can't believe it," Nolan feigned surprise again.

Nolan fast forwarded through the actual act. They then watched her leave the screen with Willy, then come back and pull the condom and wrapper out of the garbage.

Rick noticed what Nolan hadn't when he first watched it.

"Hold on," he said. "What's she doing?"

Nolan clicked rewind and they watched it again.

Her back was to the camera, but she had paused and it looked like she was fiddling with the condom.

"Back it up, let's see it again," Rick seemed curious.

They watched her one more time.

"Is she tying it shut?" Rick asked.

"I don't know," Nolan answered.

They watched her walk off camera and then the video went blank.

"So what are you going to do now?" Rick asked.

"I don't know," Nolan lied. "What do you think I should do?"

"I would spring it on them at trial. Man, what a kick in the groin that would be for Mutz!" Rick exclaimed.

Nolan hadn't told them about the subpoena. He didn't want Danny to know the dirty details yet, because there was still a chance that the videos would convince Mutz to drop the case.

"I wonder who sent it?" Danny pondered.

"Yeah, good question, Danny," Rick chimed in. "Who the hell would've sent such a thing?"

"I don't know," Nolan lied again.

CHAPTER 33

The next day, Nolan called the court and told the clerk that he needed to set up a meeting with the temporary judge who was presiding over the case. The clerk told him the judge would be in the following day. He set up the meeting for nine a.m., then called Mutz.

"Hello, this is Montgomery Mutz."

"Hey, it's Nolan."

"What's up?" Mutz asked.

"We need to have a meeting with the judge in the Bisbaine case. The judge will be in tomorrow, so I set it up for nine. Can you make it?"

"Yeah sure," Mutz answered. "Are you recusing yourself?"

"Why would I do that?" Nolan feigned ignorance.

"Because I'm going to make you a witness," Mutz gloated. "I know you got the subpoena . . . I checked."

"Oh, that," Nolan replied. "But I can't be a witness if there's not going to be a trial."

Mutz was silent for a moment.

"So, he's pleading guilty?"

Nolan laughed. "Not a chance. See you tomorrow."

"Wait," Mutz interjected. "What's this about?"

Nolan smiled and clicked the speaker phone off. "Stew on that, you son of a bitch."

* * *

Mutz and Judge Ferguson were waiting in the judge's chambers when Nolan arrived. Judge Ferguson sat on the bench up north in

Roanoke, but he came to Big Shanty whenever a temporary judge was required. He was a tall man with a half-balding head, a hook nose and piercing eyes.

Nolan heard that he had been a Public Defender when he was young, but he didn't know if it was true. It made sense though because it seemed that he was more sympathetic to the defense than most judges in southern Virginia.

"Hello Mr. Getty," the judge stood up and came around his desk.

"Hello Judge, how are you?" Nolan replied, shaking his hand.

"Have a seat," the judge waived to the chair beside Mutz.

"What's this all about? Mr. Mutz seems to be in the dark too."

Nolan retrieved the envelope with the disc then held it up.

"I received this envelope two days ago," he began, staring at Mutz to see his reaction.

"What is it?" he asked.

Nolan opened the envelope and retrieved the disc. "There are two videos on this disc," he explained as he retrieved his lap top computer. "I think you should see them."

"Let me see that envelope," Mutz interjected.

Nolan handed him the envelope, then played the first video while narrating the important details as they unfolded.

"If I had to guess, that's Jim Sanders, the man who Judge Chancey hired to install security cameras in his house," Nolan explained as Mutz feigned surprise. "Obviously, there is a hidden camera in the kitchen. He must've secretly installed it while he was working there."

Nolan then played the second video.

"And that's my client, William Bisbaine," he explained as he stared at Mutz.

The judge's face slightly reddened, but he remained silent as the video played out. When it had finished, the judge leaned back in his chair.

"So why are you showing us this?" he asked. "Why not save it for trial?"

"Well," Nolan began. "There is obviously a crime going on here. Sanders may be still recording from that hidden camera in the judge's kitchen so I thought I should report it. Besides, I thought this would also convince Mr. Mutz to drop the charges against my client."

"This doesn't prove anything," Mutz interrupted. "So what if she was screwing around. That doesn't exclude Mr. Bisbaine as the murderer."

Nolan shrugged. "Well, it certainly doesn't exclude Jim Sanders either. If I were you, I'd check into this hidden camera and get a search warrant for Sanders's house."

"Don't tell me how to do my job," Mutz shot back, like a child. "Who sent this to you?" he asked, turning the envelope over, looking for information.

"I don't know. There's no return address on the envelope."

"Well, at the very least someone needs to inform Judge Chancey and it's not going to be me," the judge interrupted, staring at Mutz.

Mutz nodded. "Yes, yes. I'll let him know and we'll investigate this whole thing."

"All right then," the judge stood up. "Good day to you both."

Mutz wasn't ready to conclude.

"I have to bring something else up," Mutz began, as if he had the weight of the world on his shoulders. "I've sent a subpoena to Mr. Getty and I plan on calling him as a witness in Mr. Bisbaine's trial."

"A witness?" the judge asked. "Of what?"

Nolan sighed.

"I have reason to believe he was the last person to see Mrs. Chancey alive . . . besides Mr. Bisbaine, that is.

"Is this true?" the judge looked at Nolan.

"The subpoena part is true," Nolan answered. "I plead the 5th on everything else."

"Huh," the judge grunted.

"So, you see, Judge, I think Mr. Getty must recuse himself because of a conflict of interest," Mutz continued.

"Oh you do, huh?" the judge seemed suspicious. "What do you say about this?" he turned to Nolan.

"I say it's too early. After all, there may not even be a trial based on this new evidence and whatever other evidence it may lead to. If you're in town next week, maybe we can revisit it then. I mean there's no sense going through all the trouble of lining up new counsel before it's necessary."

"I agree," the judge quickly answered.

"But, if we wait too long then we'll have to continue the trial," Mutz pleaded.

"It's too late already," the judge said. "Even if Mr. Getty recused himself today, the new counsel would need a continuance."

"But . . ." Mutz tried to continue.

The judge held up his hand. "But nothing. We'll have another hearing next week. Until then, you better follow up on this hidden camera thing with Judge Chancey, and I mean immediately."

"Yes sir," Mutz gave up.

CHAPTER 34

When Mutz returned to his office he immediately phoned Judge Chancey.

"Hello Judge, it's Montgomery Mutz."

"Hello Mr. Mutz, what's going on?"

"Well, a lot sir. I just got out of chambers with Judge Ferguson and Nolan Getty. Mr. Getty called the meeting and he showed us a disc with two videos on it. The videos were taken in your kitchen from some sort of hidden camera."

"What? When?" the judge asked.

"Before your wife's murder," Mutz replied.

"What's on them?"

Mutz sighed. He didn't know how or what to tell him.

"Well?" the judge prodded.

"The videos show your wife having sex in the kitchen with Jim Sanders a few weeks before her murder and William Bisbaine a week before her murder."

Silence.

"I'm sorry I have to be the one to tell you this but that's what the videos show and they're pretty clear."

More silence.

"Judge, we need to find that hidden camera. Can I come over now?"

The judge didn't respond.

"Judge?" Mutz pressed.

"Yes. I'm here. I . . . I'm not home right now. But I can meet you there in about 45 minutes."

"Okay, thank you," Mutz ended the call.

He immediately called Lieutenant Childress, briefly explained what was happening and asked him to meet them at the judge's house to conduct the investigation.

When Mutz arrived Childress was already there, leaning against his car and smoking a cigarette. He was wearing a long trench coat which appeared to be an adequate barrier against the chilly wind.

Mutz parked his car behind Childress' and approached.

"The judge isn't here," he said. "I already knocked."

"Oh, well he should be here in a few minutes," Mutz shrugged, buttoning his coat.

"What's this about a hidden camera?" Childress asked.

"We think Jim Sanders, Judge Chancey's construction guy, planted a hidden camera in the kitchen. He was secretly taking video."

"And how did you find this out?"

Somebody sent copies of the videos to Nolan Getty . . . anonymously," he added.

Childress mulled it over. "Who would possibly do that?" he asked.

"You got me," Mutz shrugged.

They both turned as Judge Chancey pulled into the circular driveway. He slowly exited his car and approached. He had a thousand-yard stare, as if he was sleep-walking.

"Where do you think it is?" he asked, fumbling at his key ring.

"It's in the kitchen," Mutz answered.

The judge opened the front door and they proceeded to the kitchen.

The house was cold, as if nobody had been living there. He must be still staying at his daughter's house, Mutz thought.

When they entered the kitchen Mutz glanced at the floor where Mrs. Chancey's body had been. The mess had been cleaned and no trace of the gruesome killing remained.

"The angle is from over there," Mutz pointed to the other side of the room.

They examined the cupboards and the tins of baking goods under them. Then Mutz noticed the clock on the wall.

"The clock," he pointed. "It's the right height."

Childress donned a pair of latex gloves and lifted the clock from the wall. Behind it there was a hole that had been sawed through the drywall, approximately 12 inches in diameter.

"Well, there's nothing here now," Childress commented as he looked inside. "Except a plug-in. Looks like someone ran a feed wire from the electrical box through the wall studs, so the camera could be plugged in. Was this hole always here?" he asked the judge.

"No. I put that clock up . . . well, at least three years ago. That hole's been cut out since then."

"So you think Jim Sanders did this?" Childress asked.

"He's the only one who could've."

"Has he ever contacted you since that day?"

"No. And I've left messages but he hasn't returned them."

"I guess we need to get an arrest warrant and a search warrant," Mutz said. "He at least violated the eavesdropping statute and possibly others. Let me know what you find at his house."

"All right," Childress nodded.

They walked to the front door and the judge left with them, locking the door behind him.

"Mr. Mutz," the judge stopped him. "I need to see those videos . . . I just can't believe it . . . I need to see it with my own eyes."

"I understand," Mutz nodded. "I'll send you a copy."

"Thank you," he looked away, then ambled to his car.

He was completely broken, Mutz thought, right down to his soul.

CHAPTER 35

Nolan was at his desk, visiting with Rick and Eric when Mutz called. Nolan put him on speaker.

"What's up?"

"You're a lucky man," Mutz stated.

"How's that?" Nolan asked.

"Your DNA did not match the unidentified sample from Mrs. Chancey."

"It didn't?" Nolan felt relief more than anything. He was pretty sure he hadn't had sex with her, but he was never absolutely positive.

"You free tomorrow morning?" Mutz asked.

Nolan rolled his eyes. "For what?"

"I'm going to nolle prosse the charges on Bisbaine."

Nolan raised his eyebrows and glanced at Rick and Eric. "Oh yeah? Why is that?"

"Because he didn't do it."

"And how did you suddenly figure that out?" Nolan queried.

"It doesn't matter. The hearing's at nine." Then the line went dead.

"Whooa, you did it!" Rick exclaimed as he stood and held out his hand for a high five. "You won again!"

Nolan smiled, slapping Rick's hand. The burden that he'd been carrying finally lifted. He now knew that he wouldn't have to disclose his indiscretions and he'd be able to keep his career in Big Shanty. Everything suddenly felt right in the world. And it felt good.

"Thank God," Nolan sighed.

"But I thought you said that Mutz acted like he wasn't going to drop the charges after you showed those videos to him," Eric commented.

"True," Nolan agreed. "I wonder what made him come to his senses."

"Maybe they found something else. Like more video from the kitchen," Eric added.

"Well, after seeing those videos, you know they would've obtained a search warrant for the guy's house, so maybe they found something there," Rick opined.

"Maybe," Nolan glanced at Eric. Rick still didn't know about Eric and Nolan's earlier search of the house that came up empty—except for the videos, that is.

"Well, it doesn't matter to us anymore," Nolan shrugged. "We did our job and Willy's going free."

"This calls for a celebration," Rick stood up. "To the basement!"

CHAPTER 36

Nolan didn't bother to call Willy. He knew from experience that things could change quickly in the legal world and he didn't want to get Willy's hopes up if Mutz suddenly changed his mind.

He entered the courtroom at 8:45, fifteen minutes before the scheduled hearing.

Mutz and one of his assistant prosecutors were seated at the prosecutor's table and a handful of people had already filtered into the gallery for the morning docket.

Nolan pushed through the swinging gate at the front of the courtroom and approached the prosecutor's table.

"You still going to nolle prosse?" he asked Mutz.

Mutz looked up. "Yes."

"What changed your mind since the other day?" Nolan sat down on the edge of his table.

"That's none of your business," Mutz answered, returning his attention to a file in front of him.

"Ohhh . . . somebody has a secret," Nolan said sarcastically. "Come on, Mutz, you can tell Uncle Nolan. I promise I won't punish you if it's something bad."

"Piss off, Getty," Mutz said without looking up.

"You sir, are an international man of mystery," Nolan smiled as he stood up. "One of these days I'm going to solve the complex enigma that runs the Mutz Machine," he added with more sarcasm.

Nolan approached the door that led to the lockup behind the courtroom. He knocked three times and waited a moment before the slot opened at eye level.

"Mornin'," he nodded.

"Mornin'," the deputy replied, before closing the slot again.

The door beeped and swung open. Nolan nodded to the deputy as he entered. "How's it going Jerry?"

"Good," he deputy replied. "Who you got?"

"William Bisbaine."

The deputy checked his chart. "Third one down," he pointed. "You need to get in?"

"Nope," Nolan answered as he approached the pen that contained Willy.

There were two other defendants in the cell with him. Both looked up and stared at Nolan with desperation in their eyes, hopeful that he was there for them. Meanwhile, Willy appeared to be asleep in the corner.

"Willy," Nolan yelled out.

Willy jumped and opened his eyes. "Yeah," he blinked.

When his eyes focused and he saw Nolan, he stood up and approached the steel bars.

"What's going on?" he asked.

"I've got some great news. They're dropping the charges on you this morning," Nolan smiled.

Willy's eyes lit up. "Really?"

"Really," Nolan replied.

Willy let out a yell. "Hallelujah! Praise the Lord!" He stomped around the cell, pumping his fists. "Yes! Yes!" he repeated. "I can't believe it! Finally!"

Then he returned his attention to Nolan. "Thank you Mr. Getty, thank you, thank you, thank you!"

"No problem," Nolan smiled, then glanced over his shoulder. Burford Hammer was waiting to talk to his client.

"They'll bring you out in a little bit," he told Willy. "Just be calm out there, and don't say anything."

"Okay," Willy agreed.

Nolan turned to leave and nodded his head at Burford. "Morning."

"Mornin'," Burford nodded back.

Nolan couldn't help himself. He paused after Burford passed him, curious as to what he was going to say to his client.

"Good morning, Mr. Stevens. Come up to the pass through here, I need to go over the guilty plea form with you."

Nolan shook his head and continued walking.

"All rise!" the deputy yelled as Judge Ferguson appeared on the Bench. Nolan paused and waited for him to sit before taking his place at the defense table.

"William Bisbaine," the judge called out.

The deputy standing near the lockup door bent his head down to his radio and spoke into it softly. A minute later the door opened and Willy appeared. The deputy escorted him to the defense table where Nolan was standing. Nolan stuck out his hand to shake Willy's, but Willy ignored it, opening his arms instead. Nolan smiled as he let Willy give him a hug.

"Just remain standing," Nolan said, pulling away from Willy.

"Go ahead Mr. Mutz," the judge instructed.

"Motion to nolle prosequi all charges against William Bisbaine," he said in his courtroom voice.

"Any objection, Mr. Getty?" the judge asked. Neither he nor Mutz expected one.

"Yes, your Honor, I do object," Nolan answered.

The judge raised an eyebrow and Nolan heard Mutz whisper, "What?"

"This is the second-time Mr. Bisbaine has been wrongly prosecuted. The first time he spent eight years in prison. On the current charges, they've been holding him for almost two months. My concern is that there may be a nefarious reason for the motion such as a delay tactic. As you know, if the motion is granted it is without prejudice and the prosecution may bring the same charges later. Section 19.2-265.3 states that good cause must be shown before granting a motion for nolle prosequi, and Mr. Mutz has yet to provide any reason."

Willy turned to Nolan and whispered in his ear. "What are you doing? They're trying to drop the charges and you're fighting it?"

"Relax," Nolan replied. "You're walking free today no matter what happens right now."

The judge turned to Mutz. "What do you say about that?"

"We have good cause, your Honor," Mutz stammered, shuffling papers on his desk.

"Well, I believe Mr. Getty is correct. And I think it takes more than a bald statement that you have good cause. The statute states that good cause must be *shown,"* the judge emphasized the last word.

"Well," Mutz stammered. "As an officer of the court I can assure you that this motion is not for purposes of delay, rather, it is based on evidence we have discovered that is exculpatory in nature with respect to Mr. Bisbaine."

Nolan was aware of cases in which the court had granted a nolle prosequi motion for little or no reason, and the appellate courts had upheld such decisions. On the other hand there were no cases where a judge's decision to deny the motion had been overturned. So, ultimately, it was up to each individual judge and whatever the judge decided would not be overturned by a higher court. And Nolan had a feeling that Judge Ferguson was a bit suspicious about Mutz, especially after he attempted to force Nolan to recuse himself.

"Does your evidence inculpate somebody else or does it just exculpate Mr. Bisbaine?" the judge pressed.

"Ah, well, it also inculpates another," Mutz nodded.

"So, is it fair to say that based on this evidence, you no longer have probable cause to prosecute Mr. Bisbaine?" the judge asked.

"Yes," Mutz answered. He thought the judge was simply leading him in an effort to help him show cause but then the judge seemed to turn on him.

"So, why not dismiss the charges with prejudice?" the judge asked.

Mutz had been boxed into a corner and it didn't appear that he liked it.

"Well, the procedure in this court is for the judge to grant a nolle prosse motion when the prosecutor's office requests one, so that's what I'm doing. If the court doesn't want to grant it then so be it. Mr. Bisbaine can go back to jail and I'll continue to prosecute until this court decides to grant my motion."

Judge Ferguson pursed his lips and furrowed his brow. It appeared he didn't like the challenge from Mutz.

"Excuse me, your Honor," Nolan interjected. "I would just like to point out one thing."

"Go ahead," the judge continued to stare at Mutz.

"Well, as you know, we all have a duty to abide by the ethical rules of the law. Mr. Mutz has a specific duty under these ethical rules and that is to only prosecute a defendant if there is probable cause. And Mr. Mutz just admitted that there is no probable cause in this case. Therefore, if Mr. Mutz continues to prosecute this case, I have a duty . . . you have a duty . . . every lawyer in this courtroom has a duty to report this violation to the Bar," Nolan turned to Mutz. "And I can assure you, I take this duty seriously."

Mutz turned to the judge. "I've shown good cause. Is the court granting my motion or not?"

"No, the court is not," the judge quickly answered. "Based on the history of this defendant and the history of this case, this court is not satisfied that good cause has been shown. Motion denied."

Judge Ferguson had called him on his bluff. Now Mutz had no choice but to fold.

"Motion to dismiss the charges with prejudice," Mutz responded.

"Granted," the judge banged his gavel.

CHAPTER 37

For Montgomery Mutz, the unfortunate turn of events in the Chancey murder case was disappointing to say the least. The problem was that Jim Sanders was on the loose and if he wasn't found soon, there wouldn't be time to bring him to trial before the special election in January. That meant he would have to find some other way to get free campaign advertising and it would have to happen soon.

Mutz had learned many things from John Keene, the former prosecutor, but the most important thing he learned was how to use the press to your own advantage. For that reason, upon returning from the Bisbaine hearing he immediately picked up the phone and called Scotty, the criminal reporter for the *Big Shanty Gazette.*

"This is Scotty," he answered.

"Hello Scotty, Montgomery Mutz here. How are you?"

"I'm great, how about yourself?"

"Just fine. Say, I haven't talked to you for a while but I saw you at the nolle prosse hearing this morning and I wanted to know if you had any questions about what had happened and why we dismissed the charges against William Bisbaine."

"Yes, absolutely. I was actually going to call you in a few minutes. Hold on one second," he added.

Mutz heard Scotty rattling some papers.

"Okay, so yeah, you said at the hearing that you uncovered some sort of exculpatory evidence and that's why you were dropping the charges against Bisbaine?"

"Yes, that's right," Mutz began. "As you know I take my responsibilities here at the prosecutor's office very seriously and when I took office I pledged to be transparent and always seek the truth in the pursuit of justice. Well, I've kept that pledge today as I do every day."

"Uh huh," Scotty mumbled. "And so why did you drop the charges?"

"Well, I believe it's very important for this office and the police department to have a sound relationship and to work hand in hand in all we do. But I will never put that relationship before the citizens of this community. You see, when a detective with the police department thinks he has arrested the actual perpetrator in any crime I will always conduct an independent investigation to make sure the detective is correct. In other words, I will never prosecute a defendant simply because the police think he did it. And that's basically what happened in this case. The police thought they had the right guy but after an exhaustive investigation by my office, we uncovered evidence . . . both physical and scientific, that absolutely absolves William Bisbaine with respect to the murder of Torey Chancey."

"Uh-huh," Scotty mumbled again. "Are you going to tell me what this evidence is?"

"I wish I could but there is an on-going investigation and I am not able to release that information at this time. I can tell you this, though: We are seeking information from the public on the whereabouts of a person named James Sanders."

"Who is he?" Scotty asked.

"James Sanders is the owner of Old Dominion Construction and he had been doing some renovation work at the Chancey's home in the few months prior to Mrs. Chancey's murder."

"Do you think he is the one who committed the murder?"

"Yes. Today I am working with the police department and we will be issuing a warrant for his arrest. But do me a favor, Scotty, please don't publish that fact as it may make it more difficult to find him. I would appreciate it greatly if you just reported that he's wanted for questioning."

Mutz didn't care whether Scotty published that fact or not, he just wanted Scotty to think he was getting inside information.

"Okay, well the arrest warrant is public information, so we probably have a duty to report it, but I'll make sure nobody knows the information came from you if that's all right."

"Yes, I understand," Mutz smiled.

"But what were you and the defense attorney arguing about in court?"

Mutz was caught off guard for a moment, but quickly recovered.

"Oh, that was just legal procedural technicalities. The important part is that I made a motion to dismiss the charges with prejudice and the court granted it."

"I see," Scotty replied.

"There is one other thing I'd like to add though. This office saved William Bisbaine's life . . . not once, but twice. And I think our office deserves some credit for never giving up in the relentless pursuit for truth and justice. Because of our determination, we made sure he was exonerated from his wrongful conviction and we stopped another wrongful conviction that may have gone unfettered in any other jurisdiction."

"Uh-huh, I see," Scotty mumbled. "Anything else?"

"That's it," Mutz seemed satisfied. "Take care."

CHAPTER 38

When Nolan entered the chateau the next morning Eric was leaning against the file cabinet, reading a newspaper out loud to Vicki.

"Good morning," Nolan interrupted him. "Whatcha reading?"

"Oh, I was just reading about our local hero, Montgomery Mutz," Eric rolled his eyes. "According to the paper his office is single handedly responsible for saving William Bisbaine's life . . . not once, but twice."

"Is that right?" Nolan asked. "Are we under his bus or did he throw somebody else under there this time?"

"Looks like the police department has the honors this time. It says here that he conducted an independent investigation and uncovered exculpatory information that absolutely absolved William Bisbaine of the crime, and . . . wait for it . . . here it is, the killer quote, 'I will never prosecute a defendant simply because the police think he did it. And that's basically what happened in this case.'"

"Ha-ha," Nolan chuckled. "And liberty and justice for all!"

"Jesus, this guy's a rat," Eric shook his head. "And the real shame is that people who read this will believe it."

"Of course," Nolan quipped. "It's in the paper—it has to be true. Got time for a cup of coffee?"

"Ah, no. I'm headed to the range. But I just thought I'd drop this off for you," he handed Nolan an envelope.

Nolan opened the envelope. It was Eric's bill. And it was a big one.

"Ouch!" Nolan winced.

Eric smiled. "Hey, I even gave you the family discount."

Nolan grunted. "Yeah, I'm sure. Looks like the in-law discount to me."

CHAPTER 39

A week had passed since Willy had been released and things were back to normal in the Big Shanty Public Defender's Office. The steady, unending stream of client files continued to flow into the factory and one, by one, they were filtered and closed out by the industrial process known as justice.

On an early Monday morning, Nolan entered the chateau and heard Rick and Danny in his office even before he reached the top of the stairs.

"Unbelievable," he heard Rick exclaim.

"Morning boys," Nolan greeted them as he entered.

Rick was on the couch reading the local newspaper and Danny was in the side chair listening intently.

"What's unbelievable?" Nolan asked as he sat down at his desk.

"They caught your boy, Jim Sanders," Rick exclaimed.

"Oh yeah?" Nolan was surprised.

"Yep, caught him in Kentucky and they extradited his ass yesterday morning."

"Oh, boy," Nolan muttered, glancing over at the pile of new client folders that Vicki had already delivered. "I suppose I should've known it was bound to happen," Nolan reached over and began sifting through the files, looking for one labeled 'James Sanders'. But it wasn't there.

"Huh," Nolan grunted. "They must not have processed him yet."

"It says he's being charged with rape, murder, burglary, grand larceny and intercepting oral communications," Rick continued. "Oh, and here it is . . . the big kicker," Rick began chuckling as he read the last sentence, "His attorney, Burford Hammer, did not respond to a request for comment."

"Oh!" Nolan winced. "What an idiot. I wonder who in the hell gave him the idea that he should hire the Hammer."

"The Lord works in mysterious ways," Rick continued to chuckle. "I mean, could this have ended more perfectly? You get Mutz to drop the charges on Willy and we don't even have to represent the real killer."

"That is a pretty clean finish," Nolan chuckled.

"You gotta tell me though, boss, were you going to finally put Danny on a murder case if the court had appointed us?"

"Possibly," Nolan smiled, glancing at Danny. "But we don't have to worry about that anymore, do we?"

"I guess not," Danny shrugged, attempting to hide his relief.

"You know, somebody really needs to put out a public service message about this dude," Rick added. "A billboard, a poster in the courthouse . . . something." Rick highlighted the words in the air with his hand, 'Do not hire Burford Hammer—he really sucks.'"

"But why did the court appoint him instead of us?" Danny queried.

"The court didn't," Nolan explained. "Jim Sanders hired him."

"I wonder how much Burford's charging him?" Rick asked.

Nolan shrugged. "Fifteen grand? Maybe twenty?"

"Jesus," Rick whistled. "And the dumb ass doesn't even realize he's going to plead guilty for that."

CHAPTER 40

Ten days later in early December, Nolan entered Big Shanty General District Court for his turn at misdemeanors and bond hearings. Although Danny and Rick handled most of those cases, Nolan wanted to stay in touch with all aspects of the Big Shanty justice system so he took on such cases and appeared in the lower court approximately once a month.

He passed the long line of citizens waiting to take their turn through the metal detector, then nodded to the deputy as he stepped through it.

"Morning Mr. Getty," the deputy ignored the alarm. "Have a good day."

"You too, Bill," Nolan smiled.

When he opened the courtroom doors, he was surprised to see a TV camera set up near the judge's bench and an unusual number of people in the gallery.

He parted the swinging gates in the front of the courtroom then sauntered to the side bench and sat down next to Danny who had an armful of files.

"Morning Danny," Nolan nodded. "You got a lot this morning?"

"Not too bad," Danny shrugged. "Two driving suspended, a domestic violence, reckless driving and a trespass."

"What's all the hub bub about this morning?" Nolan asked.

"The deputy said they're having the preliminary hearing on the guy who murdered the judge's wife."

"Well, that explains the TV camera," Nolan commented. "And I suppose they're going to do that first and make the rest of us wait."

"I guess so," Danny nodded.

"Well, I guess I have time to talk to my clients then," Nolan smiled as he stood up and turned to the gallery full of people.

"Todd Blankenship!" he yelled loudly, startling the deputy on the side bench.

Everyone stopped talking for a second, a mild curiosity pulling at them to see if anyone would answer the call. No one did.

"Esther Hamilton!" Nolan called another name from the folders in his arm. No one answered.

"Zero for two," the deputy on the side bench announced, peering over the top of his newspaper.

"Thanks for the play-by-play."

"Sherman Calhoun!" Nolan tried again. This time, an elderly gentleman in a suit raised his hand. Nolan flipped open the file and immediately recalled the circumstances of the stolen package and mental illness. He waved to Mr. Calhoun and motioned him to the door.

Mr. Calhoun met him at the door and they shook hands.

"Follow me," Nolan said.

He took him to a side room in the hallway outside of the courtroom and shut the door behind them.

"How you doing, Mr. Calhoun?"

"I'm fine."

"Are you on your medication?"

"Oh yes," he answered. "Everything's fine. No more problems . . . no more TV people telling me what to do . . . everything's just fine."

"Great. So, when the judge calls your name just come up to the front and I'll meet you there. Then we'll have a little trial."

"And you don't think I'll get jail time if the judge finds me guilty?"

"You shouldn't. But if you do, I will appeal your case and we will have another trial in Circuit Court where I'm almost positive you will not get jail time."

"Okay, that sounds good," he nodded.

"Okay, see you out there," Nolan opened the door and held it for him.

Nolan followed Mr. Calhoun back into the courtroom and sat back down next to Danny.

A moment later, the deputy yelled out, "All rise. Oyez, Oyez, Oyez, the Big Shanty District Court is now in session, the Honorable Judge William Sawyers presiding!"

Nolan and the other lawyers on the side bench stood up in unison, then the people in the gallery followed as Judge Sawyers appeared in his flowing robe and took his seat on the bench.

"You may be seated," he proclaimed. He then turned to Mutz who was approaching the bench with Burford Hammer at his side. "You going with the preliminary hearing on the murder first?"

"Yes sir," Mutz answered.

"James Sanders," the judge yelled out.

The deputy in the corner opened the lockup door and yelled out, "James Sanders."

"Good morning, Judge," Burford nodded.

"Good morning, Mr. Hammer," the judge nodded back.

Both Mutz and Burford stood at the bench waiting for the defendant to come out.

A moment later another deputy appeared, escorting Mr. Sanders into the courtroom. He was in standard issue, orange coveralls and handcuffed at the wrists with shackles around his ankles. He shuffled forward in short steps until he reached the bench, where he nodded at Burford. Burford whispered something to him as the judge continued.

"Do you want me to read the charges?" the judge asked.

"No sir, that's not necessary," Burford answered.

"Very well then, go ahead Mr. Mutz."

Nolan leaned over to Danny. "Look at this crap. Burford didn't even bother to object to the TV cameras, and he's letting everybody in the world see his client in chains and orange coveralls."

Danny nodded.

"Don't ever let that happen to any of your clients," Nolan added.

Danny nodded again.

Mutz called Detective Childress first, who approached the bench and stood between Mutz and Burford. After the judge swore him in Mutz began the examination.

Nolan surveyed the gallery and noticed for the first time that Judge Chancey was in the front row. He wondered if Mutz was going to bother to call him.

With Mutz's prompting, Lieutenant Childress described all the gory details of the murder scene and the evidence they collected, including the photographs and physical evidence. Childress explained that the swab samples taken from Mrs. Chancey were sent to the state lab and compared with a blood sample they took from Sanders when he was arrested and DNA analysis concluded that it matched James Sanders. Childress then explained that when the defendant was arrested they found a blood stain on the seat of his pickup and analysis from the state lab showed that it matched Mrs. Chancey. Mutz produced the lab reports and they were successfully admitted into evidence.

Mutz then produced more papers, which Childress explained were telephone records from James Sanders's cell phone. After the records were admitted into evidence, Childress read the tell-tale text to Mrs. Chancey, which he explained, was made right before she was raped and murdered.

Finally, Mutz asked Childress about a search warrant executed at the defendant's home. When he did, he handed Burford a piece of paper in a clear, plastic bag. Burford spent a few minutes studying the exhibit and showing it to his client before handing it back.

Mutz then handed the exhibit to Childress.

"I'm handing you a document labelled for identification as Commonwealth's Exhibit Seven. Do you recognize this item?"

"Yes."

"Is this item in the same or similar condition as when you first saw it?"

"Yes," Childress nodded.

"What is this document?"

"It is a letter I found in the garbage can, which was located on the side of James Sanders's house."

"I'd ask the court that Commonwealth's Exhibit Seven be admitted into evidence," Mutz requested.

"No objection," Burford nodded.

"Admitted," the judge said.

"And for the record, what does this letter say?" Mutz asked.

Childress cleared his throat and began to read. "It says, 'Jim Sanders. You don't know me but I know you. I know you're planning on framing that Bisbaine kid, but you are the one being framed. Torey is going to take the money in the safe and double cross you. All the evidence will show that you killed the judge. And by the time you realize what's happened, she will be long gone to Mexico and it will be made to look like you abducted and killed her. She already has a fake passport. Don't do it!'"

Nolan leaned into Danny. "Wow, I didn't know they found a letter. That's not very nice of Mrs. Chancey."

Danny nodded.

"That's our evidence judge," Mutz concluded.

"You have anything, Mr. Hammer?" the judge asked.

"No sir," Burford shook his head.

Nolan leaned into Danny. "Jesus, he's not even going to cross-examine Childress."

Danny shook his head.

"Any argument?" the judge asked.

"Yes sir, just briefly," Mutz began. "The DNA in the vaginal swab from the victim matches the defendant, and the blood in the defendant's truck matches the victim. We have shown that the defendant texted Mrs. Chancey immediately before she was murdered and indicated that he was waiting for her. And although we don't need to prove motive, the letter makes it clear why the defendant raped and murdered Torey Chancey."

"Any argument, Mr. Hammer?" the judge asked.

"No sir," Burford responded.

"Very well, I find probable cause that the defendant committed these crimes and certify this case for trial," the judge stamped the papers on his desk and handed them to the clerk.

Huh, Nolan thought. They didn't even mention the videos. But that made sense. If things went as predicted, there would never be a need to expose the embarrassing nature of those videos because Burford would most certainly convince Sanders to plead guilty.

I wonder if Burford Hammer even knows about the videos. No, he probably doesn't. And what the hell is with that letter? Who would've possibly written that?

"Sherman Calhoun," the judge yelled out, interrupting Nolan's thoughts.

Nolan stood up and met Mr. Calhoun in front of the judge's bench. Calhoun put his hand to Nolan's ear and whispered, "What was Jim Sanders doing here?"

Nolan looked at him quizzically. "You know Jim Sanders?"

"Yes. He's my next-door neighbor," Mr. Calhoun whispered.

Wow, Nolan thought. What a small world.

"He was here for a preliminary hearing, that's all," Nolan answered.

"It wasn't about me?" Mr. Calhoun asked.

"No, it had nothing to do with you. They say he murdered the judge's wife."

"Oh, okay, thanks."

Mutz's assistant prosecutor also approached the bench with a police officer and a little old lady following closely behind.

"Are you Mr. Sherman Calhoun?" the judge asked.

"Yes."

"Mr. Calhoun, you're charged with larceny—stealing goods valued at less than $1,000 from a person named Alice Henderson on November 1st. How do you plead?"

"Not guilty," Nolan cut in.

"Very well. Everybody who's going to be a witness in this case raise your right hand and repeat after me," the judge ordered.

Nolan nodded at Mr. Calhoun and tapped his arm. Mr. Calhoun raised his hand and so did the little old lady and police officer.

"Do you swear to tell the truth so help you God?" the judge asked.

"Yes," they replied in unison.

"Go ahead," the judge turned to the prosecutor.

Ordinarily, Nolan would've made a motion to separate the witnesses from the courtroom as each one testified, but in this case, it didn't matter because the only thing in question was the reason behind Mr. Calhoun taking the package.

The prosecutor waved the old lady closer to the bench, then began his questioning.

"Please tell the judge your name."

"My name is Alice Anderson," she said in a crackly voice.

"And where do you live?"

"2311 Orchard Street," she answered.

"And can you tell the court what happened on November 1st?"

"Well, I had taken a shower that morning and I guess a package got delivered while I was in the shower because usually the deliveryman knocks on the door when he delivers a package, but this time I didn't hear him. So, it's about 10 a.m. when I just happen to look out the window and see Mr. Calhoun on my porch. I then see him pick up a package and walk back across the street to his house."

"And Mr. Calhoun is the defendant right here?"

"Yes," Ms. Anderson glanced at him.

"Then what happened?"

"Well, I called 9-1-1 and told them that Mr. Calhoun just stole a package from my porch."

"Did you get the package back?"

"Yes, the police officer brought it back to me."

"And what was in that package?"

"Vitamins," she answered.

"And what did those vitamins cost?"

"About fifteen dollars," she answered.

"Thank you ma'am," the prosecutor nodded. "Please answer any questions the defense attorney may have."

"Hello, Ms. Anderson, how are you?" Nolan asked.

"I'm fine," she smiled.

"So, you never asked Mr. Calhoun what he was doing, correct?"

"No sir, I thought it was pretty clear what he was doing."

"Had you ever had a package stolen before this day?"

"No, not me," she answered.

"Are you aware of others in the neighborhood getting packages stolen?"

"Well, yes. The neighbor across the street who lives next to Mr. Calhoun told me that he had a package stolen just the week before Mr. Calhoun took mine."

"That's all the questions I have," Nolan nodded.

"Thank you, Ms. Anderson, you can either stay up here or take a seat in the gallery," the judge instructed.

"Okay, I'll just go sit down," she said, shuffling back to the gallery.

The police officer stepped in front of the bench.

"Please tell the judge your name."

"Officer Richard Bagnell."

"And could you please tell the judge what happened on November 1st?"

"Uh, well I was dispatched to Orchard Street at about 10:10 a.m. in reference to a larceny. I met Ms. Anderson at her house. She told me what had happened, and so from there, I just walked across the street and knocked on Mr. Calhoun's door."

"Then what happened?"

"He came to the door and I explained that he had been seen taking a package off the porch and I just asked for the package back. He went inside his kitchen, then retrieved the package and brought it to me."

"What was the address on the package?"

"It was addressed to Alice Anderson, 2311 Orchard Street."

"Then what did you do?"

"I placed Mr. Calhoun under arrest and read him his Miranda rights."

"And what did he say, if anything?"

"He admitted to taking the package and told me that he was holding it for Ms. Anderson so that nobody would steal it."

The judge smiled at that one.

"No further questions," he finished.

"The package had not been opened, correct?" Nolan asked.

"That's correct," the officer answered.

"No more questions," Nolan nodded.

"That's our case, your honor," the prosecutor stated.

"You want Mr. Calhoun to testify?" the judge looked to Nolan.

"Yes sir." Nolan stepped back and waved for Mr. Calhoun to stand in front of the judge, which he did.

"Mr. Calhoun, why did you take the package from Ms. Anderson's porch?"

"Because I didn't think she was home and I didn't want anybody to steal it."

"So, you were just holding it for her?"

"Yes sir."

"And why did you think somebody might steal it?"

"Because my neighbor next to me had just told me that he had a package stolen the week before."

"And just for the record, that wasn't you who had stolen the package, was it Mr. Calhoun?" Nolan gave a quick smile to the judge, who smiled back.

"No sir, it was not."

"When were you going to give the package back to Ms. Anderson?"

"When I saw her next," he answered.

"Mr. Calhoun, that's all the questions I have for you. Please answer any questions from the prosecutor."

The prosecutor cleared his throat.

"Mr. Calhoun, you know that Ms. Anderson has a car, right?"

"Yes sir."

"And you know that car was in her driveway that morning, right?"

"Yes sir."

"And isn't it true that you never bothered to knock on her door to see if she was home when you picked up that package?"

"Yes, true."

"And isn't it true that Ms. Anderson never gave you permission to pick up and hold her packages for her?"

"True."

"No further questions," he finished.

The judge allowed both attorneys to argue their case and when they were done, he found Mr. Calhoun guilty.

"$100 fine, 30 days in jail, 20 suspended."

Ouch, Nolan thought. That meant 10 days to serve and he wasn't expecting that, especially since his story was somewhat believable.

"See the clerk, Mr. Calhoun," the judge ordered.

Nolan ushered Mr. Calhoun over to the clerk and whispered in his ear. "The judge just gave you 10 days in jail. If you appeal your case today, you won't have to go and we can have a new trial in Circuit Court next month. Want to appeal?"

Mr. Calhoun nodded.

"He's going to appeal," Nolan whispered to the clerk.

CHAPTER 41

After he finished his trial with Calhoun, Nolan returned to the chateau with a nagging sense that something wasn't right. Witnessing Burford Hammer's inadequate representation was about as disturbing as watching those TV commercials with the abused, trembling pets. Nolan imagined a soft voice begging for help as the camera panned to a jail cell, showing a disheveled, shaking defendant with puppy dog eyes.

Please donate now to the state bar association. Every dollar you pledge will help James Sanders and others like him. And for a limited time, with any donation, you will receive a free American Flag lapel pin.

There were so many questions that Burford could've asked, Nolan thought. But he didn't even ask one.

And the letter . . . that was the troubling part. Who could've possibly sent such a letter? There has to be somebody else who knows and who is possibly involved. And why didn't Eric see the letter?

Nolan picked up the phone and rang Eric.

"Hey man," Eric answered.

"Hey, I just watched the preliminary hearing for Jim Sanders, and Childress testified about a letter he found when they executed the search warrant. He says they found it in the garbage can at Sanders's house."

"What did it say?" Eric asked.

"It said something to the effect that the writer knew him and of his plan to kill the judge and that Mrs. Chancey was going to double cross him and frame him for the judge's murder. And then Mrs. Chancey was going to run to Mexico and he would be left holding the bag."

"Wow, who wrote it?"

"I don't know, they didn't say. But you looked through the garbage cans and you found the DVD's. Is it possible you missed the letter?"

"No," Eric answered. "Not a chance. I looked at everything."

"100 percent?"

"110 percent," Eric answered.

"Hmmm," Nolan pondered. "That makes no sense at all."

"No it doesn't," Eric agreed. All I can tell you is that it wasn't there when I looked, so that means somebody put it there after we were there. Or, they're lying about where they found it."

"Yeah," Nolan agreed. "All right, thanks."

Nolan hung up the phone and leaned back in his chair, staring out the window. If the letter wasn't there when Eric searched the garbage then how did it get there later, Nolan wondered. It couldn't have been put there by Jim Sanders because he was in Kentucky. So, that means it was put there by somebody else. Somebody who knew Mrs. Chancey and knew about her plans. But why was it placed there so long after the fact? Mrs. Chancey had been dead for weeks so it didn't make sense.

That sinking feeling that he had at the beginning of the murder case came back to him. He knew then that he would have to talk to Burford Hammer and tell him about the videos. He also knew that he had to tell him about the letter and the fact it wasn't there when he and Eric searched the garbage. Nolan didn't like the idea of admitting such things, especially since it would make him a witness, which meant that Burford would call him to the stand and he'd have to explain what he had done. But there was no other choice. He couldn't just stand by and bury evidence that could help a defendant . . . his career wasn't that important compared to someone's life.

Nolan retrieved Burford Hammer's website on his phone, then clicked on the call button.

"Burford Hammer Law Office, how can I help you?" a female voice answered.

"Hello, it's Nolan Getty from the Public Defender's office. Is Burford available?"

"One minute please," she put him on hold.

A minute later her voice returned.

"He's not available right now. Can I take a message?"

"Yeah, tell him I need to speak to him about the James Sanders case and to call me as soon as possible."

"Okay, who is this?"

Nolan sighed. "Pay attention here now. My name is Nolan Getty and I'm with the Public Defender's office. I need to speak to Burford ASAP. And by ASAP, I mean today. Got it?"

"No-lan Gett-ee," she pronounced slowly, obviously writing it down as she spoke. "How do you spell your last name?"

Nolan sighed again. "G-E-T-T-Y".

"And your number?" she robotically asked.

"Look it up!" Nolan shot back before slamming the receiver down.

CHAPTER 42

Of course, Burford didn't return Nolan's call. So the next afternoon Nolan called his office again. Only this time he wouldn't be denied.

"Burford Hammer Law Office, how may I help you?"

"Yes, this is Judge Ferguson, I need to speak to Mr. Hammer immediately."

"One moment sir," the female voice replied, placing him on hold.

"Hello, this is Burford."

"Hello Burford, this is Nolan Getty at the Public Defender's Office."

"What? My secretary said it was Judge Ferguson."

"Yeah, well, I lied. I need to talk to you about the James Sanders case."

"What about it?"

"I have information that may help his defense."

"What is it?"

"Well, it's a bit complicated, but there are a few different things going on here. They didn't bring it up at the preliminary hearing, but when I was representing William Bisbaine on this case I received a disc with two videos on it, both of which were taken from a hidden camera in the kitchen of the judge's house. One video showed Mrs. Chancey having sex with James Sanders a few weeks before her murder. The second video showed my client, William Bisbaine, also having sex with her a week before she was murdered."

"Huh," Burford seemed to be thinking. "And so how does that help Sanders?"

"Well, that alone doesn't. Now, Mutz doesn't know this . . . he thinks the videos were sent to me anonymously, but they weren't. My investigator found those DVD's in Sanders's garbage can next to his house. We copied them and mailed the copies to both Mutz's office and myself. Well, Mutz didn't disclose them, so I disclosed them in a meeting with Mutz and Judge Ferguson. They then executed a search of Sanders's house and found the DVD's in the garbage. But that's not all they found. They also found that letter that was read at the preliminary hearing."

"Yeah, so what?"

"Well, that letter was not in the garbage when my investigator conducted his search. That means that the letter was planted in that garbage sometime long after the murder occurred."

"Well, maybe Sanders put it there later," Burford offered.

"No way. He was long gone to Kentucky. So this means that somebody else purposely put it there."

"Well, I don't know about all that," Burford cut in. "My client has basically confessed, so your theory can't be accurate."

"Confessed? To the police?"

"Well no, to me."

"Wait, Sanders told you he raped and killed Mrs. Chancey?"

"Well, in so many words, yes."

"What do you mean in so many words?"

"Well, you know how they are. He admitted to everything but the actual act. You know, yeah, I drove over there that morning; oh, and then I blacked out and then when I woke up, I had blood all over me and I fled. He did it Mr. Getty, there's no doubt in my mind about that."

"What about the letter? What did he say about that?"

"Well, I'm not going to go into any more detail about conversations with my client, but the bottom line is that you're wasting your time. Thanks for your concern, but he's agreed to plead guilty and that's it. Have a good day," Burford added, before hanging up.

"Damn it," Nolan breathed, tossing his cell phone on his desk.

It still didn't make any sense. There was something that just didn't fit with the letter. But if all that Burford said was true then the letter was pretty much meaningless. It was just some little loose end that couldn't be explained.

The rational side of his brain told him to just forget about it. He had done his job. He had disclosed the information to Burford and his conscience was clean. What else was he supposed to do? If Jim Sanders wanted to plead guilty then that was his problem. End of story, move on.

"To hell with it," Nolan said out loud. He grabbed a file on his desk and began paging through it. But the lawyer-trained part of his brain would not relent.

Jim Sanders didn't put that letter in his garbage. Somebody else put it there. So, it was written and placed there after the fact . . . not to warn him, but to implicate him.

As much as he wanted to ignore that lawyer-trained part of his brain, he couldn't. He knew it would nag at him forever, unless and until he talked to Jim Sanders himself. So, that's what he intended to do.

CHAPTER 43

"Who are you?" Jim Sanders asked as he entered the booth and sat down on the other side of the glass.

Nolan studied him for a moment. Despite the orange coveralls, he appeared to be physically fit and he was a good-looking guy, but he also appeared to be wracked with anxiety.

"My name is Nolan Getty. I'm the Public Defender in this town. I represented William Bisbaine, the person they originally charged with raping and murdering the judge's wife."

"So, why are you here?"

"I wanted to ask you a few questions—to see if there is any way I can help you."

"Why do you want to help me?"

"I think there's something weird going on here . . . some things that don't make any sense and I'm just trying to get to the bottom of it."

"My lawyer told me not to talk to anyone about my case," Jim replied.

"I'm a lawyer too, and I want you to know that anything you tell me is completely confidential. In other words, I'm ethically required to keep everything you tell me a secret. Is it true you're going to plead guilty?"

Jim stared at Nolan for a moment before answering. "My lawyer says I don't have a choice. He says the prosecution has an air tight case and if I plead guilty, the judge will sentence me and he'll be lenient because I owned up to it."

Nolan shook his head. "That's not true. Even if you don't have a criminal record the minimum you're going to get for rape and murder is 60 years . . . and that's the minimum. In reality, I can almost guarantee the judge is going to give you life whether you plead guilty or not."

"How do you know that?"

"Because that's what they do around here for murder and you're charged with rape and murder."

"Huh," Jim grunted.

"Let me ask you this. Did you rape and murder Torey Chancey?"

"Show me some i.d. that says you're a lawyer."

Nolan retrieved his picture badge from his briefcase and his bar card, slipping them both through the pass-through slot in the window.

Mr. Sanders looked them over and passed them back.

"I guess you're who you say you are."

"So, did you do it?" Nolan pressed.

Jim rubbed his face and shook his head. "I guess so. I mean, I can't believe I would do something like that, but there doesn't seem to be any other explanation."

"You don't remember being there?"

"Yeah, I was there. But for whatever reason, there's a block of time that is just gone—like I blacked out. I remember driving across town and I remember pulling into the driveway . . . I remember walking to the side door of the house and then the next thing I remember is sitting in my pickup, and I was in the garage."

"In the judge's garage?"

"Yeah. And everything was a fog but I guess I put the pickup in reverse and floored it. I remember feeling a big jolt and hearing a crashing sound, so I must have gone through the garage door. And then the next thing I remember is driving down the street."

Nolan tapped his pencil on the counter, thinking about the scenario.

"Do you remember anything about a can of paint thinner?"

Jim raised an eyebrow. "No."

"There was a can of paint thinner in the yard by the garage."

"I don't remember anything about that."

Nolan stared at him for a few moments. "The prosecution is going to say you killed Mrs. Chancey, then you went into the garage, grabbed a can of paint thinner and began breathing it and then you started your engine with the garage door closed, all in an attempt to kill yourself."

Jim grunted, then shook his head.

"And then you chickened out at the last second, drove through the garage, threw the can of paint thinner on the lawn and drove away. All the way to Kentucky."

Jim's shoulders sank and he let out a big sigh. "Damn this is all fucked up."

"Why did you go over there that morning?" Nolan asked.

Jim stared at Nolan for a few moments. "I went over there to get some work done."

"Just work?"

"Yeah, the judge hired me to install a security system and build a wine cellar," Jim answered.

"You didn't go over there to see the judge's wife?"

Jim's face flushed. "No. What do you mean?"

Nolan smiled. "I mean you were having an affair with her so I was wondering if you went over there to see her."

Jim shook his head. "No I wasn't."

Nolan chuckled and put down his pencil. "You don't know that they found the videos, do you?"

Jim's eyes widened. "What videos?"

"The videos of you having sex with the judge's wife on the kitchen counter," Nolan continued to smile.

Jim just stared at Nolan with no response, as if he was thinking intently, and then his face broke down.

"No. I did not know that. Where did they find such a video?"

"In your garbage can," Nolan replied. "Didn't the police tell you about the video?"

"No. They didn't mention it."

"Well, did they ask if you were having an affair with the judge's wife?"

"Ah, yeah . . . yeah they did."

"And what did you tell them?"

"I denied it."

"Ah, so they trapped you into a lie and now they have quite the surprise for you at the trial . . . if it comes to that," Nolan explained.

"Huh," Jim grunted.

"So, you were having an affair with her and you went over to see her the Sunday morning she was killed, correct?" Nolan asked.

"Yeah, you're right," Jim lowered his head.

"And then what happened?"

Jim shrugged, "I'm telling you I blacked out . . . I don't remember."

"Did you know the judge's wife was also having an affair with Willy Bisbaine?"

Jim blinked rapidly. "No."

"They found a video of that too. Both of them together on that same kitchen island and just a week before she was murdered," Nolan stared at him, wondering if he would flinch.

Jim slowly shook his head, as if subconsciously. "No, I didn't know anything about that."

There was something about his facial expression and mannerisms that told Nolan he wasn't being truthful again.

"Why did you videotape it?"

Jim shrugged. "I didn't."

"They found the secret camera in the kitchen and they found the DVD's in your garbage can."

"I don't know nothing about that. It wasn't me," Jim acted like he was perplexed.

"Uh huh," Nolan nodded. "So, if you didn't plant a video camera in the kitchen, then who did?"

"I don't know. It wasn't me though."

Jim wasn't very convincing.

Nolan thought for a moment. "What about that letter they found in your garbage? Did you see that?"

"Nope. That's the first time I saw that letter—when they showed it in court. And I told my lawyer that, but he just acted like it didn't matter."

"According to that letter, you and the judge's wife were planning on killing the judge and framing Bisbaine. Is that part true?"

"No," Jim answered without making eye contact.

Nolan leaned back in his chair. "I don't believe you. Listen, if you don't tell me the truth about what was going on here, I'm not going to be able to help you."

"I'm pretty sure I didn't kill her and we didn't have any plan to kill the judge, and that's that."

"So, if you didn't kill her then who did?"

"I don't know. Maybe the guy she was having an affair with before she met me."

"What do you mean a guy she was having an affair with?"

"She had an affair with a tennis instructor a few years ago. Well, let me back up. Just before she was murdered she didn't seem to be acting like herself. So I decided to follow her one day when she left the house. And I followed her to a condo complex on the east side of town. She went to a condo and knocked on the door and a Hispanic guy let her in. And it was the same guy that I had seen talking to her at the end of her driveway one day. And then about twenty or thirty minutes later she came out and I confronted her in the parking lot. And she told me that she had an affair with the guy a few years earlier and he was harassing her and she went there to confront him and tell him to leave her alone."

"Uh-huh," Nolan nodded. "How do you know she was telling the truth? I mean, maybe the letter is true and that's the guy she was going to run off to Mexico with?"

Jim shook his head. "No. When she saw me, she turned and threw a rock at the door and yelled at him to leave her alone. And then she pointed at me and said, 'You see this guy? He's going to beat the living hell out of you if you ever stalk me again!'"

"I see," Nolan nodded. He knew from Mrs. Stenson's story that the judge's wife could be very cunning and that it was just as possible that when she saw Jim, she began acting so that Jim wouldn't catch on to the fact she was still having an affair with the Stefano dude.

"So why did you run to Kentucky?"

"Man, when I woke up in that garage all dizzy and stuff . . . and there was blood on me, I just knew that something went bad. So, I went home and took a shower and packed up my stuff and just drove. And I kept driving until I got to Kentucky."

"So based on what you're saying, somebody killed Mrs. Chancey then planted those videos and the letter in your garbage in order to frame you. Is that right?"

"Yeah, I guess. I never intended to kill Torey and I've never seen those videos or the letter."

"So, let me ask you something. Do you really want to plead guilty to something you don't think you did?"

Jim shook his head. "No. Like I said, my lawyer said I didn't have a choice."

"Well, the way I see it there's no reason to plead guilty because the result is going to be the same—you'll be doing life in prison. So, would you rather take a chance and see if I can help you?"

"Absolutely. I mean, why not?"

"Exactly," Nolan agreed.

"But I already paid my lawyer. What are you gonna charge?"

"Well, Burford Hammer is going to try to keep your money so I tell you what. When all this is over I'll sue him on your behalf and whatever I get from him, that will be my payment. So all I need from you is to agree to pay for all the expenses—let's say not more than $2,500."

"I ain't got that," Jim lowered his head. "I gave everything I had and then some to my lawyer."

"You don't have to pay me now," Nolan added, knowing that he would never see a penny if Jim was actually convicted. "Just pay whenever you can."

"Really?" Jim asked. "Why are you doing this for me?"

Nolan shrugged. "Let's just say I have a bit of a grudge against the chief prosecutor and there's nothing I enjoy more than making his life as miserable as possible."

Jim thought for a moment. "What am I going to tell my lawyer?"

"Well, that's the tricky part," Nolan replied. "We can't let anybody know right now that you're going to retain me as your attorney. So, here's what you need to do. You need to tell Burford Hammer that he must set your case up for trial and that if nothing comes up that can prove your innocence, then you will plead guilty on the day of trial. It's important that you make sure he sets a trial date and not a guilty plea date though. Also, make sure you tell him to file for discovery and to provide you copies of everything he gets from the prosecutor. In the meantime, I will investigate and see if I can find anything that can help you. If I can't find anything by the day of the trial, then no harm, no foul—you can just plead guilty with your lawyer. On the other hand, if I find something that may give you a chance at winning, you can fire your lawyer and I'll step in to represent you in your trial. Sound fair to you?"

Jim nodded his head. "That sounds great."

"Okay, then. It's a deal."

Nolan stood up and exited the booth. He wasn't getting a good feeling about Mr. Jim Sanders and his truthfulness. Perhaps Burford Hammer was correct after all and this was a big waste of time, he thought. It's the damned letter that changes everything. One thing Nolan knew for sure was that the letter was put in the garbage long after the murder, so Sanders was most likely truthful when he said he had never seen it. If it wasn't for that letter this would be a no-brainer guilty plea, Nolan thought.

CHAPTER 44

Nolan had asked Eric to meet him in the office the next morning. Rick and Danny were already in their usual positions when Eric arrived.

"Do you boys actually represent anybody or do you just watch your boss?" Eric asked as he entered the office.

Rick folded his newspaper over and peered over the top. "Looks can be deceiving when you have representation without compensation. Right now, we are actually engaged in a high-level staff meeting."

"Uh-huh," Eric plopped down in the chair in front of Nolan's desk. "What's going on boss?"

"Well, you'll never guess who I met with yesterday at the jail."

"Let me try," Rick cut in. "Was it one of Danny's clients complaining about ineffective assistance of counsel?"

"Ah, no. It was Jim Sanders, the guy who killed the judge's wife."

"What?" Rick exclaimed. "Why the hell would you do that?"

"Wait," Danny replied. "I thought he hired Burford Hammer?"

"He did. But I wanted to hear his side of the story so I went up there and talked to him."

"Are you allowed to do that?" Danny asked.

"Technically, no," Nolan answered. "The ethical rules are pretty clear that you can't talk to other lawyers' clients without their permission, but who's going to complain? Certainly not Hammer. He doesn't give a darn about who talks to his clients."

"Well, I can think of some other reasons not to," Rick cut in. "Let sleeping dogs lie. Don't open a can of worms. Let every fox take care of its own tail. Don't flog a dead horse. You know, all the golden rules."

Nolan smiled. "Well, there is that, I suppose. But sometimes the worms just need to get out. And in this case, it's a letter. Somebody wrote a letter to Sanders warning him not to go through with his plan to kill the judge because Mrs. Chancey was going to set him up. Now, he says he never saw that letter. He also says he never planted a camera in the judge's house and he never saw any videos, even though the videos and the letter were found in his garbage. Whether he's telling the truth or not doesn't really matter. The letter exists, which means somebody knew of their plan and perhaps was even involved. And I'd like to find that person."

"Ah, so that's why I'm here," Eric smiled.

"That's right," Nolan nodded. "Sheila Stenson told me that Mrs. Chancey had an affair a few years ago with a tennis instructor by the name of Stefano Rodriguez. Judge Chancey caught them—not in the actual act, but riding with him in his car to his condo. The judge saw them and followed them and when she saw the judge in the rear view mirror, she pretended like he had drugged her. The judge took her home and ran Stefano out of the club."

"Wow," Rick exclaimed.

"Then Sanders told me that he followed Mrs. Chancey to this guy's condo about a month before she was murdered. And when she saw Sanders, she claimed that Stefano was harassing her and she had gone to his condo to confront him. I don't know if that's true or if she was having an affair with him as well. So, I need you to try and make contact with him and see if he's willing to answer a few questions. According to Sanders he lives in a condo on this side of town."

"So you think he may have written the letter?"

"Possibly."

"Well, he's not going to admit to it," Eric replied. "We would need to have access to his computer to see if it's on there. Could you subpoena it?"

"I suppose I could, but he would just scrub it when he saw the subpoena."

"Huh, I suppose," Eric agreed.

"When you find him, let me know. I want to go with you."

"Let's see if I can find him right now," Eric said as he pulled a laptop out of his briefcase. He opened it and began clicking the keys. "So it's S-T-E-F-F-A-N-O?" he asked, spelling it out.

"I'm not sure—try it with one F and if that doesn't work, try it with two."

Eric clicked a few more times on the keyboard. "Here he is. Fourteen Totten Trail. And here's his phone number," Eric added as he retrieved his cell phone.

"How can you find people so fast? Every time I search it says I need to pay to get additional information," Rick exclaimed.

"Magic police stuff," Eric replied. He stared at the computer screen and whispered the numbers before punching them into his phone. After he dialed the number, he nodded and smiled at Nolan as he pushed the speaker button. The phone was already ringing and it rang five more times before someone answered.

"Hello?"

"Hello, is this Stefano?"

"Yeah, who is this?"

"My name is Eric Wentz. I'm a special investigator and I've been hired by a lawyer to investigate a case that you may have information about. I was wondering if I could stop by your house and talk to you."

Silence.

"Hello?" Eric prompted.

"What kind of case?"

"The case where Judge Chancey's wife was murdered."

"Ah, no. I'm very busy. I don't have time."

"It's very important, sir. It's so important that if I can't talk to you, then we're going to have to subpoena you and you'll have to come to court and testify at trial. And I was just trying to avoid that."

More silence. After a few moments, he replied, "Can't you just ask me over the phone?"

"Um, sure," Eric nodded. "Can you hold on for a second, I need to find my notes."

"Okay."

Eric clicked the mute button on his phone. "Look up his address on your phone," he said, handing his laptop to Rick. "How far away is it?"

Rick retrieved his phone and opened the map app, quickly punching in the street address. "Ah, it's about two blocks east of here and 10 south."

"You and Danny go there now and text Nolan when you get there."

"What?" Rick asked.

"Just do it! We need you to look at his computer."

Rick looked at Nolan.

"Go!" Nolan yelled.

They both jumped up and ran out of the office.

Eric pushed the mute button again. "I'm sorry, sir. I have to run downstairs because the file's down there. Can I call you right back?"

"I can wait."

"Oh, okay, thank you for your patience. It shouldn't be more than a minute," Eric replied, clicking on the mute button again. "Well, that will give them a head start," he said to Nolan.

"What's your plan?" Nolan asked.

"Well, I'm hoping he will let us look at his computer. And if he agrees to let that happen, then Rick and Danny will be right there to do it before he can erase anything."

"Nice," Nolan smiled.

"You're going to want to record this."

"Right," Nolan opened his desk and retrieved the digital recorder. "Okay, I'm ready."

"Let's stall a few more minutes so Rick and Danny can get there," Eric smiled.

More than five minutes later, Eric punched the mute button. "Okay, sorry about that. Are you still there?"

"Yeah, I'm here."

"Like I said, my name is Eric Wentz and you are Stefano . . . what is your last name?"

"Rodriguez."

"Okay Mr. Rodriguez. And is it correct that you were the tennis instructor at Royal Oak Country Club?"

"Yes."

"When was that?"

"Oh, it was about two years ago. I've been working at the Whispering Pines Country Club south of town ever since I left."

"And why did you leave?"

"I just needed a new scene."

"Oh, okay. And did you know a person named Torey Chancey?"

"Um. Yes. I gave her tennis lessons."

"Did you know that she was married to the judge in town?"

"Yeah, I knew that."

"Did you know that she was murdered?"

"Yeah, I heard."

"Did you ever socialize with her outside of tennis?"

"Um, well, I guess we had a few drinks at the club now and then."

"Yeah, but didn't you two have a little more than that going on?"

Wow, Nolan thought. Eric's cutting right to the chase.

"What do you mean?"

"I mean you were having an affair with her, you know, like a sexual relationship."

"No."

"Mr. Rodriguez, please. I don't just make this stuff up. I've heard it from several sources."

"So? You can't prove anything. That's hearsay."

"Well, it's more than that, but maybe I should start with some easier questions. When did you last see her?"

"Um, about the same time. At least a few years ago."

Eric chuckled. "Oh, okay. Well, let me explain myself a little better. I'm just trying to conduct an adequate investigation into some loose ends and I'd really appreciate it if you would answer my questions honestly. If you don't do that, then I'm going to have to send you that subpoena and when you lie in the courtroom it's going to become a perjury charge. So, what's it going to be, an honest and polite conversation right now or a grueling cross-examination under oath?"

"I told you it was a few years ago."

"Well, that's a lie though. I'm not sure if you know him or not but a guy named Jim Sanders was doing some construction work at the judge's house and he was also getting a little side action from the judge's wife, if you know what I mean. Did you even know that she was sleeping with her handyman?"

"Ah, no. How would I know that?"

"I don't know. I guess she wouldn't tell you that. At any rate, because of this he became a little jealous and followed her one day. He followed her all the way to your house and this was about a month before she was murdered."

"Well, that's hearsay too."

"Come on Mr. Rodriguez, you're a tennis instructor, not a damned lawyer," Eric raised his voice. "If you had allowed me to come see you in person I could've showed you the pictures he took," Eric lied. "Let's see, here's one where she's knocking on your door and here's one where you are clearly standing in the doorway and here's one where she's entering your house. And all these pictures are pretty damned far from hearsay."

A moment of silence followed. Then, he folded. "Ah, well. I forgot about that, I guess."

"Oh, well that happens," Eric replied in a condescending tone. "Why did she go see you a month before she was murdered?"

"Um, just to visit."

"Oh, so you never had an affair with her but she just pops over to your house to visit?"

"Yeah. She stopped to see if I would give her private tennis lessons."

Eric laughed. "Is that your term for a sexual affair . . . private lessons?"

Silence.

"She didn't come to see you about lessons," Eric continued. "We also know about that little incident a few years ago when you drugged her and took her to your place. Do you remember that? The judge caught you and then instead of calling the police, he ran you out of the club and told you never to be around his wife again, right?"

"That was a lie. She faked everything. She didn't want the judge to think we were having an affair so she pretended like I had drugged her, but it was all an act."

"Okay, so she faked it. I already knew that. But that doesn't change anything. Because of that she would've never gone to your house to ask about private lessons, so why did she go to your house then?"

"Well, I think I'm done answering questions."

"I'm not playing, Mr. Rodriguez. If you don't cooperate right now, I am absolutely going to be forced to subpoena you. Do yourself a favor. It's not that difficult. Just answer my questions. You're not in any trouble."

"Okay, so what? We were having an affair! That doesn't mean I killed her!" he shouted.

"I didn't say you did," Eric replied.

"Well, why did you call me then?"

"Mrs. Chancey and her construction guy had a plan to murder the judge. The police found a letter in the construction guy's garbage and I was wondering if you wrote it?"

"No. Why, what did it say?"

Nolan waved his hand and pointed to his phone, mouthing the words, "They are there."

Eric nodded. "Hold on one second, please." He muted the phone, then spoke to Nolan. "Tell them to go to the front door and when you text them, tell them to knock on the door."

"Okay." Nolan texted the instructions to Rick.

Eric pressed the mute button. "Okay. Sorry. The letter said he should not go through with the murder plan because she was going to double cross him and frame him for the murder and then she was going to flee to Mexico. And it makes sense that you wrote it because you knew her and you're from Mexico. What happened, did you get cold feet?"

"No. I didn't write that letter."

"Come on, Mr. Rodriguez. If not you, then who?"

"I don't know. All I know is that I didn't write it and you can't prove otherwise."

"I suppose you wouldn't mind if we looked at your computer then?"

"Why would you want to do that?"

"To see if you wrote the letter."

"When would you do this and how long would it take?"

Eric pointed at Nolan. "Right now. There are two lawyers at your door." Eric could hear a knocking in the background.

"What? Hold on."

Eric could hear the door open. "Who are you?"

"We are defense attorneys and the man you are talking to is our investigator. May we come in?" Eric heard Rick say.

"Fuck you," Stefano yelled, then he slammed the door.

"And fuck you too," he said into the phone.

"Mr. Rodriguez, let them in and you'll never hear from us again."

"No, I'm not letting them into my house and I sure as hell am not going to let them snoop through my computer. I'm done with you. Do what you have to do."

"Wait," Eric pleaded. But it was too late, he had hung up.

"Damn it," Eric lowered his phone.

Nolan texted Rick, "Come back, it didn't work."

"Well, we tried," Nolan sighed.

"Yeah, we tried. He sure got defensive in a hurry though, didn't he?"

"Yeah. He's definitely a liar and it makes you wonder if he was in cahoots with Mrs. Chancey."

"So now what? You going to subpoena him or his computer?"

"That's about all we can do," Nolan replied, thinking intensely. "Well, there's something else you could do," he added. "You could contact the judge and see if he'd let you into his house to inspect the crime scene."

"For what?" Eric asked.

"To see if she had a computer and whether there are email messages between her and Mr. Rodriguez."

"I suppose I could do that. But I thought you didn't want anybody to know you're working on Sanders's case."

"Tell him that Burford Hammer hired you to cover the file."

Eric chuckled. "I suppose that would work."

"Oh, and I have one more theory," Nolan added.

"Another theory? Now what do you want me to do, sneak into the White House?"

Nolan smiled. "Well, it is a bit technical, but I'm sure you can handle it."

CHAPTER 45

Eric had attempted to call Judge Chancey several times but he never answered the phone. Finally, the fourth time worked, probably because he called his house during his lunch hour.

"Hello?"

"Is this Judge Chancey?" Eric asked.

"Yes."

"Hello Judge, this is Eric Wentz. How are you?"

"I'm fine, and yourself?"

"I'm great. Say, I've been hired to investigate the James Sanders case and I'm calling to see if you would give me permission to view the crime scene."

"I thought you worked for the Public Defender's office?" the judge asked.

"Well, I don't technically work for them. I'm an independent contractor and I actually do investigative work for several lawyers in town. It's just that those cases never seem to go to trial, unlike the Public Defender's cases."

"I see," the judge replied. "What exactly do you want?"

"Well, I want to see the crime scene . . . you know, look around and take a few pictures if you wouldn't mind. The lawyer just wants me to cover the file . . . you know, he doesn't want Sanders to claim ineffective assistance of counsel after he's convicted. He needs to prove he conducted an investigation so that's what I'm trying to do."

"Uh-huh," the judge grunted. "I can understand that but you're wasting your time. Everything has been cleaned up for months."

"Oh, we all know it's a waste of time but he's paying and he wants the file covered, so he wanted me to ask you for permission. I guess he wanted to avoid the hassle of getting permission through the court."

"Uh-huh. Well, I guess I don't have a problem with it. When do you want to come over?"

"How about Saturday at ten a.m., will you be home then?"

"Yeah, I can be home. See you then."

* * *

On a Saturday morning in late December Eric pulled into the judge's circular driveway at the front of his house. By then, the leaves on the trees had all dropped and everything seemed gray, including the sky. The temperature was colder than usual, hovering in the lower 40's but the high humidity made it feel much colder than that.

Eric buttoned his long coat to the top and lifted his collar as he approached the front door.

Judge Chancey immediately opened the door. He was wearing a jogging suit, which was an odd sight because Eric had never seen him in anything but a robe or a suit.

"Hello Judge," Eric smiled.

"Hello," the judge stepped to the side. "Come on in."

"I apologize for interrupting your day like this. Those damned lawyers just don't have much common sense sometimes. But I guess that's a good thing—it keeps me employed."

"It's no problem," the judge smiled. "I imagine you want to see the kitchen?"

"Yeah, I guess that's as good as place as any to start," Eric replied as he retrieved the camera from his pocket.

Eric took photos of the floor near the kitchen island where Mrs. Chancey had been killed. He then stepped back and took panoramic photos of the entire kitchen. He then nodded at the clock and turned to the judge.

"Is that where he hid the camera?"

"Yes," the judge nodded.

Eric stepped over to the clock and lifted it from its hook. The wall looked normal, as if there had never been a hole in it.

"Like I said, everything's been fixed," the judge explained.

"Yes, I suppose," Eric replied, replacing the clock. He then went to the right side of the kitchen. "Is this the side door that leads to the garage?"

"Yes," the judge answered.

Eric stepped into the small hallway and noticed a bathroom just inside the door. He took a photo of the bathroom, then turned and looked through the glass panels in the exterior door. He snapped another photo of the covered walkway to the garage.

"Do you mind if I take some photos in your garage?" he asked.

"Help yourself," the judge nodded. "It's a little chilly for me, so I'll wait here."

Eric opened the side door and a gust of wind almost pulled it from his grasp. He quickly closed it behind him and walked across the covered walkway to the garage. He took several photos of the garage including the garage door that had obviously been replaced.

When he was done in the garage he returned to the kitchen and saw the judge staring out the window, appearing as if he was lost in thought.

"Well," Eric wanted to get him out of his trance, "I'm done out there."

The judge turned and Eric saw tears welling up in the judge's eyes.

"It's a hell of thing . . . losing someone you love. Even when you find out later she's not the person you thought she was, it still doesn't change anything. You still miss her, but you also feel naive and stupid. It's not a good feeling," the judge shook his head.

"I can't imagine," Eric replied.

"Well, anyway," the judge blinked, "can I get you a cup of coffee?"

"Oh, no thanks. I appreciate it though. I think I'm pretty much done, but as long as I'm here, would you mind if I ask you a few questions?"

"Not at all," the judge poured coffee into a cup for himself. "Have a seat," he waved to the bar stool at the kitchen island.

"Thanks," Eric sat down, retrieving a pen and pad from his pocket. "As you know, some things came up after we interviewed you when I was working for the Public Defender's office . . . like the videos and that letter. And I just had a few follow up questions about that."

"Yes, I understand."

"Well, here's the deal. There's a lot of information in that letter and it seems to be a loose end that can't be explained. First it reveals that your wife and James Sanders had some sort of plot to kill you, and evidently, you had no idea any of it was happening?"

"No, not at all," the judge shook his head. "It completely shocked me as a matter of fact. And I can't help thinking how utterly ignorant I was. I mean, we had some arguments, just like anybody else, but I never thought she could or would do something like that."

"Yeah, I bet," Eric nodded. "And then there's the part in the letter that warned Sanders that she was going to frame him for the murder. That had to be what set him off and made him come after her that morning, I guess," Eric added.

"I suppose it did," the judge agreed.

"So the real question . . . the loose end that doesn't have an explanation, is who sent it?"

"I haven't figured that out either," the judge shook his head.

"Yeah, it's weird. But we know somebody had to send it, so she must've confided with this person, or perhaps this person was who she was going to run away with to Mexico, but maybe the person got cold feet and changed their mind."

"Yes, that's possible," the judge agreed.

"Can you think of any friends or anybody else she had been in contact with in the weeks leading up to her murder?"

"Well, there is Sheila Stenson, her friend that she went to the fundraiser with that night. Other than her, I don't really know of anybody else that she could've been associating with. I mean, she takes golf lessons, she does yoga, and she works out at the gym, so she would have contact with people in those places . . ." the judge paused in midstream. "You know, there was something that happened a few years ago that perhaps I should mention."

"What is that?" Eric asked.

"Well, it's a bit weird, but I was driving home early one day and I saw a car pass me on the road and it looked like my wife was in the passenger side of that car, and it looked to me like the driver was the tennis instructor at the country club. So, I turned around and followed them. I'm not sure why, I just had a bad feeling, you know, like she was in trouble or something. Well, I followed this car and it went to a condo building on the east side of town and when it parked I drove up beside it. I immediately saw that it was Stefano, the tennis instructor, and I yelled at him and asked him what was going on. He looked at me and just ran inside one of the condos. So, I opened his car and that's when my wife practically fell out. She was barely conscious, like she had been drugged or something. I carried her to my car and I took her home. After a few hours, she became coherent and she told me that the last thing she remembered was having a drink with Stefano after her tennis lesson."

"At the club?" Eric asked.

"I guess," the judge nodded.

"Did you call the police?"

"No," the judge shook his head. "She didn't want that. But I did call Stefano and I told him he better pack his bags and leave town or I was going to report it to the police and have him arrested."

"Uh-huh," Eric nodded. "Did he?"

"Yeah, I never saw him at the club after that."

"Interesting," Eric jotted down a note. "Did anybody ever check her phone? Was there any communication from this guy?"

"Well, her phone was never found, but I know Mr. Mutz did get her cell phone records, and I guess nothing stood out, except for a text from Jim Sanders. Do you know about that text?"

"Yeah," Eric nodded his head. "What about emails? Do you have a home computer?"

"Ah, yes."

"And does she have a separate email account or do you share one?"

"No. We share one. Well, at least I thought we shared one, but I suppose it's possible she had her own without me knowing about it."

"Did you ever check the email history to see if she had been in contact with anyone, or perhaps this Stefano character had been in contact with her?" Eric asked.

"No. I guess I hadn't thought about that."

"Would you mind if we looked right now?" Eric asked. "I don't mean to pry into your personal affairs, but it's probably the minimum I should do . . . you know, to cover the file."

"No, not at all. I have no problem with that. It's in my office," he said. "Follow me."

Eric followed him out of the kitchen and through the formal living room, where he opened a pair of glass paneled doors into his office.

"Here, let me open up the email account for you," he said as he bent over the desk and clicked on the keyboard. "Here you go," he said. "Have a seat."

Eric sat down at the desk as the judge hovered over him. Eric noticed that there were 1,201 emails in the in-box. He clicked on the 'Sent' box and noticed there were 900 more there.

"Okay," Eric muttered. "This may take a little longer than I thought. You know, on second thought, I could probably use that cup of coffee."

"Yes, no problem. I'll be right back."

Eric clicked on the trash folder and saw that there were only 52 emails there. All of them were dated after Mrs. Chancey's murder, which meant the trash had been emptied relatively recently. Eric quickly moved the mouse to the regular trash bin on the computer and noticed that it was completely empty. He then began searching . . . the first search was simply inputting the name, Stefano Rodriguez. There were no hits. An alias was always possible so he continued clicking and searching until the judge returned with the coffee.

"I'm not going to open every one of these, or I'd be here all day," Eric stated. "So if any one of these seems to stand out in any way, I'll just ask you about them and hopefully we can get through this relatively quickly."

"Sounds good to me," the judge placed the cup of coffee on the desk then sat down in the thickly padded armchair opposite the desk.

"Okay, here's a message to a person named Thad Jones and she's asking him what time she should meet him. Do you know him?"

"I believe he's the golf instructor," the judge answered.

"All right," Eric continued perusing the emails.

After several minutes, Eric asked the judge about another email, which turned out to be her personal trainer. The queries repeated several times, each time resulting in a dead end. Finally, he came across an email to srodtennis@cityscape.net.

"Oh, here's something," Eric stated. "It's an email to srodtennis and I guess your wife wrote, 'Don't ever email me again.'"

Eric scrolled down the email and read what had originally been sent to the judge's wife. "And that was in response to his email, which stated, 'We need to meet. Call me immediately' and the date is eight days before she had been murdered."

"Huh," the judge grunted. "So he was trying to reconnect and she evidently didn't want anything to do with him."

"I guess not," Eric commented.

Eric continued his task for another 30 minutes until all the emails had been read and there were no more emails from Stefano Rodriguez . . . even if he had an alias.

"Well, that should do it. I'd say the file is covered," Eric sighed. "I sure do appreciate your cooperation."

"Yes, no problem."

Eric stood up and made his way to the front door.

"I'm sorry I had to screw up your Saturday, especially since this guy is probably going to end up pleading guilty anyway," Eric said.

"It's no problem. I understand. Have a good day."

"You too, Judge."

CHAPTER 46

One Month Later

Nolan hadn't told either Rick or Danny about his plan and the evidence that had been collected since he had first talked to Jim Sanders. But now that it was the eve of trial he thought he should clue them in so they wouldn't feel left out, especially since there was a slight chance the next day would enfold into a spectacular, career ending implosion for him.

"Big day tomorrow," Nolan casually mentioned as he busied himself on the computer.

"How's that?" Rick asked.

"The Jim Sanders trial," Nolan replied.

"Oh, you mean the Jim Sanders guilty plea?" Rick asked.

"He's not going to plead guilty," Nolan smiled. "Tomorrow morning he's going to fire Burford Hammer and he's going to retain me."

"What?" Rick exclaimed. "Have you lost your mind?"

"Maybe," Nolan shrugged.

"How can he retain you?" Danny cut in. "You're a Public Defender. Don't you have to be appointed by the court? And doesn't he have to prove that he's indigent?"

"Yes, normally that's how it works. But there's no rule prohibiting me from having my own paying clients. It's just that it's never happened before."

"Wait, you're telling me that I could be representing my own clients while I'm being a Public Defender?" Rick asked.

"Well, it's not that easy," Nolan explained. "You can't use any Public Defender resources and you have to do everything that a private lawyer has to do, like get insurance . . . things like that, but it is possible."

"Huh," Rick grunted. "So what's your plan tomorrow, get a continuance?"

"Nope, tomorrow is going to be the big ambush and you're probably not going to want to miss this one. You see, neither Mutz nor Burford know it's coming. Jim Sanders told Burford that he wanted his case set up for trial, but that he was going to plead guilty if the prosecutor didn't give him a deal in the last second. Well, of course there's not going to be a deal, so although it's set for trial, both Mutz and Burford think it's all going to be wrapped up tomorrow with a nice little guilty plea."

"Whoa, that is awesome," Rick exclaimed. "Can you imagine the look on Mutz's face? That's going to be priceless!"

"Why the big surprise?" Danny asked. "I mean, why wait until the day of trial?"

Nolan glanced at Rick before answering. "Mutz tried to get me to conflict out of Willy's trial. He sent me a witness subpoena for the trial knowing that I couldn't be a witness and also represent him at the same time. And if he knew I was representing Jim Sanders he would try to do the same thing. But when he finds out tomorrow it's going to be too late."

Danny seemed confused. "How were you a witness?"

"He claimed that I had seen her the night before she was murdered, at that bar across from the old train depot. But the point is that he didn't really want me as a witness he just wanted me off the case. I'm sure he would've never even called me to the stand if it had gone to trial."

"Huh," Danny grunted. "So you're going ahead with the trial tomorrow but what's the point? Sanders still needs a defense and from everything I heard he doesn't have one."

"You know what makes a bad criminal defense attorney?" Nolan asked.

"Um, somebody that doesn't do their job?" Danny offered.

"Close," Nolan replied. "Someone who doesn't believe their client. And by believe, I don't mean actually believe, I mean legally believe. Do you know what it means to legally believe?"

"Um, I guess I'm not following you," Danny shook his head.

"It means that you should always assume your client is telling the truth first, then try to fit the building blocks around that foundation. Sure, sometimes it's not the truth in which case you explain to the client that the blocks don't fit. But you'll never know if the blocks don't fit and you'll never develop a defense unless you put in the effort. And that's why Burford Hammer sucks . . . because he doesn't legally believe in any client."

"I guess that makes sense," Danny nodded.

"So, here you have a defendant that was having an affair with the victim. He claims he loved her and wouldn't have killed her. But he also admits that he was at the scene of the crime that morning and he blacked out for a while, then he came out of it with blood all over himself. He also claims he never put a video camera in the house and he never saw the videos or the letter they found in his garbage. Oh, and by the way, the letter says that Mrs. Chancey's going to double cross him which is a perfect motive for him to kill her. Doesn't sound very good for the defendant, does it?" Nolan asked.

Danny shook his head. "No, that's why I'm saying he doesn't have a defense."

"And that's where you're wrong," Nolan cut in. "You don't think he has a defense because you don't legally believe him. What I'm trying to teach you is that you have to start with the assumption that everything your client says is true. In this case I had to assume that he didn't rape and kill her and that he didn't know about the videos and the letter. And if I hadn't done that I couldn't have developed an alternative theory."

"And what's that theory?" Danny asked.

"That's not important. The important part is that he's not going to plead guilty to something he doesn't think he did. And whether he wins or loses he at least gets the benefit of a trial. Besides, he has absolutely nothing to lose."

"Come on, boss," Rick chimed in. "I know you and you got something up your sleeve."

"Not really. It's just going to be an ugly slugfest . . . you know, pointing fingers, challenging witnesses . . . anything I can do to create reasonable doubt. And that's why I want y'all there . . . especially you, Danny. You need to get a feel for what it's like to zealously represent your clients, even when there's no perfect defense."

"Uh-huh," Danny nodded. "You want me to sit second chair then?"

"No. You're still a Public Defender so you can't. Just show up and pay attention."

"How about you, Rick? You got anything tomorrow?" Nolan turned to Rick.

"Hell no. Just a few misdemeanors in General District and I'll get them continued. I ain't gonna miss this!"

"I've got one little problem though," Nolan continued. "I've got a misdemeanor appeal scheduled for the other courtroom at 9:00 a.m. in front of Judge Chancey. He's going to take care of those appeals before he comes over to the other courtroom as a witness in the murder case. I need one of you to cover it. It should only take about 20 minutes and you're not going to miss anything—we'll still be picking a jury by the time you're done."

"I'll do it," Danny offered.

"Here's the file," Nolan tossed it to him. "Sherman Calhoun. He stole a package from his neighbor's porch. He claims he was holding it for her because he didn't want anybody to steal it. He says his other neighbor had a package stolen the week before. Just have him plead not guilty and hopefully Judge Chancey just gives him a suspended jail sentence and a fine if he finds him guilty. He got 10 days in General District Court, so anything less than that is a win."

"Sounds simple enough," Danny nodded.

"Well, there's a little more to it than that. He's schizophrenic and wasn't on his meds at the time. He thought the TV was talking to him and telling him to take the package. I wouldn't bring that up though."

"Why not?" Danny asked. "Sounds like a good insanity plea."

"Yeah, well, I suppose it does. But if you went with an insanity plea he'd be spending a year at the state hospital getting evaluated and probed, and I don't think that's in his best interest. He's on his meds now and he's good, or at least he was at his trial in General District."

"Don't mess it up, Danny," Rick chimed in. "Just do what the boss says and you can't go wrong."

Danny frowned at Rick. "What about a jury trial?"

"Well," Nolan answered with a question, "what do you think?"

"It might be the way to go . . . I mean, it's a relatively minor incident and I think a jury would be more likely to find him innocent than a judge."

"I agree," Nolan nodded. "The problem is that if the jury finds him guilty, they'll sentence him and you know by now that no judge in this town has ever changed a jury sentence. Juries don't see this every day like judges do, so they're very unpredictable when it comes to sentencing. By that I mean they may not bat an eye at giving him 12 months in jail."

Danny nodded. "Yeah, I suppose you're right."

"Good boy," Rick chimed in.

"There's one more thing," Nolan continued. "Don't go anywhere after the trial is continued at the end of the day tomorrow. You're going to want to see what I have planned."

"Oh boy. And what would that be?" Rick asked.

Nolan held up his finger, then retrieved his cell phone and dialed a number on speaker. The other end answered after the third ring.

"This is Scotty, Big Shanty Gazette."

"Hello Scotty, this is Nolan at the Public Defender's office. How are you?"

"I'm good, what's up?"

"Are you covering the trial of James Sanders tomorrow?"

"Well, yes. I'll be there but I understand it's going to be a guilty plea."

"You may be right. I just wanted to know because after whatever happens tomorrow in the Sanders case, I'm going to make an important public statement and I wanted you to have the exclusive coverage on it."

"What is it?" Scotty asked.

"Gotta wait until tomorrow. It's going to be big—you going to stick around for it?" Nolan teased him.

"Yeah, I guess."

"Okay, thanks. Goodbye," Nolan clicked the phone.

"What in the hell are you up to boss?" Rick perched up in his chair.

Nolan smiled. "Gotta wait until tomorrow."

CHAPTER 47

That afternoon, Nolan visited Jim Sanders at the jail for the last time. He had a few forms to go over but most importantly, he wanted to deliver a suit for Jim to wear at his trial the next day.

"I dropped off a suit that I think will fit you. Make sure you remind the jailors tomorrow morning so they don't ship you over to the court house in those orange coveralls."

"Okay," Jim replied. "So you think I have a chance?"

"You have a better chance than if you plead guilty," Nolan smiled as he retrieved some forms from his briefcase. "Here's the retainer agreement that states you're hiring me as your attorney. It also states that you agree to sue Burford Hammer for fraudulent billing and anything recovered is mine and you agree to pay not more than $2,500 in expenses. Just sign at the bottom there."

Jim signed the paper and slipped it back through the pass-through.

"Here's a statement I typed out for you. It says you wish to have me represent you at the trial tomorrow and you're releasing Burford Hammer as your attorney. Sign at the bottom."

Jim signed the paper and returned it.

"And finally, this is the 'Not Guilty' plea form. It says you've discussed your case with me, you're deciding to plead 'not guilty' of your own volition, you're satisfied with my representation, and you're ready for trial. Sign right there," Nolan pointed.

Jim signed the form.

"So, does my lawyer know all this yet?" Jim asked.

"Not yet. He's going to find out tomorrow, right before the trial starts. And it's important you don't tell him, otherwise, all this will fall apart."

Jim smiled. "Do you know that he hasn't even come up to see me since the first time, which was right after I was arrested?"

Nolan nodded. "Sounds par for the course."

"You got your family on board?" Nolan asked.

"Yeah, they're all coming to town. They'll be there tomorrow."

"Good." Nolan didn't want to tell him that their only purpose would be for sentencing. "And you told them to sit as close to the front as possible, right?"

"Yeah, I told them."

"All right. Well, like I said before I think you need to testify. You need to convince the jury that you didn't rape and kill Mrs. Chancey.

"What are my chances if I don't testify?" Jim asked.

"Not good. I can point fingers all day but none of it will be believable unless you tell them what happened. So, it's your choice, testify and you have a chance or don't testify and you're almost sure to get life."

Jim nodded. "Yeah, all right. I'll testify."

"Now, after I question you, the prosecutor is going to cross-examine you. Just answer his questions in a yes or no fashion, and don't worry about what he's trying to imply. When he's done cross-examining you, I will be able to ask follow up questions so that you have an opportunity to clear things up."

"Okay," Jim nodded.

CHAPTER 48

On an unusually cold morning in late January, Nolan climbed the marble steps of Big Shanty Circuit Court, an iconic bastion of justice built with red brick and towering white columns that supported a massive copper dome with green patina.

It had been built in 1878 . . . at least that's the year that was inscribed in a cornerstone, but the interior had been remodeled several times over the years. Twice in its history the entire exterior had been refurbished— the last time in the early 1990's, so it hid its age well.

One would never know unless a little research was conducted, the historical events that occurred inside and outside of this brick marvel over the decades. For example, over a hundred years earlier three young black men were convicted of raping a white girl after a one day trial and hung by their necks near the marble steps. Five years later the so-called victim killed herself because she couldn't live with the lies she told to cover up the consensual sex she had with them.

For several years in the early 1900's the mode of execution was by firing squad, which occurred to the left of the building in front of the brick wall that was still standing today. This was also the place where wives were convicted of adultery and were given an appropriate number of lashes via bull whip to correct their behavior.

All that was in the past though. There were no more hangings, no more whippings and justice had become modernly refined.

There was one thing that had not changed about the courthouse though . . . one thing that would never change: There had always been and would always be a cheating prosecutor hiding under the protection of its copper dome.

No one knew this better than Nolan Getty who nodded to the deputy and walked through the metal detector, ignoring the alarm.

"Good luck today," the deputy nodded back.

"Thanks," Nolan replied.

Nolan entered the courtroom which was empty. He usually didn't arrive early but he wanted to be there when Mutz arrived so he could drop the bomb on him. Of course, he would need permission from the judge so they would have to meet with the judge in his chambers which would take some time.

He had called Burford Hammer's office before he left for court and left a message that he should come to court early because he was going to be fired by Sanders. Whether Burford got the message or not, Nolan didn't know . . . nor did he care. He knew Burford wouldn't object to the change in counsel, after all, he already had Sanders's money and he would be more than happy to take it and run.

Nolan took a seat at the defense table and retrieved his trial notebook from his briefcase. As he was going through it he heard the court room doors open and shut. He turned to see Mutz coming down the aisle.

"What are you doing here?" Mutz asked as he pushed through the swinging gate at the front of the gallery.

"I have a trial," Nolan smiled.

Mutz placed his briefcase on the prosecutor's table. "Well, I already talked to the judge and he's going to call my case first. It's a guilty plea and the defense attorney is going to need that table so you may as well pack up your stuff and wait in line."

"Is it the Sanders case?" Nolan asked.

"Yeah, it's the Sanders case," Mutz grunted.

"Oh, well that's who I'm representing at trial today!" Nolan beamed.

Mutz froze in place, blinking rapidly and slightly shaking his head.

"What? How?" he stammered.

"Burford's been fired and I've been hired," Nolan grinned. "And now you and I get to play all day together. It's going to be fun don't you think?"

"He can't hire you. You're a Public Defender!" Mutz exclaimed as his face turned red.

Nolan laughed. "Not today, Mutz. Today I'm a private lawyer."

"Well, I object. Let's see the judge."

"As you wish," Nolan waved his arm. "After you."

Mutz spun around and stormed through the swinging gates, not bothering to hold them open for Nolan. He stomped to the back of the courtroom and did the same with the courtroom doors. Nolan fell behind as Mutz paced briskly to the judge's chambers. When he opened the judge's office door Mutz was standing in front of the secretary with his hands on his hips.

"You want to see him?" she asked.

"Yes," Mutz answered.

She glanced at Nolan. "You with him?"

"Yup," Nolan smiled. "I'm just a little slow."

She picked up her phone and pushed a button. "The lawyers want to see you." After a pause, she replied, "Okay, I'll send them in."

"Go ahead," she nodded to Mutz.

Mutz led the way into the judge's chambers.

"Good morning, Judge," Mutz greeted him.

"Good morning, gentlemen. Have a seat. What's going on?"

"Mr. Getty claims that James Sanders fired Burford Hammer and now he's going to represent him. But Mr. Getty is a Public Defender," Mutz whined. "I don't think he can do that."

Judge Ferguson turned to Nolan. "Is this true? You've been hired by the defendant?"

"Yes sir," Nolan nodded.

"Why can't he do that?" the judge asked Mutz.

"Well, he's not a private attorney. He can only represent clients that this court appoints him to represent."

"I disagree," Nolan cut in. "There is no such rule."

Mutz shook his head. "Well, you work for the Commonwealth so you can't use government resources in a private enterprise."

"I'm not using any government resources," Nolan turned to the judge. "Everything I will use today is paid for out of my own pocket . . . paper, pens, computer . . . everything. And I have specifically taken a day of vacation from the Public Defender's office."

"Uh-huh," the judge grunted. "You do know that private lawyers are required by the bar to have liability insurance. Do you have insurance?"

Nolan reached into his coat pocket and retrieved a piece of paper. "Yes sir, here's my policy."

The judge examined the paper then handed it to Mutz, who glared at it as his face flushed red.

"Well, Mr. Mutz? Are you satisfied?" the judge asked.

The judge's phone buzzed and his secretary's voice came over the speaker. "Mr. Burford Hammer is here to see you."

"Send him in," the judge replied.

Burford Hammer entered the chambers and greeted the judge. "Good morning, your honor."

"Good morning, Mr. Hammer. Have you heard that new counsel has been retained by James Sanders?"

"Yes, I got the message this morning. I just wanted to let you know that I have no objection."

"Okay then. Well, let me ask you this, Mr. Getty. Are you ready for trial?"

"Absolutely," Nolan replied.

"And is the defendant going to plead guilty or not guilty?" the judge asked.

"Not guilty," Nolan replied.

"Well, I'm not ready," Mutz cut in. "I need a continuance."

"On what basis?" the judge asked.

"Because I didn't know that Mr. Getty would be representing him and that he'd plead not guilty."

"Was this case set for a guilty plea or was it set for trial?" the judge asked.

"Well, it was set for trial, but I thought he was going to plead guilty at the last minute."

"The court doesn't care what you thought would happen," the judge replied. "This case was set for trial, and everybody knows that if a case is set for trial the attorneys have the responsibility to be ready for trial. Did you subpoena witnesses?"

"Well, yes," Mutz stammered.

"Motion denied then," the judge replied.

"May I have my policy back?" Nolan asked as he held out his hand to Mutz.

Mutz stood and handed the paper to him.

"Thank you, judge," Nolan smiled and exited the chambers.

On the way to the courtroom Nolan saw Danny in the lobby talking to Mr. Calhoun, so he approached them.

"Mr. Calhoun, this is my assistant, Danny. He's going to do your trial because I have another trial booked in the other courtroom."

"Yes, that's what I understand," Calhoun nodded.

"Are you still on your meds? Everything okay?" Nolan asked.

"Yes, yes, everything's fine. All is good," he answered.

"Okay then, good luck," Nolan finished.

CHAPTER 49

Nolan was waiting at the defense table when they brought Jim Sanders out of the lockup. The dark suit actually looked good on him.

They shook hands and both sat down. Nolan glanced behind him and saw that the gallery was full of people, all of whom were there to either watch or report.

"The judge is going to arraign you before the jury comes in," Nolan explained. "Stand up when he comes in and stay standing when the judge tells everyone to be seated. He's going to ask you questions about your plea, so just answer them. When he's done all the potential jurors will be brought in and we will then ask them questions until a final jury is picked. Any questions?"

"Nope," Jim answered.

Nolan heard the distinctive sound of the chambers door opening, as did the deputy.

"All rise," the deputy yelled out. "The Big Shanty Circuit Court is now in session!"

Judge Ferguson appeared on the bench in his black robe. "You may be seated," he said as he took his seat.

Jim began to sit down but Nolan grabbed his elbow, stopping him.

"Oh, sorry," Jim whispered. "I forgot."

"Good morning," the judge looked to Mutz and then to Nolan. "Are both parties ready for trial?"

Nolan and Mutz answered in the affirmative.

"Are you James Sanders?" the judge asked.

"Yes sir," Jim answered.

"Please answer the clerk's questions," the judge turned to his clerk who was sitting at the side bench.

The clerk stood, holding a piece of paper in front of her.

"Mr. James Robert Sanders, you are hereby charged with the following crimes: Count 1. Murder in the first degree, to wit, on or about October 22nd of last year, you did willfully, deliberately and with premeditation, kill Torey Anne Chancey in violation of Commonwealth statute 18.2-32. How do you plead; guilty or not guilty?"

"Not guilty," Jim croaked, his voice breaking.

There was something about the formality of a clerk's reading of the charges that really got a defendant's attention, and it was no different for Jim.

"Count 2. Rape, to wit, on or about October 22nd of last year, you did engage in sexual intercourse with Torey Anne Chancey against her will, by force, threat or intimidation in violation of Commonwealth statute 18.2-61. How do you plead; guilty or not guilty?"

"Not guilty," Jim replied.

In this same manner, the clerk continued to read each count against him, including burglary, grand larceny, and two counts of intercepting oral communications. His plea was the same to each: "Not guilty."

The clerk finally stopped reading and sat down.

"Mr. Sanders," the judge began. "I have a 'Not Guilty' plea form in front of me. Did you go over this form with your attorney?"

"Yes, sir," Jim nodded.

"Do you fully understand the charges against you?"

"Yes, sir."

"Is your plea entered freely and voluntarily?"

"Yes."

"Are you satisfied with the services of your attorney?"

"Yes, sir."

"Are you demanding a jury trial?"

"Yes, sir."

"Do you understand that when you request a jury trial, it is the jury that will recommend a sentence if you are found guilty?"

"Yes, sir."

"Do you understand that you could be sentenced to life in prison if you are found guilty of these charges?"

"Yes, sir."

"Are you ready for trial?"

"Yes, sir."

"Very well then. The court accepts your 'not guilty plea' on all charges," the judge turned to the deputy. "You can bring in the venire."

CHAPTER 50

While the venire entered Courtroom A, Mr. Calhoun sat upon the stand in Courtroom B, testifying under oath about the stolen package.

"Why did you think someone would steal Ms. Anderson's package?" Danny asked.

"Because just the week before, my other neighbor had a package stolen from his porch," Calhoun answered.

"And just for the record, the person that stole the package from the other neighbor, that wasn't you, was it?"

"Oh no," Mr. Calhoun answered. "But I think I know who did it."

"Oh?" Danny asked, surprised. Although he was trained to never ask a question to a witness on the stand that he didn't already know the answer to, he couldn't help himself. "Who would that be?"

"My other lawyer before you. Mr. Getty."

"Um, disregard the question please," Danny stuttered, afraid that Mr. Calhoun was having a short-circuit in his brain.

Judge Chancey leaned forward. "Are you talking about Nolan Getty, the Public Defender?" the judge asked.

"Yes sir."

"What makes you think Nolan Getty took the package?"

"Because I saw him and another guy go into Mr. Sanders's house next door and then I saw them take something out of his garbage can."

"Mr. Sanders?" the judge cut in. "What is his first name?"

"It's Jim. His name is Jim Sanders," Mr. Calhoun answered.

The judge raised an eyebrow. "The Jim Sanders that owns Old Dominion Construction?"

"Yes, that's him."

"And he was your next door neighbor?"

"That's correct," Mr. Calhoun answered.

"When did you see Nolan Getty at his house?"

"Um, Your Honor, I'm going to have to object. I don't think this line of questioning is relevant," Danny cut in.

"Objection noted and overruled," the judge quickly replied without even looking up.

"Should I answer?" Mr. Calhoun asked.

"Yes, you must answer," the judge told him.

"It was the week after I met with him in his office, so I guess it was around November 10th. I wouldn't have recognized him if I hadn't just met with him."

"What did he take from the garbage?"

"I couldn't really see. It was something small. It was actually the guy who Mr. Getty was with that took it, but then Mr. Getty brought it back."

"And all this happened around November 10th?" the judge asked.

"Yes. And then a few days later, I just happen to be looking out my window and I see another person in Mr. Sanders's garbage."

"Another person?" the judge asked. "Who was that?"

"I don't know. It was at night. Probably about 11 o'clock. It was too dark to see. But I don't think it was Mr. Getty. It wasn't his shape. This person was shorter."

"Do you know if it was a male or female?" the judge asked.

"Ah, no, I guess it could've been a female. I have no idea."

"Did you see any car or anything associated with this person?"

"No sir. Nothing."

"Could you pick this person out of a lineup?"

"No sir. I couldn't see a face. Just the outline of a person opening the garbage."

"Could it have been James Sanders?" the judge asked.

Mr. Calhoun shook his head. "No, I don't think so. Mr. Sanders was skinnier and I would recognize his walk."

"When was the last time you saw James Sanders at his house?"

Danny wanted to object to the continued line of questioning that had nothing to do with his client but he didn't have the spine.

"Oh, it had been several weeks. It was probably mid-October. Then all of a sudden, he just disappears and never shows up again. And before that, I saw him every day," Mr. Calhoun answered.

"I see. Did you see any other strange activity around his house, either before or after he disappeared?"

"Ah, no, not that I can think of."

"All right, thank you Mr. Calhoun," the judge finished, then turned to Danny. "Do you have any further questions?"

"No sir," Danny folded.

CHAPTER 51

In Courtroom A, the deputy opened the side door of the courtroom and the jury panel began to file in. The Big Shanty Circuit Court empaneled 42 potential jurors; all of whom had been prescreened by the use of a questionnaire to ensure that they met the minimum qualifications.

Once they were seated, the judge welcomed them to court and described the nature of the case. He then introduced the prosecution, the defense, and finally the defendant. He then asked a series of questions directed at identifying any jurors who could not serve for a variety of reasons, including, medical conditions and potential bias. With respect to bias, the judge asked if any of them were related to the lawyers or the defendant through blood or marriage; whether anybody had any financial stake in the case; and whether any of them had preconceived opinions of the case. All answered in the negative.

In Big Shanty Circuit Court, much like many courts in Virginia, the voir dire process was extremely abbreviated. The attorneys were not allowed to question the venire for days, like in California; rather, they were only allowed about 45 minutes per side. If an attorney attempted to go beyond that limit the judge was always quick to scold.

Mutz went first, asking the typical questions that were intended to identify anybody sympathetic to a defendant or distrustful of the police. Of course, he introduced Judge Chancey, who had entered the courtroom when he had finished the misdemeanor appeals. He wanted to know if anybody personally knew him.

Nolan knew that his intention was not only to identify a juror who may be biased but to also let the jury know that the murdered victim's husband was present and watching.

When nobody answered in the affirmative Mutz asked if anybody had been in a hearing with Judge Chancey or if they knew anyone who had been in a case in which Judge Chancey presided. Two jurors raised their hands. Upon further questioning Mutz learned that the first juror's cousin had sued a contractor and Judge Chancey presided over it. The outcome was favorable to her cousin. The second juror indicated that Judge Chancey had sentenced his son to ten years in prison for selling drugs.

"Will this in any way prevent you from fairly judging the facts of this case?" Mutz asked.

"No," the juror answered.

Despite his answer Nolan knew that Mutz would get rid of him with his peremptory strike. He couldn't afford to have a juror with a grudge.

Mutz spent the remainder of his 45 minutes questioning the jurors about their interactions with police. When he had finished he gave the floor to Nolan.

Nolan went through his typical questions that were intended to identify any jurors that were pro-prosecution or sympathetic to the police. There were certain types of people that Nolan generally favored and those he didn't. He liked engineers and those with science backgrounds because they were more likely to analyze evidence with a critical eye. Although it seemed counterintuitive, he also liked females when there was a female victim because they seemed to be less sympathetic than male jurors. He couldn't admit this theory though because it was illegal to strike jurors on the basis of gender. Enforcement of the rule was impossible though because he could always find a separate reason unrelated to gender if questioned about it.

Those he didn't like included teachers and government workers. The former were notorious for being sticklers for rules and unsympathetic to those who break them. The latter lacked suspicion of government and its processes.

In the end he identified one teacher, three government workers, and one person related to a police officer.

His final question was intended to remind the jurors that a defendant is innocent until proven guilty. He returned to the defense table and placed his hand on Jim's shoulder as he did it.

"As you know, in our trial system a defendant is always presumed innocent until proven guilty. So, as we sit here before trial is there any one of you who doesn't believe that Jim Sanders is completely innocent of all charges?"

Nobody raised a hand.

"Conversely," Nolan continued as he raised his own hand. "Please raise your hand if you presume that Jim Sanders is innocent of all charges."

First one juror, then another slowly raised their hands. Finally, they all caught on and everybody raised their hands.

Nolan smiled. "Thank you."

The voir dire process being completed, the judge excused everyone but the first twenty jurors. Once the excess jurors had left, he instructed the prosecution and defense to exercise their peremptory challenges. Taking turns, Mutz and Nolan each crossed off a name from the list, until they were down to 12 jurors.

The deputy handed the paper to Judge Ferguson, who read the names of the remaining jurors who were excused. Once they had left, the judge swore in the jury of 12. He then explained the process of the trial, including their role and the rules they should follow. When he finished he turned to Mutz.

Two hours and fifty-two minutes after the venire had entered the courtroom, jury selection was over and a hot, steaming pile of justice was ready to be served.

"Do you have an opening statement?"

"Yes, sir," Mutz answered as he stood and buttoned his suit coat.

Nolan stood. "Excuse me your honor, before we begin, I have a motion to separate the witnesses."

"Very well. Ladies and gentlemen, the attorneys are going to call their witnesses. When your name is called please come up to the front. Go ahead."

Mutz read his list of witnesses, then Nolan read his, which included Eric, two police officers who were at the crime scene and his own expert in collecting samples for DNA analysis. All the witnesses came to the front, including Judge Chancey. Upon seeing the judge, Nolan wondered how Mr. Calhoun had faired.

"Ladies and gentlemen, you will be excluded from the trial until your name is called, at which point you will be escorted in by a deputy. Under penalty of law, you must not discuss the trial with anybody else, either before or after you testify. Do you understand?"

They all nodded.

"This way folks," the deputy called out, opening the side door to the courtroom. The witnesses, including Judge Chancey, followed the deputy out of the courtroom.

"Go ahead, Mr. Mutz," the judge nodded.

Mutz approached the jury box and began his opening statement.

"Good morning again ladies and gentlemen. Today we're going to show that on October 22nd of last year, James Robert Sanders raped and murdered Torey Chancey in her own home. To understand why, we are going to have to take you back in time, well before he committed these heinous crimes. But I must warn you, the evidence we will show is both graphic and shocking. Unfortunately, we have no other choice but to show you this evidence. That said, the evidence will show that James Sanders was working for Judge Chancey and his wife for over two months before the crimes occurred. During this time he began a sexual relationship with Torey Chancey. Also during this time he installed a secret video camera in the Chancey home and he recorded at least one sexual encounter with her. The evidence will also show that at some point James Sanders and Torey Chancey developed a plan to murder the judge. Their plan was for Sanders to kill the judge on Sunday morning and then he was to wait for Torey Chancey to come home from an overnight trip, at which point they planned to frame a third party, William Bisbaine, to make it look like he murdered the judge then raped Torey Chancey before escaping. But their plan was circumvented because the evidence will show that James Sanders received an anonymous letter right before he was to murder the judge. We will show you this letter which was found in a garbage can at James Sanders's house, along with a secret video of his sexual encounter with Torey Chancey. You will see that this letter warned him that Torey Chancey was going to double cross him and flee to Mexico while ensuring that he would be caught and sent to prison for murdering the judge. Now, you can imagine how this must have angered him. So, instead of killing the judge he went to the Chancey home to confront her. He waited until the judge had gone on his morning jog then he entered the house and waited there until she arrived home from her overnight trip. When she did return home, he raped and murdered her and all this occurred before the judge returned from his jog. And before leaving the house, Sanders pried a safe from the wall in their bedroom and stole it and its contents, which included $10,000. We will show you with scientific evidence that Torey Chancey suffered traumatic injuries from sexual penetration before she was murdered. We will show you that the DNA of semen samples taken from Torey Chancey are a match with James Sanders. We will show you that the DNA of a blood stain found in Sanders's pickup is a match with Torey Chancey."

Nolan leaned into Jim and whispered, "He's going to come over here and point his finger at you. Just shake your head and don't say anything when he does."

Jim nodded.

"We will show you that James Sanders fled to Kentucky where he was eventually arrested and brought back to Big Shanty," Mutz continued as he began his approach to the defense table.

"And all this evidence is going to prove that this man!" Mutz raised his voice and pointed his finger directly at Jim. "This man raped and murdered Mrs. Torey Chancey."

Mutz returned to the prosecutor table as the judge looked to Nolan.

"Mr. Getty do you wish to make an opening statement?"

"Yes sir," Nolan stood and put his hand on Jim's shoulder while facing the jury.

"Jim Sanders is innocent. He is not the person who raped and murdered Torey Chancey. Now, he doesn't know it," Nolan pointed to Mutz, "but the prosecutor's own evidence is going to show that Mr. Sanders is innocent. Most importantly, I will show you evidence which will prove that someone else raped and murdered Torey Chancey. So, although I want you to examine the prosecutor's evidence carefully, I'd like to ask you to keep an open mind and to reserve judgement until all the evidence has been presented. Only then will you see the truth. Only then will you understand that somebody else committed these awful crimes. Thank you."

"Okay," the judge looked at his watch. "It's pretty close to lunch time, so let's just break for lunch right now before we get into the prosecution's case." He turned to the jury. "You will now go into the jury deliberation room where lunch will be provided. You are free to leave the building but you must be back in the deliberation room by one o'clock. Do not discuss the trial or anything that has occurred with anybody other than your fellow jurors. Do not read or view any newspapers, magazines, video sources or other news stories that could be related to this trial. Do not access any news based web sites or any other web site that may have information about this trial or events leading up to it. Does everybody understand this?"

The jury nodded.

"Very well, follow the deputy please."

The deputy waved his hand and led them to the deliberation room. Once they were gone the judge banged his gavel. "This court is now in recess."

"All rise," the deputy yelled out.

Everybody stood as the judge exited the bench.

After Sanders was escorted by the deputy to the lockup, Nolan turned to leave and immediately saw Danny standing by the swinging gate.

"How did it go?" Nolan asked.

"We need to talk," Danny breathed.

"Okay, let's go out to the lobby and find an empty room," Nolan suggested. They went to the lobby and found an empty meeting room.

"What's up?" Nolan asked.

"Mr. Calhoun said some things during his trial that were pretty bizarre," Danny began.

"Like what?"

"Well, it went like this. I asked him about his other neighbor's package being stolen the week before and if that was the reason he was holding Ms. Anderson's package and he said it was. Then when I asked him if he had anything to do with stealing the other neighbor's package he said he did not. But then he just blurts out that he thought it was you who may have done that."

"Me?" Nolan asked.

"Yeah. And Judge Chancey then cuts in and asks him why he would think such a thing, and he says because he saw you and another guy go into his other neighbor's house when he wasn't there and that you also took things out of his garbage."

Nolan flushed. "Huh, I guess he stopped taking his meds, maybe?"

"I guess. But anyway, you'll never guess who his neighbor is. It's Jim Sanders!"

"Oh, yeah he mentioned that at his trial in General District Court. So then what happened?"

"Well, the judge then got curious and started asking him questions about when this happened and Mr. Calhoun told him. Then the judge asked him if he had seen Mr. Sanders around his house or acting weird after October 22nd and Calhoun said he had not seen him since about that time. But Calhoun says that after he saw you at his house, a night or two later he saw somebody else at Sanders's house and that person was also messing around in the garbage. Well, the judge was real curious then and asked him a bunch of questions about the person but Calhoun didn't know what he looked like because it was dark. Apparently he just saw a shadow of a person and that's it."

"No car description?" Nolan asked.

"No, nothing. All he saw was the outline of a person—it could've been male or female, he didn't know. But he was pretty sure it wasn't Jim Sanders because the person was much shorter."

"Huh," Nolan grunted. "Then what happened?"

"Well, the judge found him guilty of larceny and gave him 30 days suspended."

"Nice," Nolan smiled. "You won!"

"I guess," Danny smiled.

"Well, thanks for the info and good job," Nolan told him. "Why don't you go get some lunch and then come back and watch the trial."

"Okay. You're not getting lunch?"

"No, I've got some things to think about and get ready for trial."

"You want me to bring you anything?"

"No, I'm good."

During lunch Nolan thought about Calhoun's statements. One thing was certain, he was not hallucinating about Nolan's presence at Sanders's house, so chances were he was not hallucinating about the shadowy figure in Sanders's garbage a night or two later. And it was the presence of this shadowy figure that fit perfectly with Nolan's theory that somebody planted the letter after he and Eric had been there. The problem was that if Calhoun testified he would also reveal that Nolan and Eric had been there first and unless Nolan confessed to that, it was unbelievable, especially because of his history of mental illness.

Nolan really wanted to have a face-to-face with Mr. Calhoun and grill him on the details of what he had seen. Unfortunately, he couldn't have Eric hunt him down because Eric was a sequestered witness and he wasn't allowed to have contact with him. Perhaps I'll just go to his house tonight and see if I can find him, Nolan thought.

The only other option was to ask for a continuance so that Mr. Calhoun could be sent a subpoena, but that amount of time would allow Mutz to send his own subpoena to him, which would force him to recuse himself. No, Nolan thought, the better option is to wait until after he had an opportunity to grill Calhoun.

CHAPTER 52

"Call your first witness," the judge instructed.

"The Commonwealth calls Lieutenant Jack Childress of the Big Shanty Police Department," Mutz said in a loud voice.

The deputy opened the side door of the courtroom and leaned into the corridor. "Lieutenant Childress!" he yelled.

A few moments later, Childress entered the courtroom. He was wearing a blue suit with a red tie. Usually his gray hair was unkempt, but today, he had combed and slicked back perfectly. Even his gray mustache looked trim.

"Raise your right hand," the clerk turned to him. "Do you swear to tell the truth so help you God?"

"Yes," Childress answered.

After he was sworn in, Mutz led Childress through his background as a police officer. He then moved to the crime scene and what he'd found. He introduced photos of the house, the missing wall safe, and Torey Chancey's body, which the judge admitted into evidence. Mutz waited until all the members of the jury had seen each photo before introducing the next one. This process took over thirty minutes.

"This photo shows a video camera on the front porch. Was it working?" Mutz asked.

"Yes," Childress explained. "It was the only camera that was working. We found the DVR in the closet upstairs."

"And did you make a copy of the recording?"

"Yes."

"I'm handing you an item marked for identification as Commonwealth's Exhibit 9. Do you recognize this item?"

"Yes," Childress answered.

"What is it?"

"It's the DVD copy of the recording on the porch camera."

Mutz asked the judge to admit it into evidence, which the judge did.

Mutz wheeled a stand with a projector to the middle of the floor and pointed it at the screen. He then placed the DVD into the machine and played it. The video showed the judge going out for his jog, then returning over an hour later.

"Did you make an arrest of a person who was not James Sanders in relation to these crimes?"

"Yes. A person named William Bisbaine was initially arrested but he was later released."

"Why was he released?" Mutz asked.

"Because we discovered new evidence that exculpated him and inculpated James Sanders."

"Can you explain to the jury how you discovered this evidence?"

"Yes. I received a call from you and you indicated that Mr. Getty, the defense attorney, had received a DVD from an anonymous person. The DVD contained two videos and he showed those videos to you in the judge's chambers. Based on the angle from where those videos were taken, it was obvious that they were from a hidden camera in the kitchen of Judge Chancey's house."

Nolan didn't bother to object to the hearsay because he wanted the jury to see the videos.

"What did you do then?"

"Then we met Judge Chancey at his house and we searched the kitchen."

"What did you find?"

"We found that a hole had been cut in the wall behind the kitchen clock. There was no camera in the wall, but there was an electrical outlet that had been run through the wall studs and attached inside the wall. Presumably the outlet powered the camera that was once there."

"Based on the videos and the hole in the wall, did you then suspect who had installed that camera?"

"Yes. Because James Sanders had been doing construction work at the judge's house, we suspected that he had planted the camera. So, we obtained a search warrant for his house."

"Did you conduct the search at his house?"

"Yes."

"What did you find?"

"We found two DVD's in a garbage can next to his house. We also found a letter."

Mutz approached the witness stand.

"I'm handing you an item that's been marked for identification as Commonwealth's Exhibit 10. Do you recognize this item?"

"Yes."

"Is this item in the same or similar condition as when you first saw it?"

"Yes."

"What is it?"

"It's the letter we found in James Sanders's garbage can."

Mutz asked the judge to admit the letter into evidence, which he did.

Nolan didn't object to that either because he wanted the jury to see the letter.

"What does this letter say?"

Childress read the letter in its entirety. When he was done, Mutz handed the letter to the jury and waited for each of them to look at it.

"Do you know who this letter is from?" Mutz asked.

"No, it doesn't say."

Mutz then handed Childress another DVD.

"I'm showing you an item identified as Commonwealth's Exhibit 11. Do you recognize this item?"

"Yes."

"What is this item?"

"It's one of the DVD's we found in James Sanders's garbage."

Mutz then asked the judge to admit the exhibit into evidence, which he did.

"Your honor, due to the sexually graphic nature of this video, I'd like to move the screen so that only we and the jury can see it, but the gallery cannot."

"Any objection, Mr. Getty?"

"No objection," Nolan responded.

A voice interjected from the gallery then.

"Your honor, may I address the court?"

Nolan turned and saw Scotty from the Big Shanty Gazette.

"My name is Scott Adams, from the Big Shanty Gazette, and I believe we have a First Amendment right to view this trial and the evidence presented, including this video."

"Mr. Jones, the press has a right to view this trial but this right does not include the inspection of evidence," Judge Ferguson stated loudly. "And if you or anyone else disrupts this trial again, I'll have you charged with contempt of court." He then turned to Mutz. "Go ahead Mr. Mutz."

Mutz moved the screen so that it faced the front of the court, then played the video of Sanders's sexual act with Mrs. Chancey in the kitchen. Some of the jurors looked away during the graphic part.

Mutz played the entire video including when the judge came home.

"And for the record who is the female that is with James Sanders on the video?"

"That's Mrs. Chancey, the judge's wife," Childress answered.

"What did you do after you finished your search at James Sanders's house?"

"We obtained an arrest warrant for him."

"And obviously he was later arrested. Where did this happen?"

"In Paducah, Kentucky."

"What was he driving?"

"His construction pickup."

"What did you do with that?"

"We impounded it and had it hauled back here."

"Did you search his pickup?"

"Yes. We took a sample from the seat of the pickup where it appeared there was a feint blood stain."

"Did you interview James Sanders?"

"Yes."

"What did he tell you?"

"He said that he didn't commit the crimes he was charged with. He said he wasn't at Judge Chancey's house on the day Mrs. Chancey was murdered. He said the last time he was at the house was on the Friday, two days before she was killed."

"What else did you ask him?"

"I asked him if he was having an affair or if he ever had sex with Mrs. Chancey and he denied it. He also denied having a plot with Mrs. Chancey to murder the judge."

"At that time, did he know you had the video of him having sex with Mrs. Chancey?"

"No."

"Did he tell you why he fled to Kentucky?"

"Objection, leading and speculation," Nolan interjected.

"Sustained," the judge quickly responded. Then he turned to the jury and said, "Please disregard the question from the prosecutor."

"Did he tell you why he was in Kentucky?" Mutz tried again.

"He said he was visiting family."

"At some point, did you obtain the cell phone records of James Sanders and Mrs. Chancey?" Mutz asked.

"Yes."

Mutz approached the witness stand and handed him papers.

"I am showing you an item marked as Commonwealth's Exhibit 12 and 13. Do you recognize these items?"

"Yes."

"Are they in the same or similar condition as when you first saw them?"

"Yes."

"What are they?"

"They are the cell phone records of James Sanders and Torey Chancey that we obtained from the phone companies."

Mutz asked the judge to admit the exhibits into evidence, which he did with no objection from Nolan.

"Was there a text made from James Sanders on the morning of Mrs. Chancey's murder?" Mutz asked.

"Yes."

"What time was this text?"

"9:17 a.m."

"What did it say?"

"It said, 'Where are you? I'm waiting.'"

"Who was that text sent to?"

"It was sent to Mrs. Chancey."

"Thank you, that's all the questions I have for this witness," Mutz stated as he walked the cell phone records over to the jury box and handed them to the foreman.

"Mr. Getty," the judge nodded to Nolan.

Although Nolan had numerous questions for the detective, or more aptly, numerous statements that he would require the detective to make during cross-examination, it was too early to expose his theory. So, his plan was to take baby steps then re-call him to the stand later when the puzzle pieces would look more obvious.

"Good morning Lieutenant," Nolan nodded.

"Good morning," he replied.

"Is it true you don't know when the DVDs were placed in Mr. Sanders's garbage can?"

"That's true."

"Is it true you were unable to find any fingerprints on the DVDs?"

"True."

"So despite the fact that the DVDs were found in Mr. Sanders's garbage can, there is no other evidence that proves Mr. Sanders was the one that put them there, correct?"

"Correct."

"You said there were two DVDs in the garbage can. Is it true that the second DVD showed Mrs. Chancey having sex with William Bisbaine?"

"True."

"Is it true that Judge Chancey had found William Bisbaine guilty of raping a 13-year-old approximately eight years ago?"

"Yes."

"And is it true that William Bisbaine was later exonerated and released after DNA proved his innocence?"

"Yes."

"And this sexual encounter between William Bisbaine and Torey Chancey occurred about one week before Mrs. Chancey was murdered, correct?"

"Nine days to be exact."

"Is it true that Mr. Bisbaine used a condom when he had sex with Mrs. Chancey?"

"True."

"Is it true that Mrs. Chancey placed this condom in the kitchen garbage can after they were done?"

"True."

"Is it true that after Mr. Bisbaine had left, Mrs. Chancey retrieved this condom from the garbage can."

"True."

"Is it true that she then moved off camera towards the side door of the house with the condom still in her possession?"

"True."

"Is it true that there were three different semen samples collected from Mrs. Chancey's body?"

"Yes."

"One matched Judge Chancey, correct?"

"Correct."

"One matched James Sanders, correct?"

"Correct."

"And one matched William Bisbaine, correct?"

"Correct."

"Can you explain how William Bisbaine's semen was still in Mrs. Chancey nine days after they had sex?"

"No, because I'm not a doctor."

"If I told you that Mrs. Chancey saved the condom that Mr. Bisbaine used and then put the contents of that condom on and inside of herself on the morning she was murdered, is there any evidence to refute this?"

Childress thought for a moment. "No."

"Would this be consistent with the theory that Mrs. Chancey and Mr. Sanders had a plan to murder Judge Chancey, then frame William Bisbaine for the murder and the rape of Mrs. Chancey?"

"Yes, I suppose it would."

"Thank you. No further questions."

"Any rebuttal?" the judge asked Mutz.

"No sir," Mutz replied.

"Can this witness be excused?" the judge asked.

"Yes," Mutz replied.

"No sir," Nolan stood up. "I may call him during the defense."

"Very well," the judge turned to Childress. "You may not be excused at this time. As you know, you are still under sequestration, therefore you may not discuss the case with anybody else."

"Yes sir," Childress responded.

"This way," the deputy directed.

Childress stood and followed the deputy through the side door.

"Call your next witness," Judge Ferguson instructed.

"I call Dorothy Turner," Mutz said loudly.

"Dorothy Turner!" the deputy yelled in the hallway.

A moment later, a short, plump woman with brown hair entered the court room. She was wearing pink nurse scrubs and white sneakers. Nolan knew already that she had to be the sexual assault nurse examiner.

After she was sworn in Mutz led her through her examination of Mrs. Chancey's body. She testified that she collected several samples from Mrs. Chancey and packaged them to be sent to the state lab. Mutz led her through each sample, assuring that the proper chain of custody was followed. She then testified that she observed abrasions and other signs of trauma that were consistent with sexual assault.

Nolan had only one cross-examination question.

"Would you agree that if Mrs. Chancey had sex with a man nine days before she was murdered, the chances of that semen still being present in her body would be very low?"

"I can't say one way or the other. There are too many factors involved in any one person's body and personal hygiene. What we do know is that sperm can survive up to five days inside a vagina."

"Thank you," Nolan finished.

Mutz's third witness was the evidence technician who collected a sample from the seat of Sanders's pickup truck. He established the proper protocol and chain of custody for the sample, which was sent to the state laboratory.

On cross-examination the officer admitted that no other evidence of the crime was found in the pickup.

Mutz's fourth witness was the scientist from the Department of Forensic Services who analyzed the samples sent by the nurse and the evidence technician. The scientist explained the type of testing that he conducted including a brief explanation of how DNA analysis is performed. He then testified that samples collected from the body of Mrs. Chancey showed the presence of semen and DNA analysis of this semen indicated that it was from three different individuals, one of whom was James Sanders. As usual, the scientist testified that the chances of somebody other than James Sanders having the same DNA were about 1 in 1 billion.

The scientist then testified that the sample taken from the seat of the pickup contained blood that was a DNA match to Torey Chancey with the same remote chances of it belonging to somebody else.

Nolan didn't want to put up a fight with respect to the accuracy of the analysis. On cross-examination he had only one question.

"Is it true that part of the semen collected from Mrs. Chancey was a DNA match to an individual named William Bisbaine?" Nolan asked.

"Yes."

"Thank you. No further questions," Nolan finished.

As was typical in a trial, the day had melted away . . . at least from the lawyers' perspective. But it probably didn't seem to go so quickly for the jury.

"Well, it's 4:45 and since we're not going to finish today, we will adjourn for the day and continue the trial tomorrow," the judge stated. He then gave the same instructions to the jury that he had given earlier and then told them to report to the jury room at 8:45 the next morning.

"How do you think it's going?" Jim whispered.

"As good as can be expected," Nolan replied. "We'll see you tomorrow."

"Okay," Jim replied.

Once the jury had left the courtroom the deputies escorted Jim to the lockup.

Before Nolan left the lawyer's tables, he stepped over to Mutz and whispered in his ear, "I have an important announcement that you're not going to want to miss outside of the courtroom right now."

Mutz raised an eyebrow. "What is it?"

"Come outside," Nolan stated before turning and walking through the gallery. On the way out he noticed Scotty sitting in the gallery and nodded to him.

"You ready for that statement?" he asked.

"Sure," Scotty answered.

"Let's step out in the lobby," Nolan waved him ahead.

Rick and Danny met them in the lobby between the courtrooms where there were also others milling around.

Nolan turned to Scotty. "Let's wait for Mutz to come out—he's going to want to hear this."

Nolan glanced at Rick, who was smiling and shaking his head, completely confused as to what was about to happen.

Mutz came up behind them. "What's going on?"

Nolan nodded to Scotty. "You may want to record this and ask me about my big announcement."

Scotty turned on a recorder and put it in front of Nolan. "I understand you have an important announcement to make," Scotty proclaimed in a rather loud voice.

Those near them stopped what they were doing and turned their heads.

"Yes I do," Nolan began. "Today I am officially announcing my candidacy for Commonwealth's Attorney in the next special election."

Rick's mouth dropped open as Nolan continued.

"It's time the people of Big Shanty had a quality prosecutor; one who seeks justice; one who does not prosecute innocent citizens; one who has the ability to protect the community by convicting those defendants who are actually guilty of serious crimes. Far too long I have witnessed the incompetence of Big Shanty's prosecutors and I am willing to change that. And with the help of this community, we will change that in the next election."

Nolan glanced at Mutz. His face was deep red and his lip was quivering.

"What do you mean by incompetence?" Scotty asked.

"Well, I'm not going to get into details about any specific cases at this time, but the special election is a little more than a month away and

I will let the community judge the current prosecutor with respect to cases he is handling right now. If he wins them, you should vote for him. If he doesn't, you should vote for me. Thank you," Nolan added. He spun around and stepped quickly to the doors with Danny and Rick close behind him.

"Holy crap, what in the world are you doing?" Rick asked as they bounced down the steps.

Nolan chuckled. "I'm going to be the next Commonwealth's Attorney. And I'm going to recommend that you be hired as the Chief Public Defender."

"What?" Rick exclaimed, unable to believe it.

"You heard me."

"Boss! You're a Public Defender. You were born to be a Public Defender. You can't go to the dark side!" Rick exclaimed.

"It's only the dark side because of who's there now. It can be the light though . . . when I run the show."

Rick continued to walk beside Nolan with Danny at their heels. He was stunned an unable to wrap his head around Nolan's plan. Especially the bold statement about winning the case. And then it dawned on him.

"Wait. You're going to win this trial, aren't you?" Rick asked.

Nolan smiled. "I better after that statement."

"So, you got something up your sleeve, don't you?" Rick pressed him.

"I do," Nolan answered.

"Well, what is it?" Rick asked

"Why don't you come to court tomorrow and find out? I'd like you to see what happens before you know it's going to happen. That way we can discuss it after the trial and you can tell me whether you agree with the jury or not."

Rick shrugged. "I can do that."

Nolan went straight to his truck once they reached the chateau. "We'll see you boys in the morning."

CHAPTER 53

As Nolan drove the ten blocks to his house on the edge of Old Town, he couldn't help but notice the lack of activity on the streets. This was the slow season for drug dealers. January in Big Shanty was like July in Arizona—everybody either left or stayed in their homes as much as possible because of the weather. That didn't mean that less drugs were being sold though, they were just not being sold on the street corners and in parking lots. Instead, they were being sold at night clubs, nip-joints and carwashes. The latter being the most popular conduit.

As he drove by the Bubbly Car Wash at the edge of the business district he saw five cars in line and knew that at least one of those five was there to either sell or buy drugs. Car washes were perfect for this because dealers could deposit drugs in cars while they were cleaning them and drivers could hand the workers a "tip", and the undercover police would have no way of knowing, even if they were surveilling. It also worked the other way around—workers could leave money inside the car in exchange for drugs that were within the car—like a climb in vending machine.

As Nolan continued down the street into the residential area, he noticed a former client standing on a porch wearing a parka. He was smoking a cigarette and he nodded to Nolan as he drove by. Nolan nodded back.

This was Old Town. Located near the center of Big Shanty, it was the first high-end housing area to be built in the city after the Civil

War. Back then, the area was defined by majestic mansions that lined cobblestone streets with gas lanterns on every corner. Today, many of the old mansions were abandoned and boarded up, occupied only by crack-addicts and meth-heads, who like vampires, only came out at night.

The decaying neighborhood didn't bother Nolan though. He just wanted a cheap house close to the courthouses. Besides, the drug dealers and gang bangers pretty much left him alone—probably because they saw him as an ally. After all, he had represented many of them at one time or another.

His house was a two-story, Federal style, brick manor built in 1897. It was in rough shape when he bought it. The roof and windows needed replacing, all the electrical was bad, and the kitchens and bathrooms all needed a face lift. He began hiring contractors to renovate it, but quickly realized that he could do many of the things they did, he just needed the right tools. So, he began doing the work himself and it eventually turned into a hobby for him—a way for him to stop thinking about criminal defense and the tragedies associated with it.

Nolan turned his pickup into the driveway and parked it beside his house. He gathered up his briefcase then took the sidewalk to the front door. On the steps to the porch, he avoided the missing board and creaked across the porch to the door. He paused at the door and surveyed the porch. He couldn't wait for spring because that's when he planned to replace the entire front porch.

As he entered his house his cell phone rang. He didn't recognize the number but he thought he'd answer it anyway.

"This is Nolan Getty."

"Hello Mr. Getty, it's Judge Chancey."

"Hello Judge, how are you?"

"I'm good. Say, I was wondering if I could have a word with you tonight?"

"Um," Nolan thought for a second. "I'm pretty sure we're not supposed to be communicating."

"Oh, sorry. I should explain. It's not about the trial. It's about something that Mr. Mutz is planning on doing to you and I think you should know about it before it happens."

"Oh, well that sounds sinister," Nolan replied. "You can't tell me on the phone?"

"It's a pretty sensitive issue that I don't think should be spoken about over the phone, if you know what I mean."

"Sure," Nolan replied. "Do you want to meet somewhere?"

"I have to go check my lake house tonight because of the cold weather and I thought I would just stop by your house on the way. You live in Old Town, right?"

"Yeah," Nolan replied. "Twelve Jackson Way."

"Is eight o'clock okay?"

"Sure."

"Okay, see you then," the judge hung up.

Well, that was weird, Nolan thought. What in the world could Mutz be up to?

CHAPTER 54

Nolan saw the judge's car pull to the curb in front of his house. He waited by the front door until the judge neared his porch before opening the door.

"Watch that step, there's a missing board," Nolan warned him.

"I see," the judge looked down then skirted around it.

Nolan held the door open and the judge stepped into the foyer holding a bottle of Scotch.

"I thought we may as well have a little something to warm us up," he said.

"Oh, great. Have a seat in the study there," Nolan pointed to the small room to the right of the foyer. "I'll get some glasses."

Nolan returned with two glasses a minute later and set them on the coffee table before sitting in the chair opposite of the judge.

As the judge poured the whiskey in each glass, Nolan noted his hand was shaking. Whether it was the light or the cold temperatures from outside, the judge also looked older and more weathered than usual. And his gaunt-looking face held a pensive grimace.

"Cheers," he said, holding up his glass.

Nolan placed his cell phone on the coffee table and picked up his glass. "Cheers," he replied, clinking his glass against the judge's.

Nolan took a sip and felt the whiskey warm his insides.

"This is good," he nodded.

"Yes, it is," the judge agreed, looking around the study. "Looks like you've been doing a good job fixing this old relic up."

Nolan shrugged. "Baby steps. I might have it done by the time I retire."

"Uh-huh," the judge grunted. "Anyway, I wanted to let you know that I had an interesting conversation with Montgomery Mutz last night. You probably know this but he thought James Sanders was going to plead guilty this morning."

"Yes, I figured that," Nolan nodded. "I thought it would be fun to surprise him."

"Oh, you did more than that," the judge smiled. "The trial stopped him from doing what he planned on doing after the guilty plea."

"And what was that?"

"Charge you with a few different crimes, like breaking and entering, tampering with evidence, and making false statements to a judicial officer."

"Why would he do that?"

"He knows you broke into James Sanders's house."

"How does he know that?"

"They found a fingerprint inside his house. Did you know that the fingerprints you took for your background check to become a lawyer are stored in a database? Well, they are and the fingerprint inside the house matched you. So, he put two and two together and figured out that you found the videos in the garbage, copied them, and sent them to yourself. And then you lied to the judge when you said you didn't know who sent them."

"Huh," Nolan grunted. "That's interesting."

"Yes, it is," the judge agreed. "I guess he's sick and tired of you beating him up in court so that's his desperate attempt to get rid of you."

"I guess. But I'm not too worried. He can't prove anything, even with the fingerprint."

"Maybe not, if that was all he had. But your former client ratted you out this morning in Courtroom B. Mr. Calhoun was Jim Sanders's neighbor. He said he saw you go into Sanders's house and also take something from his garbage."

"Oh yeah?" Nolan feigned surprise. "Did you know he's mentally ill?"

"Well, apparently, that didn't stop him from seeing the reality of what happened. I don't know why I didn't think of this before but it all makes sense now. You really were at Mr. Sanders's house and you were the one who found those DVD's in his garbage can, which means you sent them to yourself or just pretended that they were sent to you."

"Well, that's quite the theory," Nolan sipped his whiskey.

"It's more than a theory. The fingerprint, the eyewitness testimony—it's something that can be proven in court."

"But Mutz doesn't know about Mr. Calhoun," Nolan replied.

"Oh, but he does," the judge responded. "You see, I had another conversation with Mr. Mutz after the trial today."

"Oh yeah?" Nolan asked.

"Yeah. He called me and said his assistant told him what Mr. Calhoun had said on the stand . . . that he had seen you at Sanders's house. He wanted to know if it was true."

"Did you tell him?"

"Of course."

"Huh," Nolan grunted. He didn't like the fact that the judge just admitted to violating the sequestration rules.

"Anyway, he's going to bring charges and there's no doubt he'll be able to prove his case, so you're on borrowed time."

"We'll see," Nolan shrugged.

"The other interesting thing that Mr. Calhoun stated was that he saw another person in Sanders's garbage and that was after he saw you there."

"Oh yeah?" Nolan asked.

"Do you know who this person was?" the judge asked.

"No," Nolan lied.

The judge chuckled. "Oh, I think you do. You see, when I learned that you had been at Sanders's house, it finally dawned on me that you were the one who had found the videos and exposed them. And then this morning it all came together when Mr. Calhoun revealed the timing of when you were there. I knew right away what must have been going on in your mind. You knew that the letter was planted well after the murder because it wasn't there when you searched the garbage. So, that means whoever planted the letter wasn't trying to warn him, he was trying to frame Sanders for the murder. Wouldn't you agree?"

Nolan nodded. "Yes, I would."

"Who is it Mr. Getty? Who did Mr. Calhoun see planting the letter in the garbage just a few days after you had been there?"

Nolan shrugged. "I have no idea. Perhaps Stefano Rodriguez?"

The judge chuckled again. "Don't be so coy, Mr. Getty. I know things that you don't think I know. Come on, just say it . . . I want to hear you say it."

Nolan's cell phone buzzed and he noticed it was a call from Eric. As he reached for the phone on the coffee table, the judge yelled, "Don't touch that phone!"

Nolan looked up and watched the judge pull a black revolver from his coat pocket and point it at him.

Nolan's eyes widened. At first his mind couldn't process the fact that the judge was pointing a gun at him. It seemed like he was in some sort of weird dream . . . that this could not actually be happening.

"Hold on now," Nolan held up his hands. "You can't be serious. You're a judge."

"Why don't you fill your glass and drink some more Scotch?" the judge asked.

Nolan remained motionless, staring at the judge.

"Please, fill your glass," the judge repeated, waving the revolver at him.

Nolan reached over and filled his glass. As he did, he heard his cell buzz again. It was a text from Eric.

The judge told me he wanted to meet us at your house. I don't like it. I'm almost there. Be careful and don't trust him.

At least there would be a record of the judge being at his house, Nolan thought. If anybody would think to look at Eric's cell phone records, that is.

"Go ahead. Drink up."

Nolan took a gulp of the whiskey and winced as it went down.

"I don't get where this is going," Nolan said as he took another gulp. He stared at the barrel of the gun and noticed that it was small caliber, probably a .22.

"You've boxed me into a corner and leave me no other choice," the judge explained. "When you figured out the letter had been planted later you began to suspect that I was the killer, which is why you sent your investigator to my house. Well, of course, if Mr. Calhoun had not testified this morning I wouldn't have even thought to check into it and I would've never even seen it coming. You had me dead to rights and I didn't even know it. When were you going to spring it on everyone, after the prosecution closed its case?"

"Spring what?"

"Stop playing dumb. I know what you did. Because of Mr. Calhoun's testimony, I knew what you were thinking. You were thinking that I wrote that letter and planted it after you had been there. So, that's why I checked my computer and do you know what I found?"

"No," Nolan lied again.

"I found a software program called 'Retrieve It' which was installed the same day that your investigator was at my house. Your investigator installed that program on my computer and ran it while he was pretending to be checking Torey's emails. But you knew that, didn't you?"

Nolan remained silent.

"Fill the glass again," the judge waved his gun. "And when he ran that program it recovered the letter that was supposed to be permanently deleted."

"That's right," Nolan replied, knowing the cat was out of the bag. "And the letter was created on your computer after your wife was murdered."

"Drink it," the judge ordered.

Nolan took a gulp and grimaced again.

"I tried to think of some explanation . . . some way to maintain my innocence, like someone had broken into my house and framed me but there is no plausible reason how such a letter could get on my computer, except if I wrote it. So, here I am, left with no other choice but to confront you."

"Uh-huh," Nolan grunted. "He was supposed to delete the program after he ran it."

"He did but he forgot to empty the trash. But now it's your turn. I'm curious as to how you think all this happened," the judge said.

Nolan smiled. "You installed the video camera in your kitchen. And then you saw that Jim Sanders was screwing around with your wife. Eventually, you found out that they were planning on killing you and you probably learned that from the videos you were recording. Regardless, you knew Jim Sanders was coming to murder you. So, you hatched your own plan to kill your wife and frame him for it."

"Take another drink," the judge ordered.

Nolan took another gulp. "You probably planted those videos in Jim's garbage the day or night before. Then, on Sunday morning, instead of going jogging you returned to the house through the side door and probably put on coveralls and a ski mask. Then, I'm thinking you used a rag or something else soaked in paint thinner to overcome him, after all, you are quite older and weaker than him. That was probably the toughest part of the job—jumping him from behind and keeping that rag over his mouth and nose until he went down. Or did you simply get the jump on him with a gun? I guess that makes more sense—you held him at gunpoint, made him restrain his own wrists, then knocked him out with paint thinner. Then you moved his pickup into your garage, put him in the driver's seat and kept the rag over his face so he wouldn't regain consciousness. How am I doing so far?"

The judge smiled. "Keep going."

"Well, then you raped and murdered your wife when she got home. Then you put her blood all over him and in his pickup, then started the engine and put the can of paint thinner in his lap. You did this so it would look like Jim killed himself in your garage. After it was all set up, you took the coveralls and everything else off, hid them somewhere, then returned to the front porch, as if you had been jogging the entire time."

"Keep drinking," the judge ordered.

Nolan ignored him.

"But somehow Jim regained consciousness and barreled through your garage door, smashing it to bits and throwing the can of paint thinner into your yard. He sped away with blood all over him and no memory of what happened. So, of course, he panicked and after cleaning himself up he fled to Kentucky."

"I said drink up," the judge raised his voice.

"I don't think so. What's your plan? Get me to pass out then put me in my car in the garage with the engine running? It's dumb. Why would I kill myself?"

"You're not going to kill yourself. You're going to get in a heated argument with your investigator, Eric Wentz. You've been drinking and things are going to get out of control. You will draw your gun, which I'm holding in my hand and shoot Eric, but he will also shoot you and unfortunately, neither of you will make it out of this gunfight alive."

"That's dumb," Nolan chuckled. "Ballistics will show it's the same gun."

"It's not the same gun. I have a .38 in my pocket which is his designated gun."

"Huh," Nolan grunted. "But Eric's not here."

"He's on the way. He said he would meet us here," the judge smiled.

Nolan shook his head. "Seems pretty far-fetched to me."

"Well it's all I have. People do desperate things when they learn they will be arrested and imprisoned for life, especially if you're a judge. It's risky but I can't just sit back and let you prove your case against me."

"Well, it's too late. Everybody in my office knows about the letter, so you're wasting your time."

The judge chuckled. "I know you better than that. You wouldn't take a chance on someone leaking something like that, so you haven't told anyone. Only you and Eric know, and that's how it was going to stay until the trial. Besides, I have to assume this because I have no other choice. I either act today, or I get exposed tomorrow."

Nolan lifted his glass. "Maybe I will have some more," he said, wanting to stall.

CHAPTER 55

When Nolan failed to take his call, Eric quickly texted him, then flipped his flashers on in his car and accelerated down Main Street. Blowing through a red stoplight, he glanced at his watch and knew that he was still at least five minutes away from Nolan's house.

He had thought about calling the police after the judge had called him, but knew it would've been premature. There was no evidence the judge knew he had found the letter on his computer and so he was still holding out hope that the judge truly wanted to talk to them about some plan Mutz was hatching against them. He also didn't want to ruin Nolan's surprise at trial, which they figured was the best way to expose the judge.

Still, his instincts were telling him something was wrong. He didn't like the fact that the judge wanted to meet them in person, especially since they were the only ones who knew he had raped and murdered his own wife.

Three minutes later, Eric found himself in traffic which was backed up due to a red light. Seeing that nobody was coming in the opposite lanes, he pulled around them and gunned the engine, speeding down the oncoming lanes until he got to the light where he slowed to make sure no cross traffic was present, then gunned the car again, speeding through another red light.

He glanced at his watch one more time. Almost there.

CHAPTER 56

"You know what else tipped me off?" Nolan continued his stall.

"What?"

"Your wife went through with her end of the deal, just like she and Jim had planned. She put Willy's semen in her when she got home from the fundraiser so that told me that she wasn't going to double cross Jim, which also told me the letter was a fake."

"I suppose," the judge replied.

"You knew they were going to murder you but you didn't know they were going to set up Willy, did you? You must have been very surprised when Willy's DNA showed up on her and they charged him with the crimes."

The judge grunted.

"Speaking of Willy, how shocked were you when you saw the video of your wife doing him too? That had to be the final straw. I mean, she did it so that she could frame him but it sure did look like she enjoyed it."

"Don't push me, Getty."

"All of this would've gone a lot smoother if your wife had just had her phone on her. When Jim had passed out, you texted your wife from Jim's phone and you thought she'd have her phone on her when she came home but she didn't. If she had the police would've seen the text and immediately known that Jim did it. But they didn't. Jim escaped from your garage and then Mutz charged Willy. So, then it was too late for the text to matter. We both know what Mutz would've done when he saw that text in the phone records later. He would've either buried the records or he would've argued it was just a coincidence and Jim was waiting somewhere else for her. Well, he buried the records . . . we both know he's a cheater. By the way, I sent him the videos and he buried them too. Did you know that?"

"No," the judge answered.

"When he failed to disclose the videos I had to disclose them myself."

"Huh," the judge grunted.

"But I should've known what you already knew . . . it was too late. You knew Mutz had a hold of Bisbaine like a pit bull and he wasn't about to let go. Once Bisbaine was charged, you knew the videos would not be enough either. After all, they didn't prove that Willy was innocent. Mutz probably had to change his theory though and the new theory was that Willy murdered her because he caught her and Sanders together, or something along those lines. At any rate, you knew you needed something more than the videos to inculpate Jim. So, you planted the fake letter in the same garbage can. Only you didn't know that Eric and I had already been there."

"You've put a lot of thought into this," the judge smirked.

"And what a letter!" Nolan exclaimed. "The whole Mexico thing was really clever because you knew that a smart person would suspect that Stefano Rodriguez wrote it, especially after you had told Eric that you had caught him with your wife in a compromising position a few years ago. Talk about killing two birds with one stone—you implicated both Jim Sanders and Stefano with that one letter. Impressive."

The judge smiled.

"Did you really believe your wife when she told you that Stefano had drugged her?"

The judge frowned. "What do you mean?"

"Well, it didn't take much investigation to find out the truth. She saw you following them, so she faked the part about being drugged. It was all a scam that was designed to cover up the fact that she was actually sleeping with him on a regular basis."

"How do you know that?" the judge asked him in a sharp tone.

Nolan smiled. "I have my sources." And then he quickly changed the subject. "But the one thing I can't figure out is what you did with the wall safe? I mean, if it was still on the property, the police would've no doubt found it—you know they search everywhere and everything."

"Not behind another painting," the judge smirked. "I pried that safe out the day before and installed it behind a painting in the hallway. And even if they had found it, I would've explained to them that I had two wall safes, and the burglar only found one."

"Ah," Nolan nodded. "Very clever."

"And now you also know where I hid the coveralls," the judge smiled. "Let's have another drink."

"And if I don't?" Nolan asked.

"I can shoot you right now. It will take a little more prep to stage the gunfight, but it can be done."

Nolan lifted his glass and this time faked as if he took a gulp.

"Oh no you don't," the judge scolded. "Drink it empty."

Nolan shrugged and raised his glass as if to make a toast, then downed the remaining whiskey.

"Do you know why your wife didn't have her phone cell on her? Her cell phone," Nolan quickly corrected himself. The whiskey was taking affect.

"No, I don't."

"It fell out of her pajamas when I took them off."

"Come again?" the judge seemed confused.

"I picked her up at the bar that night she was supposed to be at the fundraiser . . . the night before you killed her. Or I guess it would be more accurate to say she picked me up. Imagine that. In the middle of plotting to murder you she still craved other men. And you had no idea she was that promiscuous. Crazy."

The judge's face flushed but he didn't respond.

"Well, long story short, we went back to my office and things got a little carried away. We had some drinks, ended up taking our clothes off and then I rocked her world like you never could," he lied. "And I mean *rocked* her world. She's quite the tigress . . ."

Nolan felt the sting in his chest before he even heard the shot ring out. He saw the puff of smoke drift into the air above the gun as he collapsed forward.

"Damn it!" he heard the judge yell. "I didn't mean for it to go off yet!"

CHAPTER 57

As Eric bounded the front steps of Nolan's house he heard the shot from within and knew his worst fears had come true. He drew his semi-automatic pistol from his shoulder holster, held it near his chest pointing outward and then tried the door handle to see if it was unlocked.

It was.

He opened the door then quickly stepped in and moved to the left, away from the silhouetted opening.

"Jesus!" he heard Nolan yell from the study right next to where he was standing. "You frickin' shot me!"

Eric whipped around the corner with his pistol in shooting position and saw the judge standing over Nolan.

"Drop the gun!" Eric yelled, and then began firing.

The judge whirled around as the first bullet entered his side. Eric continued firing as the judge managed to lift his arm and fire back, but the inaccurate shot merely sent a bullet careening into the wall. The judge collapsed as Eric's 7th bullet entered his chest, followed by two more when he was on the floor. The only movement from the judge after that was his right foot, which quivered rapidly.

"Damn that hurts," Nolan writhed on the floor. He looked across the room through a haze of gun smoke and saw Eric on his cell phone.

"This is retired detective Eric Wentz. I've shot and killed a criminal suspect at Twelve Jackson Way. Another citizen is wounded. Send EMT's."

He paused, then yelled out again. "Twelve Jackson Way!"

"What took you so damned long?" Nolan asked in a slurred, raspy voice.

"Take it easy," Eric set his gun on the coffee table, then approached him. He placed his thumb over the bullet hole in the left side of Nolan's chest and applied pressure to stop the bleeding.

"Roll over on your side, let's see if there's an exit wound."

There was.

Eric put pressure on the exit wound with the heal of his palm while at the same time he kept his thumb over the hole in Nolan's chest. "You're gonna be fine."

"I don't feel very frickin' fine," Nolan groaned.

"Don't be a wuss. It looks like a .22 straight through and it obviously didn't hit your heart."

Nolan chuckled, which turned into a cough. He could taste the iron tang of blood in his mouth.

"My phone's on the coffee table. I had my video camera recording the whole time. It should've picked up our entire conversation," Nolan wheezed.

"That's good," Eric replied.

They could hear the sirens from a distance.

"He was going to kill us both and stage it so it looked like we killed each other," Nolan breathed. "Pretty crazy, huh?"

"Yeah, that is crazy," Eric agreed.

Nolan began to take short breaths, like a panting dog.

"I . . . I can't breathe."

"Stop talking. Your lung is collapsed, that's all. You'll be fine. The EMT's are almost here."

Two minutes later somebody banged on the front door.

"Police! Open up!"

"Come in!" Eric yelled. "It's all clear!"

Eric heard the front door open, then heard the slow steps of officers.

"We're in here! It's all clear!" Eric yelled. "Get an EMT in here!"

A police officer peeked into the room with his gun raised.

"Goddamn it! Get the fucking EMT in here!"

The police officer yelled towards the front door without taking his eyes off Eric.

"It's clear! Send in the EMT's!"

A moment later, two EMT's entered the room. One checked the pulse of Judge Chancey.

"This one's dead," he said.

The other EMT knelt down beside Nolan, at which point Eric released his pressure and moved away.

"Get your hands up and turn around," the officer barked, pointing his gun at Eric.

Eric did as he was told. The officer placed him in handcuffs, then frisked him. He pulled his phone from his shirt pocket and a wallet from his back pocket, tossing them both into the chair.

"What's your name?" the police officer asked.

"Retired detective Eric Wentz. My badge is in that wallet."

The officer opened the wallet and saw the badge.

"What happened here?"

"That's Judge Chancey on the floor there. He shot this guy," Eric pointed with his head, "who is Nolan Getty, the Public Defender. So, I shot and killed him. It's all recorded on Nolan's phone—right there on the coffee table."

"Have a seat over here," the officer directed. Eric sat down where the judge had been seated.

The officer picked up Nolan's phone and looked at the display.

"It's still recording," he said.

"Go ahead and push the stop button," Eric instructed. "And then watch the video. You probably won't be able to see anything but you'll hear what happened."

The EMT's put Nolan on the gurney. One of them squeezed a bag that was covering Nolan's face.

"See you later, boss," Eric yelled out.

Nolan held up his thumb.

CHAPTER 58

Nolan laid in the hospital bed staring out the window. The surgery to repair his lung had been a success and they had removed the ventilator earlier that morning.

He thought about all that had happened but it seemed like a dream. His mind had a difficult time grasping the fact that Judge Chancey actually tried to kill him. And the elaborate steps he took to murder his wife and frame Sanders were almost too weird to believe. But if they hadn't found that letter on his computer nobody would've believed it and Judge Chancey would have gotten away with it.

Nolan heard voices outside his room. He turned to see Eric, Rick and Danny enter.

"Hey, what do you know, he's alive," Rick smiled.

"Hello boss," Danny said. "How are you feeling?"

"Not too bad, actually," Nolan glanced at Eric.

"Hey numb nuts," Eric nodded. "I got you a teddy bear," he said, holding up a small, pink stuffed bear. He squeezed it several times, making its head nod up and down.

"Nice."

"When are you going to get out?" Danny asked.

"The nurse told me two more days if everything stays the same."

"Eric told us everything," Rick said. "I still can't believe Judge Chancey tried to kill you. If this was a movie it would be too far-fetched to believe."

"Yeah," Nolan replied. "Hard to believe. If I had known that he knew Eric had retrieved the deleted letter from his computer I would've never even met with him."

Nolan turned to Eric. "Nice job. Next time don't forget to delete the program."

Eric shrugged. "I deleted it. I just forgot to empty the trash."

"So that's how you knew the judge did it," Danny said. "Because of the letter."

"Yep. The letter was computer dated weeks after the murder so we knew it was written and planted to frame Sanders. And once we knew that all the other pieces just fell into place."

"Oh, by the way, they finally nolle prosse'd the charges against Sanders this morning," Rick added.

"Huh," Nolan grunted.

"Oh, I almost forgot," Danny said as he reached into his pocket. "Jim Sanders dropped this off right before we left."

He handed Nolan an envelope.

Nolan tore the end and opened it. He reached in and pulled out a check.

"Well, what do you know? It's a check for $2,500," he said, chuckling. But then he began coughing and wheezing. It took several coughs before the congestion cleared.

"I guess he did have some money left over after Burford raped him. I think we all have a steak dinner and a night on the town in our near future."

"Nice," Rick said. "Eric told us what the judge said about Mutz and how he was going to charge you with B&E and other stuff. You think he's still gonna do that?"

"Um, I don't know," Nolan thought a moment. "Hey, do me a favor and get him on the line for me."

"Right now?"

"Yeah."

Rick retrieved his cell phone from his pocket and dialed the Commonwealth Attorney's Office.

"Hello, Nolan Getty calling for Montgomery Mutz. Is he in?"

"Okay," Rick handed the phone to Nolan.

Nolan looked at the screen, then pushed the speaker button. Classical music emanated from the phone.

After a few moments Mutz clicked on.

"Hello this is Montgomery Mutz."

"Hey Monte, it's Nolan Getty. How are you?"

"It's Montgomery. I heard you're still in the hospital."

"Yeah, but I'll be all right," Nolan smiled.

"Did you hear that I nolle prosse'd the charges on Sanders this morning?"

"Yeah, I heard."

"It's quite the turn of events. It's almost unbelievable."

"Yeah, it's pretty crazy," Nolan agreed. "Hey, before the judge shot me he said he had talked to you and you told him you were going to bring charges against me. Something about breaking into Sanders's house and lying to a judge. What's that all about?"

"Um, well, we found your fingerprints in his house and the neighbor says he saw you entering the house. So, that means you broke into it and you were the one who made copies of those videos and sent them to yourself. Then you lied when we were in the judge's chambers and said you didn't know who sent them."

"Uh-huh," Nolan grunted.

"But you don't have to worry about that right now. I'll wait until you get out of the hospital."

"Well, that's mighty kind of you but I think you better wait longer than that."

"Why?"

"Well, two things, really. If you bring charges, I'll be forced to tell everyone about how you failed to disclose the videos that I sent you, which is a violation of *Brady*." Nolan was referring to a famous case in which the Supreme Court ruled that a prosecutor must disclose exculpatory evidence to the defense.

Mutz chuckled. "That's weird, I never got any videos. They must have been lost in the mail."

"I thought you would say that. There's one more thing. Judge Chancey told me that you had called him after the first day of the trial and you asked him about Mr. Calhoun's statements that he had seen me at Sanders's house. And that's a violation of the sequestration rules. You cheated, Mutz. You weren't supposed to talk to Judge Chancey because he's a witness. And that's the kind of thing that gets lawyers disbarred. But I tell you what, let's make a little deal. You forget about the charges and I'll forget about your violation."

"Huh," Mutz seemed to be thinking. "That's hearsay. You won't be able to bring it up."

"Oh, come on now, Monte. This is why our office whips up on you in court. You don't have a competent understanding of the rules of evidence. Look up Rule 2:804; exceptions to hearsay when the declarant is unavailable. I think it's the second or third paragraph down."

They could hear clicking on a keyboard.

"It's the one about statements against interest. If a declarant is unavailable, and I'd say the judge is definitely unavailable," Nolan added, "then any statement which the declarant knew at the time of its making would subject him to civil or criminal liability will not be excluded by the hearsay rule."

"Huh," Mutz grunted.

"The judge knew it was wrong and that he could be criminally charged but he talked to you anyway. And nobody would make such a statement if it wasn't true. So, that's why a statement against interest is an exception to hearsay. Pretty good stuff, huh?" Nolan asked.

"Huh," Mutz grunted again. "I see."

"Okay then, Monte. You have a good day!"

"It's Montgomery!" Mutz yelled as Nolan clicked the face of the phone and ended the call.

Nolan handed the phone back to Rick, smiling.

"Nicely done," Rick nodded as he turned to Danny.

"You get all that, Danny? If you start doing what the boss does you might just turn into a good lawyer someday."

"Does that include fooling around with a judge's wife?" Danny snapped back.

Nolan coughed several times as a wheezing sound emanated from his lungs. He turned on his side, which helped stop the coughing attack.

"I wish I had never licked-ed her," he croaked.

The author may be contacted at:
PatrickCleveland@gvtc.com

Made in the USA
Coppell, TX
07 June 2020

27062309R00173